Back Time
On Love City

David Culberson

**CALUMET
EDITIONS**

Minneapolis

**CALUMET
EDITIONS**

Minneapolis

THIRD EDITION DECEMBER 2022

10 9 8 7 6 5 4 3
ISBN: 978-1-960250-08-7

Cover design by David Culberson
Book design by Gary Lindberg

Amazon Reader Praise for
Back Time On Love City

Written by an old friend about a time and place that takes me back to before I ever knew the place but had heard some of the stories from the author's mouth... If you've EVER been to USVI and St John in particular, it's a must read.

James M. Kirsh

I was totally engaged, drawn into the story from the first page. David brings this magical story alive with the many vignettes and characters (and characters they are) he brings to life on every page of the book. I could not put the book down.

Stan Kaufman

Loved this book-. Easy to enjoy and imagine- this book is a must read for any St. Johnian!

Isla Monroe

This idea is explored on St. John's when it was still a "virgin" island and through the captivating, action-packed rapport between Captain Jay and the Rookie. Certainly, on the surface their friendship is exciting if not reckless, but in the depths we find symbolic twists and the irony to some of life's big questions. I thoroughly enjoyed the story and similar to a good movie it has provided great insight and lasting effect. Written in the style reminiscent of Hunter S. Thompson, I was reminded of a time when rules were made as you went along or perhaps never made at all.

BYC Reader

This is a book that draws you in slowly but once you're in the dreamy place it takes you, you want to stay there. We have no idea what will become of our main character, a young neophyte looking for adventure beyond the dreary cornfields of the Midwest. Will he be the consummate rookie lured by the pirates or, will he choose a better path? ... It's a fun read with a great moral: We can swim with the sharks, as long as we know when to get out of the water. I think it would make a great film.

Michael Garber

It's rainy up here in Illini country and I just finished reading this very refreshing book. For just a few bucks, I could spend a few hours imagining I was in solace of the Virgin Islands. I could actually feel the heat beaming from the pages of this funny, poignant book. I can't wait for the movie.

Justa Ghion

By the time I reached the end, I was fully immersed and was ultimately sad to reach the end. I felt somehow wistful of people in a time and place that I will never experience.

Rebecca St. George

A fun, witty read. Dave Culberson does a top notch job transporting the reader to a very special time in a very, special place--you won't want to put this story down! If you liked Hunter S. Thompson's Rum Diaries (minus the excessive drinking!) you'll love this book.

Jordan Alexandra

Great read focused on a young man's coming of age among locals on St. Johns Island. Narrative infuses ambition and realization of what the future holds. Takes you from reality of every day living to the beauty underwater.

Janet Stanton

A joyful yet poignant retrospective examination of a life filled with verve and colorful characters. Most autobiographies bore me to tears; this one certainly did not! It's certainly worth reading.

Michael Riley

This book is dedicated to my children in the fervent hopes that all my crazy living somehow imparted something good within them, even if purely by accident.

Acknowledgements

Thanks to all who helped me with this effort at Calumet Editions and special thanks to Amy, Jordan, Mike and Jeff, who are always available to read and critique clunky first drafts.

Also by David Culberson

Alterio's Motive

Back Time On Love City

David Culberson

Chapter One

"It's better to be silent and thought a fool than to open one's mouth and remove all doubt."
Mark Twain

I stepped down to my basement and turned on the TV, hoping to pass the time on my Stairmaster listening to news of the world—North Korea, Syria, Iran, Russia. Most news channels continued to report the aftermath of a crowded cruise ship that had been towed to port somewhere in the Gulf of Mexico. It had lost its engines and had to rely on backup generators for power. For the past three days, each time I tuned in for meaningful news, this was all that I saw. Watching a one-hundred-thousand-ton ship being towed to port at five knots per hour was like watching grass grow. Where was the real news?

Other than a few broken toilets and a flooded lower deck, everything on the ship functioned normally. By the number of channels covering it and the sensationalized reporting style, you'd have thought the cruise ship was being chased by a herd of Somali pirates, and the passengers were fighting for their lives. It wasn't, and they weren't. News helicopters flew over the ship and panned the scene, showing passengers having the time of their lives—some toasting the helicopters from deck chairs, others playing basketball on the topside courts or swimming in the pool; all enjoying a few more days of sun, free drinks and food.

When the ship finally docked and reporters flocked around it looking for blood and gore and horrible tales of survival at sea, the cameras caught passengers laughing as they disembarked, some grouped together feigning incredulity at the situation while waving drinks in plastic cups at the cameras. One reporter found a disgruntled passenger who complained that he could only get cell phone reception to check his email when other ships came by every day to bring additional food. That must have sucked.

Soon after the ship made port the shock of the "disaster at sea" had run its course, and the reports of the distressed ship no longer dominated the airwaves. The dramatic background music that had accompanied them was gone. It seemed the news channels were moving on to their normal snippets of news and discussion panels loaded with trendy experts—mostly bloggers who butchered the King's English once in front of the camera.

Having lived outside the US for most of my adult life, I hadn't realized how many news channels had cropped up on cable television in my absence and how scarce good journalism was. Slap and tickle journalistic spin in this new competitive environment had become the norm. Networks looked for stories anywhere they could find them, and on slow news days they made things up. The cruise ship event was newsworthy? Twenty-four hours a day?

Tired of television to accompany my evening workouts, I turned the TV off and glanced at the collection of old books stored on shelves in my basement. A Stairmaster is a great place to read. Of the hundreds of titles on the shelves, *Me and My Beloved Virgin*, written by Guy Benjamin, a long dead educator on St. John in the United States Virgin Islands (USVI), stood out. I'd read it years ago and had sat with the author many times at the Sputnik Bar in the little village of Coral Bay, on the eastern side of St. John, while he told delightful tales of his experiences growing up on the island when donkeys were the island's only transportation.

Something about the cruise ship disaster nagged at me. Opting not to read, I stepped onto my Stairmaster with the heavily accented second and fourth beat of reggae music pounding into my head through a pair of earbuds. I entered my weight, resistance and time and pushed start. Five minutes into a fast-paced climb, as my thoughts settled into a familiar rhythmic pattern, I started to figure out what had been nagging at me earlier—*Cruise ship disaster; St. John.* Two seemingly unrelated subjects, separated by space and time, brought together in my mind through continuous, unremarkable news reporting in an era of instant global coverage. I smiled at the irony. Far worse and more catastrophic events were common on or near our little island when I lived there, and they were barely a blip on anybody's radar screen—and none made news.

When I'd returned to the US after having lived in the Caribbean for many years, I told stories of the island and its characters—mostly to blank expressions or sighs of disbelief. No one could relate, so I stopped telling the stories. I hadn't thought much about St. John recently. But, that evening on my Stairmaster, memories of the island came flooding back. The more I reflected, the more I remembered. The more I remembered, the more I laughed. For the next couple of hours, while my heart maintained a pace of 140 beats per minute, my brain went on an historic journey of my life long ago on the little island of St. John—before it had become a *destination*; when it was an unassuming and unhurried island that had a peculiar personality, made that way by the cast of characters who lived there, especially one larger-than-life modern day pirate by the name of Captain Jay.

***

1978 – Pillsbury Sound, between St. Thomas and St. John, USVI

One in the morning and moonlight sparkled off the water of the sound that separated St. Thomas and St. John—four miles of beautiful Caribbean Sea with two to three-knot currents that moved the water north to south then south to north, changing direction every twelve hours.

A twenty-two-foot, baby-blue Seabird powerboat passed by me about a hundred feet to my right. Behind the Seabird was a sixty-foot ski rope, and at the end of the rope was a handle that danced and skipped at twenty knots along the surface of the calm sea. It was the second time in the past ten minutes it had sped by me.

I saw the familiar silhouette of the driver standing at the center console, holding on to the steering wheel with one hand and his other hand on the ass of a long-haired woman standing to his left. The woman held on to the aluminum frame of the fiberglass center console with one hand and held a beer in the other. Two women and a man sat tightly together on the fiberglass seat that had been molded into the front of the center console. I couldn't hear them above the sound of the 150 horsepower engine running at full throttle, but their heads and bodies gesticulated in drunken laughter.

The Seabird continued its irregular, high-speed trek throughout the sound.

The two men in the boat were my roommates, Captain Jay and Chuck. Earlier in the evening we had gone to one of the four bars on the island, the only one that stayed open past ten at night. On Wednesday and Friday nights people of all ages, colors and backgrounds—local St. Johnians, tourists and continentals, people from the US who called the island their home—gathered at the bar to dance to calypso and ska music and drink stale Heineken beer. The green Heineken bottles couldn't protect the hop molecules from being ripped apart by the intense Caribbean sun while stacked on docks waiting to be transported by freight boat to bars and restaurants on multiple islands, causing the beer to taste *skunky*. But it still tasted better than the alternative… Old Milwaukee.

I'd known my roommates for a year. The three of us were continentals. They were seasoned pros, having lived on the island for a few years. I was the rookie. We were not *bawn* there, as the locals would always remind us, but we lived there. We and the other continentals on the island represented a 7 percent minority of the population and were an integral part of the island's cultural fabric. Not all continentals got along, but the thing we had in common, other than being from the US, was that each of us effortlessly engaged the primitive comforts offered by the island's natural environment and the strong friendships offered by the local West Indians.

Chuck worked at Caneel Bay, an island resort built by Lawrence Rockefeller. His Hollywood good looks, along with his thick, black-rimmed glasses and his quick, dimpled smile made him quite popular with women on the island. The house we lived in was Chuck's, as long as he managed the resort's books.

Captain Jay, the instigator of all mischievous things that I would get involved with for the foreseeable future, owned the SCUBA diving concession at the resort. We were so different that Jay and I would never have become friends if we had met anywhere other than a small Caribbean island. We would never have crossed paths.

Jay grew up on the Florida Panhandle and, barely out of high school, headed off to work on fishing boats, barges and oil rigs in the Gulf of Mexico and eventually found his way to the Caribbean. He was a couple of inches over six feet and two hundred pounds of muscle and gristle. His body had as many knife and bullet scars as it had years. He talked and looked like a blond Elvis but with a personality more similar to Steve McQueen. His natural charisma allowed him to get away with referring to the women he came in contact with, those of breeding age anyway, and breeding age to Jay was just about any age, as *Puddin'*, *Sugar Plum*, or *Darlin'*. The vast majority of the women loved it.

Captain Jay couldn't hold an intellectual conversation. He was all about doing, all about the moment. His survival instincts were molded by past insular experiences that required a more animalistic approach to life. He never reflected, told few stories about his past and he never planned a future. Being around him was like watching a movie with him in the starring role, with no boring parts. He had one of two reactions to everything—joy or anger. He never sat in the corner at a party—he *was* the party. He was the loveable dog that trots into the house, tail wagging as if saying, "We can start the party now." Captain Jay was quick to lend a hand to anybody who needed one. But he was reckless—dangerously so. And his recklessness eventually caused him to make mistakes—mistakes that would complicate his life and cause me to focus on mine.

The Seabird sped past me again, its occupants still partying and paying no attention to the empty ski rope.

The three women in the boat worked at the resort in various capacities. They'd come into the open-air bar late in the evening. Chuck's dimpled smile and Jay's catcall had brought them scrambling to our picnic table near the far end. We drank and laughed until last call. We were young enough, stupid enough and drunk enough to want to continue our party elsewhere and had decided, on Captain Jay's recommendation, to do so in one of his boats—the Seabird. I knew it well, having spent hours on it since first meeting Captain Jay months earlier.

We bought several bottles of beer and piled into Captain Jay's baby-blue Willys Jeep and drove out of Cruz Bay and over the mountain to Caneel Bay, on the northwest side of the island. Jay parked in the resort's employees parking lot, and we staggered down a concrete path surrounded by tropical vegetation and dimly lit with lights low to the ground and painted green to match the plants. We passed a security guard who smiled and said "Okay" as we filed by. He'd recognized we weren't lost tourists. We wore island wardrobes, which consisted of T-shirts, cut off shorts and worn flip-flops; except Jay—he'd shed his shorts and shirt in the Jeep and wore a Speedo and flip-flops. We were definitely locals.

We walked out onto the main dock, passing the brown and white Caneel ferry boat, and stepped down onto a small dinghy dock that ran perpendicular to the main dock about halfway to the end. Several rubber dinghies were tied up, lightly bouncing into each other as they rode the gentle surf. Captain Jay jumped into the dinghy that he used to get out to his boats when anchored in the bay. He primed the engine by squeezing a black rubber ball in the gas line that connected the engine with a small, red, portable gas tank that sat in an inch of sea water at the bottom of the dinghy and pulled the starting cord. The motor sputtered to life. By habit, I untied the dinghy from the dock, threw the line into the boat and shoved it into the open water. Captain Jay sank into one of the half-inflated pontoons near the stern and, with a big Elvis grin, twisted the throttle on the end of the handle that steered the motor. I watched the dinghy speed off into the moonlit bay.

Many dinghies in the Caribbean had affectionate names painted on their sterns or their sides that were meant to indicate a sense of belonging to the mother boat they served. Captain Jay's always half-inflated Avalon dinghy was named the *Rumpled Foreskin*, which had no relevance to its mother ship, or anything else, as far as I knew.

A few minutes later Captain Jay brought the center-consoled Seabird back to the dock, having left the *Rumpled Foreskin* tied to the mooring where the Seabird had been anchored. We threw our beers and ourselves into the boat in a stumbling heap. I fell, face first, on top of one of the women, and the other two women and Chuck fell on us. In front of me, stashed into one of the soffits running along the side of the boat, was a water ski. I had never seen it before. From the bottom of the heap I made a very dumb comment about my skiing ability that I would later regret.

"Hey, you have skis? I've never seen skis on your boats. Where'd they come from?"

"They? You mean *it*. Where did *it* come from? Right, Rookie?"

"Uh?"

Captain Jay laughed and said, "I took it out of my storage shed a couple of days ago. Thought I'd do some skiin' sometime while the sea is still calm. Tonight would be a good time."

I looked around, as best I could with three bodies on top of me, and asked, "Where's the other one? I'm a pretty good skier."

Captain Jay, who grew up in Florida, the water skiing capital of the world, looked at me with an incredulous smirk and said, "Don't tell me you need two skis."

I could slalom ski, but normally, in the Midwest, we started with two skis, got comfortable, and then dropped one as we passed near the dock on the way around the lake. Chuck and the two women that fell on top of us stopped laughing long enough to start to untangle themselves and get to their feet. I stood and helped the woman whom I fell on top of up and to the seat in front of the center console. She laughed and fell into the lap of one of her friends. I looked around for a place to sit. There were none left. I stepped to the side of the center console where Captain Jay stood.

Jay cocked his head, shrugged his shoulders and said, "Well?"
"Uh?"

"What? You gonna wuss out, Rookie?"

I meant to say "Yes," but beer and youth inspired a more bravado viewpoint. "I can ski better than you," I said.

That was enough for the captain. With a big smile, he grabbed
the ski and shoveled it onto the dock.

"Get your ass up on the dock," Captain Jay said, his smile having disappeared.

"And take off from there?"

"You got a problem with that?"

I looked at the others in hope of support. They were busy talking
and laughing. I looked at Captain Jay. He glared back, challenging
me.

I stepped back up on the dock and grabbed the ski. I threw my
T-shirt and flip-flops back into the boat and sat on the end of the dock
trying to remember which foot I used to put forward on a slalom
ski. Jay untied the boat, throttled gently forward and brought it back
around so the stern faced me. He slipped the gear into neutral, tossed
me the handle end of a ski rope he had pulled from one of the stern
holds and tied off his end to the stern on either side of the motor.
Sitting on the dock with my ski in the water, I caught the rope and
grabbed the handle. Captain Jay pushed the gear forward and slowly
took the slack out of the rope. I had to lean back to keep from being
pulled into the water prematurely. The captain pulled the gear in reverse to keep me on the dock. His passengers fell into each other,
spilling freshly opened beers.

"Shouldn't I be taking off from the water?" I yelled.

Captain Jay had turned his back to me. His shoulders heaved up
and down as he laughed and barked orders for everybody to sit down
and hold on. I could hear the kathunk of the transmission as he pushed
the gear to the neutral position, then it kathunked back into forward.

*Where is my life jacket? What about all of those sailboats in the
bay? I know they have anchor lines. How am I supposed to see them?
It's dark.*

Captain Jay looked back with his Elvis grin.

"Don't sharks feed at night?" I shouted.

"Ready?" Captain Jay shouted back.

"No."

"Here we go!" he shouted and pushed the throttle forward.

Shit.

Everybody in the boat watched me navigate around the anchored boats out of the bay and out into the vast and mostly empty sound, where they lost interest in me and busied themselves with partying. A few minutes later I'd skied into the heavy wake of a passing freight boat, and the impact left me floundering in the sea—just me and my ski. I was perfect shark bait, silhouetted on the surface by the bright moonlight. The Seabird sped on.

I had watched the running lights get smaller as the Seabird headed south, then made a wide turn back to the north and continued to maneuver in irregular loops throughout the sound, passing dangerously close to me several times. Each time the boat approached I hollered and waved my ski high above my head. Each time the boat passed I blindly stabbed at the water below me with the ski, hoping to keep the menacing sharks, which I was convinced were swimming below me, at bay.

This wasn't the first time I'd allowed myself to be tested by Captain Jay. I wasn't too worried. I might get tired. Maybe a jellyfish would sting me. Maybe a shark would try to take a bite, but I wouldn't die. At that age I was immortal. I had no doubt that I'd either be rescued by the Seabird or I'd make it to shore somewhere where I'd be able to wave down a passing charter or freight boat the next morning. My biggest fear was failing Captain Jay. Not surviving would have been failure.

I started to think of all of the stupid things I'd done since meeting Captain Jay—things I'd not have done without his encouragement. Another fifteen minutes passed. Maybe it was time to exercise a little more caution. I would have a conversation with Jay later when I was back in the boat or on the dock or maybe at our house later than that. I would talk to him about the risks he took and the danger he put himself and those around him in. I would talk to him about the numerous sordid activities he was involved with.

I turned to see the Seabird make another turn to the south. It would be back. I looked to the north, in the direction I was drifting. A rogue wave crashed into me, and I almost lost my grip on the ski. After coughing up another few teaspoons of seawater I realized there would be no meaningful talk with Captain Jay about anything, especially ethics or morals, which didn't seem to penetrate this part of the world, anyway. Somewhere out there to the north was an imaginary glass wall that deflected the concept of ethics and warped any moral code as it passed through on its way to the Caribbean.

I tired and stopped poking my ski in the water and lay it flat on the surface in front of me. I placed my palms flat on top of the ski as far apart as I could reach and slowly pushed the ski under the water. That gave me temporary buoyancy and allowed me to rest my legs. I repeated this several times, until my right leg bumped into something—a large something. Could have been a dolphin, but it would have surfaced and laughed at my predicament. Could have been a large turtle, but turtles avoid humans at all costs, and an accidental bump would have been almost impossible. More likely it was a curious shark.

I started to think about all I'd learned about sharks since meeting Captain Jay and spending hundreds of hours underwater. I hoped there weren't any tiger sharks lurking. Most other sharks might take a bite. It would hurt and probably require stitches—but a bite by a large tiger would be certain death. My sense of immortality started to waiver.

There wouldn't have been any dusky or silky sharks, which I knew to be fairly harmless. They were pelagic and stayed in the open water far offshore. They would come sniffing around when I drifted another twelve miles north and over the Puerto Rican Trench, a twenty-eight-thousand-foot-deep valley on the floor of the Caribbean Sea just north of the Leeward Islands and Puerto Rico. Lots of sharks hung out in the Trench.

There could have been bull sharks or Caribbean reef sharks nearby. They looked almost identical until the bulls grew over seven feet long or so and became much bulkier than the reef sharks. But what difference did it make if I knew which shark was which? They all had sharp teeth.

There were probably no hammerheads, we didn't see them around St. John much.

A mako? Maybe. The mako shark and its cousin, the great white, were mackerel sharks. The tops and the bottoms of their tail fins were equal sized, allowing them to swim very fast. Mako sharks liked to swim near the surface and had mouths full of jagged teeth. Shit!

I returned to poking my ski down into the sea and started to poke the ski sideways as well.

I just didn't want it to be a tiger.

Another ten minutes passed. The Seabird approached and passed me again, and I heard the engine throttle back to idle. They'd stopped. I took a moment to catch my breath. Treading water with no life jacket or flippers, even in the buoyant, salty ocean was exhausting. The Seabird was close. All I had to do was shout. They would certainly hear me. I could hear them.

"What the fuck happened to the rookie?" a muffled voice asked in the distance. It was Captain Jay.

"Thought he was a good skier," somebody in the boat said.

I tried to shout, but the wake from the Seabird hit me, and I swallowed water. All I could do was cough.

"Anybody see where he went down?" a female voice asked with a laugh.

"Damn! Guess we better find him," a male voice said. It was Captain Jay. "Hey Rookie, where are you? See any sharks yet?"

He laughed, and the others laughed with him. What great entertainment—at my expense.

I cleared the water from my throat and started to shout again, just as the Seabird's motor revved and pushed the boat in the opposite direction. Where the hell were they going? Damn! The Seabird was gone. I poked my ski into the water and wished sharks had evolved the ability to bark or hiss or rattle, anything that would give me some warning of their presence.

I followed the running lights of the Seabird through Pillsbury Sound. It began to move in widening concentric circles, signaling that common sense had finally broken the seal of drunkenness, and they had started a proper search. They only had twenty-four square miles to cover—unless I drifted out of Pillsbury Sound. The current had picked up, making it impossible to control my course, even a few degrees left or right. If the Seabird didn't find me and if I couldn't maneuver close to one of the small cays that made up the north side of the sound, I would drift out to the Trench, where another current would take me west. I looked north and back toward the running lights of the Seabird, which were well south.

This was going to be a long night, and I realized I might have to poke and wave all the way to Puerto Rico.

Chapter Two

"I've never let my schooling interfere with my education."
Mark Twain

It's been many years since I lived in the Caribbean. I've been back to visit, and it's not the same. The sand is still sugary and white, the water is still blue and tourists flock to it, mesmerized by its tranquil beauty, but in a one-week visit how much do they really see? On the surface it's paradise—a booze-filled la-la land, perfectly suited for people who want to kick back for a few days to escape reality, or the weather, of wherever they're from. Scratch the surface, though, and you'll find a group of islands that have been inundated throughout their history with evil heaped upon them by man: cannibalism, slavery, piracy, revolts, political persecution, corruption and a host of dangerous characters—all as tumultuous as the volcanoes, earthquakes and hurricanes that Mother Nature has thrown their way.

For several hundred years, the Caribbean was populated by wandering tribes from South America, the Caribs and the Arawaks, who hunted and gathered their way through the island chain—until the Caribs ate most of the Arawaks. Then the Europeans came and, for a couple of hundred years, managed a culture based on slavery and piracy. It was during that time that many of the islands were raped of natural resources, which were used to build ships that would carry molasses from the sugarcane plantations, built where great mahogany forests once stood, to Europe or America. The ships would then sail to Africa, fill their holds with slaves and sail back to America or the Caribbean—another lap of their triangular trade route completed.

In spite of the destruction of much of the Caribbean's forests, the beauty of the islands was undeniable, and after the emancipation of black slavery in the mid-nineteenth century, the islands stagnated before slowly creeping into a culture of tourism. The invention of modern jet airlines and the rise of affluent travelers in the middle of the twentieth century pushed the Caribbean toward total immersion in tourism. By the early twenty-first century, the islands had become identified by the corporate hotel chains and crowded open air surrey buses filled with day-trippers from passing cruise ships, leaving a be-wildered local population wondering how much longer they could survive on their native lands before the cost of living and increasingly high property taxes forced them into the sea. For them, tourism had become a different kind of slavery.

For a short time, though, just before its picturesque beaches filled with overweight tourists, before a multitude of island bars started to boom Jimmy Buffett songs from speakers that hung from wooden rafters and served mixed rum drinks to wall-to-wall patrons who wore brightly-colored clothing, before air conditioned shops were built to sell duty-free goods to thousands of tourists who disembarked daily from the scores of cruise ships that lined the harbors of many of the islands, before sports cars and SUVs replaced Mini Mokes and Willys Jeeps and before hotels with glossy lobbies lined once remote beach-es—there *was* a different Caribbean. For those of us who were lucky enough to be there and patient enough to embrace its inconveniences, its imperfect social structure, its mixed bag of quirky characters and a surface beauty that belied its bruised underbelly, it was an unforget-table place.

As a traveler, if you're lucky enough to have had good timing, you might have stumbled into a similar place that captured your heart. You know the places I'm referring to. These are the special places that, if you allow their personalities into your soul, help mold your character. Maybe it was the place you spent your honeymoon. May-be you traveled there during your college days. Maybe you found it during a short side trip—a footnote on a tourist brochure. It's that magical place that was so sparkling fresh the first visit that it kept calling you back. But return visits were a little less sparkling. Something was missing or different.

The unfortunate truth is that these places don't last. This is because all places share one thing—change; a continuous stream of developmental evolution. Physical and environmental changes are the most obvious. Populations grow, more and different buildings arise, ecosystems diminish or disappear. These are the things everyone can see. However, special places share a more fleeting characteristic that only a fortunate few ever experience—personality. Some call it a *sense of place*, something most short-term visitors never feel, only seeing the physicality of the place. Others don't realize the specialness of the place while there but, upon reflection, understand it much later. Fewer still embrace it immediately, sometimes never going home.

Residents of these places always feel the personality. In fact, they are an important ingredient. When the recipe of personalities, unspoiled physical beauty and quirkiness are just right, a place is perfect—if only for a while.

Many places exhibit their best personalities early in their evolutionary cycles, before the modern gloss arrives to spread like a rapidly growing fungus, affecting everything in its path. This is also the time when it is most difficult for most people to live there, particularly if the place is a small tropical island.

The things that tourists fail to notice during a one or two-week vacation become alarmingly apparent to a wannabe full-time resident after a month or two. Forget shopping. Medical services—barely; a first aid station at best. Power—maybe, sometimes. Roads only a goat could climb. No change of seasons. The same people sit on the same bar stool and tell the same story—day after day. It's these types of things that drive people to leave soon after their attempt to call the island *home*. For those few who are a little more open-minded, or half-crazy, or if they possess the right frame of mind and a great sense of humor, these places are highly livable, maybe preferable, particularly if the new resident hasn't been spoiled by the conveniences of the first world. It isn't so much that ignorance of the outside world is bliss; rather, indifference to the outside world is bliss.

***

The St. John I stumbled onto in the late seventies was one of those places. I was young, wide-eyed and naive. The island was in the perfect place in its evolutionary cycle, though I wouldn't realize this until many years later, and only after I'd matured enough to understand what I'd witnessed while living there and how the changes in the island and its residents, barely noticeable in the moment, would permanently affect its personality. Some would say for the better, but those who would say that didn't live there then. They could never miss what they never had.

Having grown up in the Midwest I knew nothing about oceans or islands, but I knew that, as soon as I could, I would move anywhere to get away from the flat, cold landscape of corn and soybean fields. I left the Midwest to attend college in the South where the terrain improved but where I failed to collect my degree, withheld because I owed over seven hundred dollars in parking tickets to the university. I wasn't going back to the Midwest, and I wasn't going to stick around to pay the fines, which I couldn't afford. A degree would have been worthless to me, anyway. I was too young to know what I wanted to do or where I wanted to go. Curiosity and an invitation from friends to come to visit them at their vacation home on St. John gave me a new direction. I sold my VW van, packed a bag and headed to the airport, so eager to start the adventure I didn't take the time to look at a map.

When I boarded my inaugural flight from Tallahassee to Miami, where I would connect to a flight to St. Thomas, it dawned on me that I didn't really know where St. John was. I figured it was somewhere in the Caribbean Sea, which was south of the United States.

That was all I knew.

Chapter Three

"The secret of getting ahead is getting started." Mark Twain

It had been two hours and fifteen minutes since we had taken off in bad weather and into thick cloud cover above the Miami International Airport, and conditions hadn't improved. I could tell by the jet's long descent and the soft bump caused by lowering the flaps that we were well into the glide path of the Harry S. Truman Airport on St. Thomas. The view outside my window was rain and clouds with no sign of land or ocean. Even though Eastern Airline jets were equipped with modern avionics I wasn't sure that a landing in zero visibility was possible. A moment later I felt the thrust of the engines and the nose of the jet power upward. The captain announced that the heavy rain created too much of a risk to land. That was all he said. I learned later that he, or any pilot, would be concerned that the jet wouldn't be able to stop by the time it reached the mountain at the end of the short, 4,700-foot runway, which had recently claimed a couple of American Airline flights. We diverted seventy miles west to the San Juan, Puerto Rico airport, which had just as much rain but a longer runway and no mountain at the end of it.

The rains stopped during the night, and all of the passengers from the Eastern Airline flight were shuttled from San Juan to St. Thomas the next day on small commuter planes. My destination was

St. John, and after collecting my bag from a clunky carousel in the middle of the terminal, a cavernous WWII hangar with a few kiosks set up around the perimeter of its interior, I exited the building and asked taxi drivers how to get there.

"Take dat bus der," one driver told me.

Another said, "I go to Charlotte Amalie, me son. You go der and take de shuttle to Red Hook. Eh teasy, mon."

"You wit a group?" one asked, looking behind me. "I only take dem dat are groups," he said.

I know they were speaking English, but it was not any English a kid from the Midwest understood. Fortunately, a thin lady dressed as though she'd stepped out of a time warp from the late sixties overheard my questions and pointed to a Ford truck with six rows of benches built onto the frame behind the cab. An aluminum-framed canvas awning covered the benches. She called it a surrey bus and told me it would take me to Red Hook, on the other side of the island, where I could take a ferry to St. John. I thanked her and walked to my ride.

The drive across St. Thomas was eye-opening. The surrey bus driver insisted on driving in the left lane of the narrow two-lane road. All of the passengers, me included, leaned right at the first sight of an on-coming surrey bus, hoping that our body English would steer the taxi into the proper lane. It didn't. The two vehicles passed each other, each driving their left lanes, the drivers honking and smiling in recognition. Some of us shrugged and smiled, quickly understanding one of the many differences between the US and the US Virgin Islands. Others turned slack-jawed and wide-eyed to look at the next on-coming vehicle. It was a dump truck.

Outside the airport, we headed east through a mile of slums. Traffic was heavy and consisted of other surrey buses, many small pickup trucks, a few small cars with taxi lights on top and a few Jeeps. None looked new except the surrey buses, with freshly washed and waxed metal bodies reflecting the bright sunlight.

We passed through Charlotte Amalie, the only town on the island, with its large harbor on the right and scores of stone and wood stores on the left. Hundreds of houses clung to the mountainside that reached far above the stores.

Several small, wooden freight boats and a tourist boat with a large sign above it, naming it the *Kon Tiki,* were tied along the bulkhead of the harbor. Shirtless men offloaded crates of bananas and other goods from a few of the freighters' open decks into trucks that had driven over the curb and onto the apron and were parked next to the boats. The *Kon Tiki* was packed with tourists and was readying for an excursion. Calypso music blared from bad speakers placed somewhere on the boat. Six cruise ships were anchored in the harbor. A larger cruise ship sat at anchor outside the harbor in the open ocean. On the far side of the harbor, near its entrance from the sea, was a long pier that ran parallel with the opposite shore. Three cruise ships were tied alongside the pier, and there was room for at least one more. Charlotte Amalie was a bustling Caribbean town and far too crowded for my tastes. I hoped to find St. John a lot more tranquil. I didn't have to wait long to find out.

Thirty minutes after leaving the crowded town we arrived at Red Hook. I was ready for the last leg of my long journey to St. John. I climbed down from the back of the surrey bus and waited behind the other passengers to pay five dollars to the driver, then followed the group to a kiosk near the dock and paid two dollars for a one-way crossing to the island that I could see a few miles in the distance. It looked like a dark-green lump poking out of the sea, cartoon-like in its symmetry. Crew members took suitcases from the tourists and stacked them in the middle of the boat on the floor. They took boxes of provisions from the locals and stacked them, along with other island staples, on the wide bow. We boarded a steel-hulled, blue and white boat with hard plastic benches lined up behind the wheelhouse and a metal rail around the sides of the ferry to keep passengers from falling overboard. A small sign hung on the exterior wall of the wheelhouse stating that the US Coast Guard allowed a maximum capacity of forty persons. The captain sounded a horn, and a few stragglers rushed onto the boat from the dock while the crew untied the boat, and we motored out of the harbor and toward St. John.

Chapter Four

"When I was young I could remember anything, whether
it happened or not."
Mark Twain

The powerful diesel engine was loud, and exhaust fumes permeated the back of the boat where the passengers sat. I was sure that I wasn't the only person on board who felt nauseous. Fortunately, it was a short trip to St. John, and fifteen minutes after we departed Red Hook the dark lump of volcanic island that was St. John transformed into clearer shades of green that stretched from the beaches to the top of its mountains. A few brightly painted homes were sprinkled in a kaleidoscope of colors, most of them near a small village that took up a few hundred yards of beach in the center of the bay the ferry had been motoring toward since it left St. Thomas. The captain pulled the throttles to just above idle, and the boat settled to a soft crawl as it entered the harbor. The diesel fumes that lagged behind the boat caught up with us, and I had to cover my mouth to keep from breathing them in. As we edged closer to the dock and were enveloped by the bay's lush slopes, I could see that the darker green colors on the island belonged to tall deciduous trees, the lighter hues to the smaller flowering trees and bushes. The fronds of the palm trees that lined the beaches shone in the sun.

When parallel with the dock, the captain slowed and spun the boat around so that the stern pointed to shore. Several locals who had boarded the ferry in Red Hook stood and shuffled to the opening in the rail where we would exit onto the dock. I followed their example, as did a few of the other tourists. The captain performed a series of forward and reverse thrusts that brought the one-hundred-ton boat within inches of the dock, eventually kissing the hard, concrete edge and jostling those of us who stood off balance. We were forced to grab for the nearest object fixed to the boat, or the person in line ahead of us, to keep from falling. The locals laughed it off. The rest of us looked around, let out nervous laughs and continued to hold on to whatever we had grabbed.

The crew tied the ferry to the dock, and we disembarked. I made the step from the gently rocking boat to the solid pier with my only travel bag hanging from my shoulder. The tourists behind me disembarked and had to wait for their luggage, which was unloaded and stacked on the dock by the crew after everybody was off the boat. While the tourists scrambled for their luggage, the crew went to the bow of the boat to unload island provisions—boxes of food, hardware items and a sofa. A couple of thin local men and a fat lady who had been on board waited for their boxes and were joined by other locals who had backed Jeeps and beat-up trucks out onto the dock to pick up provisions. A few taxi drivers mingled with the tourists, soliciting fares and helping with their luggage. The tourists hurried and wore serious frowns. The locals didn't. They took their time, wore big smiles, slapped backs, shook hands and joked with each other in their strange English.

The intensity of the sun reminded me that I would need to buy a hat and maybe a pair of sunglasses, but it was not unbearably hot. A mild, swirling breeze cooled my skin and kept my sweat to a minimum. Each time the breeze came from the direction of the island, steel drum music wafted by, then faded as the breeze shifted.

The fat West Indian lady who'd been waiting for her sofa to be off-loaded shouted orders to two men who struggled to load the sofa onto the back of a small Toyota truck. They had successfully loaded one end of the sofa on the tailgate. While moving it further onto the truck the sofa slipped off and banged onto the dock. Both men laughed. The fat lady shook her finger and hollered at them, causing them to laugh harder. I walked toward the truck and was joined by two of the crew from the boat. We helped the two men load the sofa, which was far too large for the truck. The two crew members left with a barely perceptible nod to one of the men who'd been trying to load the sofa, who turned to me and said, "Tanks, mon," before he and the fat lady climbed into the cab of the truck. With one end of the sofa in the bed and the other hanging over the roof of the cab, and the truck riding low and leaning a little toward the passenger side, they slowly drove off the dock. The other man who'd helped load the sofa tried to jump onto the bed of the truck as it left. He failed and the truck slowed. He waved the truck on with a laugh, walked to the end of the dock and greeted smiling friends.

The activity on the dock slowly shifted to shore. I turned to look out into the bay where several sailboats were anchored. Some had dinghies behind them, indicating to me that people lived on them. A thin man with long blond hair tied into a ponytail and wearing only shorts pulled the dinghy tethered behind his boat to the stern and jumped in. He untied the dinghy line, pulled the starter on the small outboard motor and sped toward the dock. At the last moment he veered to the beach to the south side of the dock and ran the dinghy up onto the sand next to several other dinghies, hopped out and sauntered barefoot up the beach to greet a couple that had disembarked from the ferry.

Three children sat and fished at the end of the dock. I walked up behind them and looked over their shoulders into the water, which was so clear it was like looking down into a large aquarium. The depth must have been seven or eight feet to accommodate the ferry boats and other sea craft that supplied the island, but the sandy bottom seemed only a couple of feet from the surface. A few two-inch fish that I'd seen in saltwater aquariums in people's homes in the US swam close to a conch shell that rested in the sand a few feet from the end of the dock. Black and yellow-striped sergeant major fish darted around the concrete piers. A small barracuda was parked a few feet away, motionless except for the very small pectoral fins fanning excessively on either side of the fish. Its mouth was open slightly, showing a set of canines that a junkyard dog would die for. I asked the children what they were fishing for and one of them proudly said, "Ole wife."

I nodded and said, "Great," having no idea what an *ole wife* was.

I heard a large splash and turned in its direction. A pelican had dive-bombed the bay a few feet beyond the bow of the ferry boat. Its body didn't completely submerge, like that of a cormorant I'd seen on fishing trips to the Upper Midwest. Instead, its head and neck remained underwater for just a few seconds before resurfacing, its neck stretching upward to a disarming length, then gulping down a large fish it had captured and stored in the pouch on the underside of its long beak. Two other pelicans came in for a bombing run and bounced into the water a couple of feet from their buddy, both gobbling up their targeted meals.

The vehicles had left the dock, and the ferry boat crew checked the lines and walked to shore. I followed. At the end of the dock was a funky wood sign that read, "Welcome to Love City." Next to it was a small kiosk. Snuggled into the little kiosk was a large woman who wore a blue uniform and was selling ferry tickets. Either she was very large or the kiosk was very small—or both. She looked as though she could have been wearing it. I had no idea how she squeezed in and out.

Next to the fat lady wearing the kiosk was a lean-to structure, about the size of a large run-in shed for horses. Half of it was closed and had the universal red and white dive insignia on the door. The other half was open and housed a car rental agency. The cars parked around it were little, beat up, go-cart-looking things with nameplates that read "Mini-Moke" and "Gurgel."

There were no crowds or traffic jams on this island. What a difference four miles of ocean made.

I hadn't told my friends when I would arrive. They wouldn't be around to meet me, and I wasn't sure where to go to find them. They'd mentioned that the island was small, and all I had to do was ask around. I was in no hurry, so I stood at the end of the dock and watched island life, which seemed, at least from my limited exposure, to center around a compact area near the dock and the arrival of the ferry. If I stayed near the dock long enough I'd probably see just about everybody on the island.

"Yo, me son. Yo need to move outta deh way."

I turned around to see a smiling face with a missing front tooth and a baseball cap on top lean out of the driver's window of a yellow Ford surrey bus filled with tourists and luggage. I moved, and the driver backed his taxi out into the road, smiling the whole time.

"Tanks, mon. Okay?" he said as he drove by.

I thought it a strange question, coming from somebody I'd never met. Of course I was okay.

A narrow road ran parallel to the beach. On the other side of the road was a small park, if a few tall palm trees and a couple of wooden benches in a small muddy spit of land that comprised the southeast corner of a very small city block could be called a park. It couldn't have been more than five hundred feet square. Passengers from the ferry joined others who waited on the wooden benches and stood in small groups laughing and slapping backs. The south side of the park was bordered by a ten-foot-wide, paved, one-way road. Nestled on the south side of it was a small concrete building that had been painted pink, though most of the paint had faded. The upper level of the building had a large portico and jalousie louvered doors that led to a residence. The lower level had one large opening at street level with two large, wooden, pink doors open and swung back against its walls. Above the opening was a hand-painted sign that read "Mooie's Bar."

An orange Volkswagen van was parked cock-eyed on the narrow concrete apron that separated the bar from the road, blocking half of the entrance. A very large black man sat on one of two large speakers that sat on the pavement just outside the side door of the van. An extension cord ran from the interior of the bar to an amplifier in the van. While the speakers blasted distorted steel drum music the man held up a handful of 45 LP records wrapped in plain white paper jackets and occasionally shouted, "One dollah." I wondered if the distorted version of the music was helping or hurting his sales.

A few rusted out CJ Jeeps and Toyota trucks drove by followed by what looked like a WWII Willys Jeep. Its metal body had been replaced with marine plywood. The corrosive atmosphere of the Caribbean was obviously not friendly. The only vehicle that passed by that wasn't rusted was a golf cart driven by an older lady who wore a flowered dress, her hair tied up into a tight bun with a pink hibiscus flower attached to the side of her head. She drove through the tropical background with a tight smile and stiff posture, looking like a librarian on the movie set of *South Pacific*.

I walked across the road to the park. It was bordered on the north by a raised wooden shack with a weathered, lime-green painted finish and a corrugated metal hip roof. The structure listed at an angle that defied gravity. It was built on wooden piers, and a tiny travel agency had set up shop under one corner of the building. As soon as I was convinced that the upper level was abandoned a person came out of the door and hopped down the stairs, shaking the building with each step. I stood back and waited for the building to fall. It didn't. I walked to the front of the building and saw a small wooden sign tacked on the exterior wall by the door on the upper level—"Customs Office." I looked up through the open door and saw at least three people inside. I was sure that one more person would have tipped it over and was glad that St. John was US territory and that I didn't need to clear customs—and I wasn't going to check on flights at the travel agency anytime soon.

Just past the customs office to the north was, according to the sign on the outside, "The Morris F. de Castro Clinic." It was a small concrete building that had a typical nineteen seventies, *built by the government*, look. I walked to the entrance and peered inside to see a reception room with a small metal desk and a file cabinet. An interior door led to another room, which I assumed was the examination room. Based on the size of the clinic there couldn't have been more than the two rooms. An old-style vending machine sat on the flat concrete entrance to the clinic. For fifty cents I could pull out a Pepsi, a Vita Malt or an Old Milwaukee beer.

I walked back toward the pink bar, close enough to see inside the windowless room. Several local men leaned on the fifteen-foot-long bar that took up the entire back of the room. The only light came from the garage-door-style opening at the entrance to the bar and one bare light bulb that hung from the low concrete ceiling. Five or six tables in front of the bar were filled with men playing dominoes, slapping the polka dotted rectangles on the table, laughing and taking swigs of Old Milwaukee and shots of rum.

The music from the VW van had stopped abruptly in mid-song, and the light in the bar went out. Nobody seemed surprised. The bartender lit a candle to light the bar in the back, and the patrons continued to drink, not missing a beat.

The big man got up off the speaker and put the LPs back in the van. "It gonna a be long time befoh the power come back," he told a couple of locals standing at the entrance of the bar.

"Wha?" one of them asked.

"Aubrey be off-island foh the week end. He de onliest mon who can fix de generator, me son."

One of the men nodded and said, "For true, mon."

"I gonna take deez speakers and my music and go to home," the big man said grinning, and loaded his speakers into the van.

A rusty truck with its right front quarter panel attached with bailing wire stopped in the middle of the narrow road, though there wasn't much middle. The driver used his left arm to wave in a downward motion as if to signal to anybody behind him that he was stopping for a while. He spoke through a wide grin to the large man loading up the speakers.

"Tiny, wha you doin?"

"Wha?"

"I aks why you quitt*in*?"

Two beater cars lined up behind the truck. Nobody honked or hollered. The driver of the beater truck didn't look back. A policeman stood in the park across the street and said nothing, laughing at the conversation between the driver and the man loading the speakers.

"Wha?"

"I aks if you quittin? You sell all dem records, me son?"

"Everyting okay, mon. Power gone."

"Gone fo a while?"

"Gone til Aubrey go to come back from seein' his woman on St. Croix."

"Fo true?"

"Yeah. No problem, doh. He be back tomorrow."

"You go to come back?"

"No. I gonna see my boys. Deh wanna learn to play de pan," the large man said and pointed to a steel drum on the floor of his van.

An attractive lady with color-coordinated running attire jogged past them.

"Okay," the driver said to the man loading the van.

"Okay," the big man replied.

The driver drove a few feet down the one-way road and slowed when he caught up to the jogger. He honked, startling the jogger, and stuck his head out his window. "Pssst. Where yo be runnin to? Dis is an islan." He laughed and drove on.

The lady frowned and watched the truck drive on. She turned her head around and looked to see if any more traffic was coming her way before she crossed the road and jumped down from a small retaining wall and onto the beach to continue her jog.

I was starting to understand the language—a little. I wondered, though, if they understood each other. They used, *Okay,* a lot—at the beginning of a discussion, at the end, and sometimes it was the only word spoken.

"Okay?"

"Okay."

"Okay."

A baby-blue CJ Jeep drove by occupied by two white guys who looked to be a little older than me. They seemed to be canvasing the people in the park. The driver of a small truck in front of the blue Jeep stuck his left arm out of his window, waved it in a downward motion and stopped to talk to friends. Two cars came to a stop behind the Jeep. I sat on my bag at the edge of the road near the blue Jeep and waited for the fight. Somebody had to be pissed off about traffic coming to a stop because of a conversation. Nobody was. Instead, they, in turn, greeted people they knew in the park with laughs and *okays*.

I heard a loud *thump* come from the direction of the park. Nothing seemed out of place, and no one else appeared to have heard it, but I saw a couple of people who had been sitting on a bench stand and move to another bench, looking at the ground next to the bench they had been sitting on. I looked up at the sixty-foot tall coconut palms and the coconuts clustered at the tops.

"You lost?" asked the driver of the blue Jeep, looking directly at me. He had curly, dark hair and a dimpled smile that made him look like a famous movie star from the sixties, whose name I couldn't remember.

I smiled and wondered if he had mistaken me for someone else.

His passenger was a rugged-looking guy who resembled Elvis, only blond, complete with a shit-eating grin, like he had just been caught doing something he had been told not to do a hundred times and knew he would do another hundred times.

He looked at me with his grin and said, "You look like a rookie. Need a ride?"

They were both wearing T-shirts and shorts and flip-flops, which seemed to be the uniform for most white people in the islands. I had noticed the same thing while passing through St. Thomas. The West Indians had more formal dress—long pants with a heavy crease and dress shirts for the men; flowered dresses and fancy hair for the women.

"I'm just looking for friends. They have a house somewhere on the island and invited me down a few months ago," I answered.

"Do they know you're here?" the driver asked.

"No, but they knew I was coming this week."

"Where's the house? What part of the island?" blond Elvis asked.

"Don't know."

"What are your friend's names?"

"Condon. Dave Condon and his wife Joan."

"Don't know them," the driver said.

"You need a ride?" blond Elvis asked again.

All I needed to do was find a place to park my bag, and then I would be able to travel a lot lighter while looking for my friends. The driver started a conversation with a local who had stopped to talk. Blond Elvis nodded to the local with an *Okay* and turned back to me.

I said, "I just need to find a place to stay. I heard there is a campground on the island."

"The campground is at Cinnamon Bay. We're headin' there anyway. You want a ride or not?"

I guessed it couldn't hurt to get a free ride to a campground.

"Okay, if it's no problem," I said, thinking how much this guy even sounded like Elvis.

I heard a very loud thump from the park again and looked over just in time to see a coconut bounce up a few inches before settling into the sandy mud.

I threw my bag in the back of the Jeep, climbed over the tailgate and sat on the metal wheel well. The cars ahead of us had moved on, but we remained parked in the middle of the road.

"Are you guys looking for someone?" I asked.

"It's tourist season."

I didn't know how to reply to that. They looked at each other and laughed.

The driver said, "The only places to stay are Caneel Bay, which has its own ferry, or the campground. The campground guests use this ferry. Every weekend new groups of ladies come to the island for a one week vacation. After a few days of mosquitoes and cold showers at the campground they're ready to leave. We introduce ourselves when they get here and tell them that we live on the island in a house with screens and hot water. By mid-week we go back out to the campground and walk the beach. We end up with a house full of girls."

Sounded like bullshit to me but maybe it worked. "Sounds great."

"That's not the best part," blond Elvis grinned.

"What's the best part?"

The driver smiled and said, "They're tourists. They always leave at the end of the week."

There didn't seem to be any young lady tourists wandering around looking for rides.

I said, "I think you missed them. I saw several young ladies on the back of a yellow surrey bus. It left a few minutes ago."

"Let's go," blond Elvis said to the driver, and we drove away, both of them waving and saying *Okay* to everybody they knew as we passed by, which was everybody but the tourists, who they greeted with an *Okay* anyway. I looked back up at the tall palms as we left the park.

"Those are tall trees. What happens if a coconut falls?"

"If you are standin' under it, you're in trouble. There's a guy on the island who climbs the trees and cuts off all of the ripe coconuts before they fall."

"I saw one fall, well, actually heard it fall, but I saw it bounce. It was really loud."

Blond Elvis turned around and said, "It's best not to stand under those trees."

We drove away from the dock, past Mooie's Bar and continued on a one-way loop that brought us back to the center of the village and to a road that led north. Cruz Bay consisted of rickety wooden shacks and clunky concrete buildings, none more than two stories tall, and all had metal hipped roofs. The structures were built so close to the narrow roads that there were no sidewalks. Pedestrians had to walk in the roads and move to one side when cars and trucks passed. Between many of the buildings and shacks was bushy jungle. Twice we had to stop to allow hens with broods of chicks to safely cross in front of us and duck into the bush. There was one stop sign in the village and three main roads, all paved. One led out of the village to the north. One led east and up the mountain and toward the center of the island. The third ran south along the bay and into a residential area before petering out at the south edge of the island. There were no alleys and only a couple of secondary roads that I could see.

The buildings of the village abruptly stopped, and the jungle started when we reached a steep hill several hundred feet from the village center. At the beginning of the steep hill on the right side of the road was a brown sign with white letters that read "The Virgin Island National Park." The well-maintained Department of Interior road was a narrow, asphalt-paved swath through dense jungle, with trees providing a thick, continuous canopy in many places. There were no cleared aprons on the sides of the roads and no guard rails. One hairpin turn was so steep I had no idea how the Jeep, or anything short of a goat or a tank, would make it up to the top. I thought that if you ever had to stop on the way up with a manual transmission you would never be fast enough to work the foot pedals without rolling back down the hill and would certainly fly off the edge of the road and dance through the trees, bouncing and ricocheting all of the way to the ocean, a hundred feet below. I was to learn later, via on-the-job training, that the trick was to use your emergency brake instead of the brake pedal. The emergency brake on just about every vehicle on the island was a hand brake between the two front seats. You could control the clutch and the gas with two feet and the brake with your right hand. It took a bit of practice.

I never learned why vehicles drove in the left lane in the United States Virgin Islands. Nobody seemed to know. It took time to get used to it. I found out months later that the real challenge was returning back to the US. It wasn't so much with driving, but, rather, walking. In the US, one tends to first look left, instead of right, when starting to cross a street. On St. John, you better look right first. During my first visit back to the US after months on the island, I found myself jumping back to the curb several times while almost being hit by oncoming traffic because I looked the wrong direction when starting to walk across streets.

Twenty minutes after leaving the village we arrived at a flat spot on the island and turned into a graveled parking lot on the beach side of the road. I noticed during the ride on the curving, steep roads the Jeep never saw anything higher than third gear.

We walked down a path with tall tropical forest on either side, so thick little sunlight shone through. A couple of mongooses frolicked near the path. Mosquitoes buzzed around my ears. A couple of minutes later I heard the muffled sound of heavy waves crashing on the beach. A minute later the jungle opened to bright sunshine, a fresh ocean breeze and a view of the Caribbean Sea and its multiple hues of blue. Large waves crashing next to us won a portion of the beach that curved to the south. The noise was deafening. I stepped out onto the soft sand and took my shoes off. My two new companions took their flip-flops off, and we trudged through the sugary sand and down the long calm part of the beach with smiles. Up and down the beach were small groups of tourists lounging on beach towels, including several groups of young ladies.

I felt the weight of my bag and said, "Guys, I'd like to put my bag somewhere."

Blond Elvis, smiling at a group of young women, pointed inland and, without looking at me, said, "If you want to rent a tent the office is just down that path."

"Great. Thanks for the ride."

"Okay," they said in unison and continued down the beach.

I put my shoes on and followed the path that the blond man had pointed out. A short walk through the dark jungle canopy led me to the main office of the campground where I rented a small tent for a week. I was given a map and found my way to a tent fifty yards or so from the office. There was a canvas lean-to with a small picnic table below it next to the tent. I opened the canvas flap of the tent and tried to adjust my eyes to the dimly lit interior. A torn screen was rolled up and secured to the top of the flap. I threw my bag on the canvas floor next to a small, sheet-covered cot with a blanket and pillow on it. Something skittered off the pillow. I walked over to the edge of the cot and saw what I thought was a scorpion. I had only seen them in books, but I was pretty sure that's what it was.

I left my tent and toured the area. There were several other tents hidden in the bush. I walked past a concrete structure that housed common baths and entered the one with the "Men" sign over the door. No frills there. No privacy doors and no hot water. I followed a wide, well-used path and found a small provision store. Beyond the store was the parking lot we'd parked in. I walked to it in time to see the baby-blue Jeep careen out of the lot with my two new friends in the front and three young women in the back. The women had big smiles as they left the campground, making me think that they weren't willing to wait until mid-week to find a warm shower and screened doors.

I walked back to the store. It had a little bit of everything you would expect to find in a campground provisioning store but more tropically oriented—lots of bug spray and mosquito coils. I looked at the price of a can of Off, which was three times more than I paid for the last can I had bought in the US. Everything was expensive, but I guess it was better than the alternative of no provisions. I picked out some beer and a sandwich to take back to my scorpion-infested tent.

"Are there scorpions here?" I asked the lady behind the check-out counter.

"No, de not be in here, me son. Bu dem could be in yo tent." She laughed. "Bu de d'own keel you. Jus sting a bit."

"Anything else I should know about critters and such that I might be sharing my tent with?"

She laughed and said, "No, me son." On my way out the door she added, "Jus watch out fo dem Jumbees."

I nodded as though I knew what she was talking about and started to walk out of the store with my provisions. Curiosity, or maybe fear, got the best of me. I turned toward the lady and asked, "What's a Jumbee?"

"Tis an evil spirit."

"Oh." I shrugged and turned back toward the door thinking more about her strange English than her superstitions. She had a stronger accent than the taxi drivers I'd talked to. Maybe she was from a different island.

"Yo best leave dem shoes outside yo tent while yo sleep."

I looked down at my tennis shoes, then to the lady and asked, "Why's that?"

"Cus dem Jumbees are real tall and have no feet. But de tink dat deh do. Sometimes deh spen so much time tryin to put yo shoes on dat deh forget all 'bout goin inside."

I responded with a weak "Okay" and then asked her where she was from.

"I from Dominica," she said proudly.

I hesitated for a moment and asked, "Is English your native language?"

She tilted her head, placed her hand on her cocked hip and, with raised eyebrows, said, "Of course, it tis. Yo got sand in yo ears?"

I left her shaking her head and walked back to my tent thinking about Jumbees and looking out for scorpions. All I saw were mongooses and lizards. When I returned to my tent I spent thirty minutes searching for the scorpion, which I couldn't find, so I sat at the picnic table and drank my beer. When the mosquitoes became a burden I retreated to the tent. I left my shoes outside and reminded myself to check them to see if they had been moved in the morning. I then unrolled the torn screen and secured it as best as possible against the canvas opening. I used the pillow to sweep any hiding scorpions off my cot and spent a sleepless night swatting at real mosquitoes and imaginary, I think, scorpions.

The sound of waves crashing on the beach in the distance woke me in the morning. After a swim I decided to go to town and track down my friends. The same yellow surrey taxi that I had seen at the dock when I arrived was parked in the lot next to the provision store. A few passengers sat on the benches in the back.

The same round face with a missing tooth and a baseball cap on it came out of the store and walked to the taxi. The driver introduced himself as Beaver and told us that he'd be leaving for town in five minutes and that the fare was two dollars per person. I handed him a couple of bills and asked him about his schedule. He told me that he came to the campground every hour about half past the hour with tourists coming from the ferry and returned to town thirty minutes later, in time to make the next ferry to St. Thomas. The last ride from town to the campground coincided with the last ferry from St. Thomas—seven o'clock at night.

I eventually found my friends dining at a restaurant in the village, and we spent the day and most of the night together, well past seven o'clock. It was more like ten when I told them I needed to leave. They didn't have room for me to stay in their small home and didn't have a car, which was a good thing because they were too drunk to drive. We all agreed that if I walked to the park near the dock I should find a taxi. I said my goodbyes and left for the short walk to the park. The taxi drivers had retired for the night and had either gone home or were playing dominoes in the pink bar. I walked to the entrance and looked in. Even if I could understand their broken English to ask for a ride, which I couldn't, I didn't think any of them were sober enough to drive the mountain obstacle course to the campground. I decided to hitchhike.

I walked to the north edge of town and up the steep hill to the only road that would take me to the campground. There was no moon and it was dark, so dark that a few times I walked off the pavement into the thorny understory of the jungle at the edge of the road. I found myself having to stoop over so I could see the yellow line marking the center of the road. I alternated between looking down to keep my eyes on the yellow line and watching for headlights of cars coming from either direction that could easily hit me as they rounded the blind curves in the road. It turned out that I didn't need to worry about any passing cars—there were none.

After an hour I heard a vehicle coming from behind and stopped when it pulled next to me. It was one of those little go-cart Mini Mokes I had seen earlier in town.

A thin, white-haired man probably well into his seventies leaned out of the Mini Moke, which put his head about thigh level, and said, "Looks like you need a ride."

I stepped into the Mini Moke and plopped down in the passenger seat. I felt like a Flintstone. My ass couldn't have been five inches off the road. "Thanks."

He was friendly, in an indifferent way, as though he'd seen this and people like me hundreds of times before. He told me his name, which I forgot, something Italian. Turns out he was the island doctor and was heading out to the resort on a call. He told me that he had been a medic in the Pacific during WWII and landed in the Caribbean after the war, trading doctoring for goats and, sometimes, money.

At the resort entrance he pulled over.

"Think I can get a ride to the campground from the resort?" I asked.

"You missed the last taxi. There aren't many people on the road this time of night. If you want to wait I can give you a ride back to town."

"No thanks, I'll take my chances finding another passing car."

"Good luck."

I got out at the resort entrance and started looking for the yellow line in the road. Not a single car passed by me. I kept walking. The sound of insects, or frogs, I wasn't sure which, was deafening. The mosquitoes were bad in some areas, mostly on the low parts of the mountains, near the sea, which I could only hear in the darkness. Still no cars passed. I started to wonder if Jumbees really existed. Three hours later I arrived at my scorpion den, where I repeated the routine of the previous night—shoes outside, screen loosely secured against the canvas opening and a quick sweep across the top of the cot with my pillow.

I went to sleep thinking this was the last time I'd ever stay at the campground.

Chapter Five

I awoke to the sound of heavy surf muffled by the fifty or sixty yards of thick jungle between my tent and the beach. I opened the flap and looked at my shoes, trying to remember what exact position I'd left them in the night before. I couldn't. I left them where they were and started down the well-worn dirt path to the beach barefoot. Three and four-foot waves crashed loudly onto the beach, where they quickly dissipated, the mass of water turning into a bubbly sheet that continued up the slight incline of the beach and, in a few places, made its way to the jungle. Tourists stood and watched, not willing to risk injury in the heavy surf. Fifty yards down the beach two local teenagers waded into surf, diving under three and four-foot waves until they were bobbing in chest-deep water. When the largest wave came in from the deeper water, one or both turned their bodies to shore and, with a timed jump, surfed the wave by holding their arms out in front of their bodies and allowing their torsos to ride on the mass of rolling water until it crashed on the beach. I'd never seen this before, and it looked like a lot of fun, so I ran down the beach and joined them. I never learned their names, but we laughed through a couple of hours of body surfing, each of us taking the brunt of more than one crashing wave and suffering minor damage to our shoulders and the skin on our elbows and palms as we were pushed onto the beach by tons of water that fell on top of us when we failed to crawl out of the way quickly enough to escape it.

Late in the afternoon I took Beaver's taxi to Cruz Bay. This time I brought my bag. I didn't know where I would stay, but a park bench would be better than walking back to the campground—unless a coconut fell on me. I spent the evening walking around and enjoying Cruz Bay and was surprised that the sound of the insects or frogs, I didn't know which, I'd heard the past two nights at the campground permeated the village as well. Mixed in with the cacophony of people, music and vehicles, it wasn't as deafening. I asked a couple of people who dressed as though they lived on the island what made that noise.

"What noise? What noise?" they asked in a staggered response.

I shrugged and continued down the middle of the road near the park with a cold Heineken in my hand and heard, "Hey, Rookie!"

I turned around to see blond Elvis coming up behind me in the baby-blue Jeep. He stopped the Jeep so that the opening on the passenger side was even with me.

"Who? Me?"

"Yeah, hop in. You can help me with somethin'."

I wasn't doing anything else and couldn't see that this would be a bad thing. After all, he had given me a ride to the campground a couple of days earlier. Maybe I'd get another ride back to the campground.

"Okay."

I tossed my bag into the back of the Jeep and settled onto an ancient seat on the passenger side. I felt springs on my ass and instinctively reached out to close the door. There was no door. There wasn't a windshield either. Or, rather, it had been lowered and secured to the top of the hood. Off we went—to where, I had no clue.

We left Cruz Bay on the same road we had taken the first time I'd been in the Jeep, the road on which I'd walked to the campground, and turned into the resort entrance where the doctor dropped me off the night before. Lights along the resort road illuminated manicured lawns and old plantation ruins on either side. The Jeep pulled into a parking lot near what looked to be the laundry and maintenance buildings for the resort.

"What is this place?" I asked.

"This is Caneel Bay. Come on," blond Elvis replied as we climbed out of his Jeep.

The sound of forest was deafening.

I started to grab my bag and asked, "Will my bag be all right here?"

Blond Elvis snorted and said, "You kiddin'? Who the hell would take it?"

I shrugged, left my bag and followed.

"Are those frogs?" I asked.

"Where?" blond Elvis asked and looked around his feet.

"*That* noise," I said and pointed to the trees. "That loud chirping noise. I've heard it every night."

"What noise?"

I started to wonder if everybody on the island was deaf.

We walked down a wide path that led beyond the maintenance buildings and into the more manicured public area of the resort. A light-green, stretch golf cart with four rows of empty seats behind the driver passed us on a parallel road. We entered an open-air lobby and bar that opened up on the other side to a beach and the Caribbean Sea and sparkled in the moonlight like a flayed disco ball lying flat on top of the water. Just beyond that, about four miles away, was the island of St. Thomas, which looked like the animated shape of a child's drawing that depicted a mountain rising out of the sea. At night the lights from the homes started at the broad base of the island and rose up the narrowing slope to the top, giving it the triangular shape of a Christmas tree decorated with white and yellow lights. I had to stop for a moment and take it in. It was an imposing sight—one that you always remember seeing for the first time and never tire of seeing; similar to the first glimpse of the Grand Canyon or of the nighttime view of the Mall in Washington, DC.

Blond Elvis had walked ahead. He looked back and said, "Come on, Rookie. I don't have all night."

"Why are we here?" I asked.

"I need to move one of my boats out to anchor. The wind's pickin' up, and it'll get beat to hell along the dock. I need you to follow me with my dinghy and give me a ride back here to the dock."

"Oh," I answered, wondering if he was concerned about my ability to operate a boat.

We walked the short distance from the lobby to the dock. A ferryboat was tied up taking much of the resort side. It was white with the name "Caneel Bay" painted on its side and stern in brown. Next to the name was the resort's logo, a squiggly double "u" that looked like the end of a cinnamon stick.

A big guy who looked like Santa Claus in a captain's uniform stepped off the Caneel boat and asked, "Hey, Captain Jay, you going out on a night dive?"

"Nah, I am takin' the boat to anchor. I hear the wind's gonna pick up tonight."

"Yeah, I'm waiting for the last guests heading to St. Thomas, and then I'm going to leave this boat in Red Hook. It might get rough here."

Blond Elvis had a name—*Captain Jay.*

Captain Jay led me to the end of the dock and a baby-blue outboard powerboat. The manufacturer's nameplate on the side near the stern read "Seabird." He pointed to a smaller dock built at a lower level on the opposite side of the ferryboat. Several dinghies were tied up to the dock, rolling with the fairly heavy waves and continuously banging into each other, competing for space.

"The one on the end is mine. That's what you'll take to pick me up."

I looked at the half-inflated rubber dinghy with a small motor attached to its stern.

Captain Jay nodded to the Caneel ferryboat captain, turned to me and said, "Let's go, Rookie." He jumped into the Seabird, started the outboard and untied the boat from the dock.

I stepped into the dinghy and just about fell into the water when it collapsed under my weight. I'd driven plenty of boats, but never a dinghy. I never saw one in the Midwest, but I'd driven plenty of aluminum fishing boats. This boat seemed to be set up similarly. After regaining my balance, I sank into one of the rubber pontoons. Captain Jay looked at me and shrugged.

"You comin'?" he shouted above the idling engine.

I stood up and pulled the starting cord. Nothing. I pulled it three more times then heard, "Prime the damn thing, Rookie."

I'd forgotten about the need to pump the ball in the line from the small gas tank to the motor. I squeezed it a few times and pulled the cord. The little motor sputtered to life, and I followed the Seabird.

We motored out to a buoy that was attached to a mooring. It was the only empty mooring I saw. About a dozen or so other boats were anchored in the bay, some on similar moorings. Captain Jay shut down his engines and stepped to the bow with a hook he used to gather in the buoy. I pulled the dinghy next to the Seabird and hung on its side.

After securing the anchor line to the bow cleat, Captain Jay climbed into the dinghy. He smiled at me and pointed to a larger, dark-blue, fiberglass-hulled dive boat tied to a mooring near the far shore.

"That boat over there is mine," he said and frowned. "What the fuck?"

There was a light on in his other boat and a dinghy tied up to the stern.

"Get me over there—now."

I motored over as fast as I could, dodging anchor lines along the way, those I could see in the dark. As we got closer we could see someone getting into the dinghy, readying to leave. He looked directly at us and took off.

"Chase him. Move it, Rookie," Captain Jay shouted.

Captain Jay turned to look at me, and I saw pure anger and tensed muscles that could do a lot of damage. I was glad that I was on his side, but I guess that depended on my ability to catch up with the other dinghy. With my limited experience and two of us versus the other guy's much lighter dinghy I knew it was going to be a challenge.

I thought that the other guy would speed to shore by the dock and turn it into a footrace. Instead, he weaved through the boats anchored in the bay toward the sea. In the pale moonlight, I saw waves crashing on the rocks near the entrance of the bay. If he went out into the open ocean it would be a long, wet trip to Cruz Bay, or wherever we were going—if we made it without capsizing. He turned back into the bay, and I followed as fast as I could.

"Goddammit. Faster! He's gettin' away."

I started to get the feel of the dinghy in the heavy swells that penetrated the bay, but how either one of us didn't fly out of the boat when I made sharp turns at top speed, I will never know. We weaved in and out of the anchored boats, passing areas we had just been, hitting our wakes, causing the dinghy to jump out of the water, the propeller cavitating in frothing surface.

The lighter dinghy put more distance between us and circled to the starboard side of a sailboat anchored closest to the mouth of the bay, its stern facing the sea. We had chased him around this boat twice before, and both times he had maneuvered around the stern and circled back into the bay, running up the port side of the boat. He rounded the stern, and I maneuvered our dinghy toward the bow and anchor line of the sailboat, planning to give the bow wide enough birth to clear the anchor line, which I couldn't see.

Captain Jay shouted, "Go under the anchor line."

"I can't see the anchor line."

"Just go close to the bow, we'll make it."

We skirted the bow, almost hitting it at full speed. The other guy didn't see us, and we had successfully cut him off. Rather than ramming his rubber dinghy, which would cause us to flip over, I planned to turn to starboard and bring the dinghies alongside each other. I saw it in my head as a kiss—but it turned out to be a crash, just as Captain Jay started to jump into the other dinghy. The collision catapulted him onto the man in the other dinghy, who had landed face down on the wooden floorboard on impact. I cut our engine and hung onto the other dinghy as Captain Jay straddled the man, grabbing both ears and repeatedly slamming his face into the wooden floor.

"Hey, he's done. You want to kill him?" I yelled.

Captain Jay's face showed no emotion. He kept pounding.

I was about to jump into the dinghy to see if I could stop Captain Jay when he turned the guy over, probably to make the damage he was inflicting on the guy's head symmetrical.

"Stu Black! What were you doin' on my boat?" Captain Jay shouted.

The bloodied face was too dazed to say anything. I found out later that it belonged to the man who owned the sailboat charter business at Caneel Bay. Most of the sailboats anchored in the bay were his. I would also learn later that Captain Jay and Stu Black were bitter enemies, though I never learned why. Nobody seemed to know except the two of them.

Recognizing his nemesis, Captain Jay's anger seemed to melt away, replaced with a smirk. He jumped back into our dinghy and said, "Come on. Let's go."

As we motored away Captain Jay shouted, "If you did anything to my boat I'm comin' for you."

I looked back at the bloody face in the other dinghy. The man wobbled to his knees. I was sure that he understood nothing Captain Jay had said.

"You going to call the police?" I asked.

Captain Jay turned his head to me with a big Elvis grin and said, "Hell no."

We went back to Captain Jay's big boat. I shut the motor down, and Captain Jay tied the dinghy up to the rail. He moved around the boat looking for anything missing or out of place. I continued to look around topside while Captain Jay went down below to check the engine room. We couldn't find anything out of place, but I couldn't be sure, I had never been on his boat. Hell, I had only been on this island two days.

On the way back to the dock I seriously thought about shortening my visit and returning to the US.

Chapter Six

"The human race has only one really effective weapon,
and that is laughter."
Mark Twain

Being a tourist in a tourist destination is easy. Being a resident isn't. Tourists notice things they're supposed to notice—other tourists, shops, bars, beaches, music and the indigenous locals—but they rarely notice the transplants who call it home. Those people blend in so well they disappear in plain sight, camouflaged in their environment. It's partly their dress, but it's mostly an attitude—confidence bolstered by a sense of belonging.

I learned this because, after the high-speed dinghy chase around Caneel Bay, I was invited to stay with Captain Jay and his roommate, Chuck, indefinitely, and I quickly made the transformation from tourist to local. One of the first signs was the unconscious decision of a more practical wardrobe. I traded my tennis shoes for flip-flops, my collared shirts for T-shirts, threw away my underwear and forgot about haircuts. A rubber band stretched around my driver's license, and a few bills became my wallet.

I'd lived at Chuck's house for a few months, and he never asked for rent, so every couple of weeks I bought provisions for the house. St. John was not a place where you'd find proper provisions. Grocery stores were limited. Two sisters owned competing stores in small buildings about fifty yards apart, one up the hill from the other. The stores might have had names on a moniker that hung over the entrance doors, but we simply called them Upper Smith's and Lower Smith's. They sold the same things. You could go for a week on the island and not see fresh bread or milk at any of the four small grocery stores, including the commissary at the National Park Campground. Forget fruit and vegetables. Nobody on the island at that time grew or sold them. There was always beer, as long as you liked Heineken or Old Milwaukee. Or Vita Malt, an unbelievably sweet drink loved by the locals that tasted like beer mixed with Aunt Jemima's syrup. There was salt fish, but dried local fish was always available. But it smelled so bad you avoided the section of the store where it was displayed at all costs even if it meant sacrificing what you came in for. Johnny cakes were displayed near the cash registers in all of the stores. They were fried bread pastries. When filled with mystery meat, sometimes labeled as fish or beef or pork, but always tasting like salty chicken, they were called a paté.

If you needed food not available on St. John, or if you needed clothing, other than tourist T-shirts, or if you needed a book or a US newspaper, you had to take the ferry to St. Thomas, *the big island*, to a real store—sort of.

It was time for me to go to the big island, so I walked down the hill to catch the ferry. I was early and sat on a park bench, looking up to make sure I wasn't sitting below any coconuts. It had rained heavily a week earlier, and the mosquitoes had sufficient standing water and time to go from egg to larvae to pupae to flying blood fiends. They were everywhere. Aside from bats, which only came out in the evening, one other animal on the island chased down and ate mosquitoes. They were little lizards known as anoles, often misnamed chameleons. They came in interchangeable brown and green colors and were everywhere. Several scampered around my feet. One eyeballed a mosquito that landed on my ankle. Instead of swatting the mosquito I waited to see what the lizard would do. It approached, stopping every few inches to cock its head to one side and do a few pushups. When the lizard was close it hopped on my ankle and ate the mosquito, licked its lips, cocked its head toward me as if to say *thank you* and bounded away to do another pushup. I scratched at the bite left by the mosquito and wished the lizard would have been quicker.

A tall, barefoot white man with broad shoulders and long, scraggly blond hair had walked up to one of the sixty-foot palm trees and peered upward. He carried a canvas bag and a machete and looked like Tarzan. Accompanying him were two locals in stiff, khaki shirts with "Dept. of Public Works" embroidered on the front pockets. Tarzan talked to the two uniformed men using the local vernacular English, which still confused me. The conversation stopped when the tall man dropped the bag to the ground, slung the machete over his shoulder using what looked like a strap made from thin jute rope and started climbing, using just his hands and feet. The men in uniform stood back from the tree and watched him climb. He made it to the cluster of brown-green coconuts at the top of the tree with little effort and managed to hang on to the tree with one arm while using the machete to cut away the coconuts one by one with the other, dropping them safely around the base of the tree.

My engrossment in the show of athleticism was broken when I heard, "Hey, Rookie. What's up?"

Captain Jay had stopped his blue Jeep in the middle of the road next to the park, waving his left arm to stop the small truck behind him.

I walked over to the Jeep and said, "I'm heading to St. Thomas to get some things. Who's the guy climbing the palm tree?"

Captain Jay looked over at the coconuts being dropped from the top of one of the trees. "That's John. Good man."

"He talks like a local."

"He is. He's one of the few white guys *bawn* here, *mon,*" Captain Jay said with a laugh. "He and his siblings grew up on the north shore."

"He looks scary. He's big enough to play tight end in the NFL."

"Probably could. Nobody else can climb the trees, and the island doesn't have the equipment to reach the coconuts. The government has been threatnin' to cut those trees down because they're afraid of a lawsuit when a coconut falls on someone. Everybody's pissed off that they want to cut 'em down. So they hire John to remove the coconuts when they're ripe."

I looked over and saw John climb down the palm tree as easily as he had climbed up.

Captain Jay said, "Listen, Rookie, I need a couple of things from St. Thomas. Can you get them for me? You can use my car in Red Hook."

"You have a car in Red Hook?" I asked and looked at the truck that waited behind the Jeep. Another Jeep had driven up and patiently waited behind the truck.

"Yeah, it's a Jeep like this." He reached into his pocket and handed me a key. "It's in the old shed across from the ferry. You know which one I'm talkin' about?"

I wasn't sure. I started to take the key and stopped. "But, wait," I said. "I don't know my way around St. Thomas."

Jay shook his head. "Jesus, Rookie. It's an island. How can you get lost on an island? Just ask any taxi driver for directions."

I wasn't sure about his logic but took the key, put it in my pocket and asked, "What do you need?"

"I need a black light. You can get that at a place called Lockhart's. Across the street is a bakery. I need some of those special rolls they make. The chef at Caneel is cooking for a party we are going to have and I need…" He counted the names from a list. "Let's see, there are forty-three, forty-four, forty-five, forty-six people coming. You had better get a couple extra. Make it forty-eight." He handed me his chicken-scratched list and asked, "You need cash?"

"No. I should be able to handle it until I see you tonight." I started to walk away from the Jeep toward the ferry dock. Captain Jay didn't move. He was hailed from the park by a tall, thin local man with a big grin. I looked behind the Jeep. There were four vehicles waiting.

After a couple of steps I stopped and turned back to Jay. "How much is a black light?"

"Hell if I know, Rookie." He reached into his other pocket and brought out a wad of cash. "Here, you'd better take this."

"I'll take some of dat, mon," the local said as he reached the Jeep.

One of the drivers honked. Jay turned around and sneered at the line of waiting vehicles.

"Fuckin' rude. Must be a tourist," he said to the local. They both laughed and continued their conversation.

I walked onto the dock as the ferry started its engines and wondered why Captain Jay trusted me with his car on St. Thomas. I boarded the boat and watched St. John grow smaller as we crossed Pillsbury Sound. I reflected on my limited experiences on the island so far and laughed. I had become familiar enough with the island and its people and had met most of those who wanted to be met. The local West Indians were always friendly. Many of the continentals weren't. I couldn't tell if they wanted to protect their privacy, or if they didn't want to befriend someone who they thought wouldn't be around long, or if it was that they didn't want any more continentals making the island their home. I suspected it was a combination of all of those things.

It was the names of some of the locals that made me laugh. The more ordinary were called by their last name. First names were reserved for the very few who offended no one and were revered on the island, or for those very few who were really bad people. They tended not to be around long.

The colorful names went to those who were truly special—and not necessarily in a good way. They didn't have the opportunity to name themselves. Their names came about by happenstance. Sometimes names were simply assigned by what the person did or looked like. One day somebody would make up a name with sufficient humor and rhythm to stick, and once christened with island names, real names were forgotten, if they were ever known.

There was Rowboat Wayne, who lived on a small cay a couple of miles away from St. John. He had built a teepee on top of the mountain of a small cay a mile from Cruz Bay and traveled to and from the island with a rowboat—no motor, just two oars. He was an aging hippie and looked the part, other than the huge upper body muscles built up by rowing several miles a day and carrying everything he owned up or down the mountain to his teepee.

Chainsaw Phil looked like he was an escapee from St. Elizabeth's mental hospital. Nice enough person, but with wild eyes and scars all over his arms and always wearing a white T-shirt that was torn in several places. Many times blood seeped through the rents in the shirt. The island was in a tropical thorn-zone. The more arid parts of the island, typically the south and east parts, were covered with impenetrable shrubs and small hardwood trees with names like casha bush and catch-and-keep, all of which had sharp thorns or zipper-like leaves that cut into your skin and never let go. When land needed to be cleared of its unwanted thorn population, several locals with machetes gingerly cut their way through the bush. This hard and painful work ramped up to a new level when Phil showed up on the island with his chainsaw. He would sharpen his chain, oil the bar and *bam,* relentlessly cut into the bush cussing and yelling with no regard to the thorns tearing at his clothes and body. Sometimes you could be driving down a road, and somewhere, hidden behind the thick brush along the side of the road, you'd hear a chainsaw and, above the noise of the chainsaw, Phil cussing and yelling all kinds of obscenities.

Mash Up was a local mechanic who drove the island roller coaster roads too fast and crashed, 'mash up' in local vernacular, everything he drove at least once. Chicken Wing Joe was an Asian who came up from Trinidad and sold fried chicken wrapped in foil from the side of a VW van. And there was Tommy No Legs. He had no legs. He got around a very non-ADA-compliant island with a wheelchair and introduced himself with a smile as Tommy No Legs.

The ferryboat lightly bumped the dock in Red Hook and brought me back to my mission—finding Captain Jay's Jeep and finding my way around the big island for provisions. The crew tied the boat off and we disembarked. I walked across the street to the shed where Captain Jay told me his car was stored. It appeared ready to fall at any moment. I opened the hinged wooden doors that faced the street and saw why Captain Jay trusted me with his car. It wasn't a car. It was an old WWII Willys Jeep chassis with a marine plywood body—just like the one I'd seen my first day on St. John. It didn't have doors or a windshield, let alone any lockable storage. With multiple stops I was going to have to strategically park to keep things from getting pilfered. Fortunately, after asking directions from a few taxi drivers before I left Red Hook, I learned that most of the stores I needed to visit were in the same area on the island, about halfway between Red Hook and the busy port of Charlotte Amalie. The decision I needed to make was to go right or left from Red Hook. I chose right—it's an island. A few circuitous routes later, I found the shopping center.

I was hungry, so I decided to go to the bakery first. I walked in and looked around. It was a normal Caribbean bakery, I guess, though this was the first Caribbean bakery I had been in. I pulled out the list Captain Jay had given me as I walked to the counter. The local man behind the counter stared at me. If I was waiting for a *May I help you?* I would be waiting forever. Not once during my time in the Caribbean did I get a *please* or a *thank you* or a *may I help you?* from any local behind a counter of a retail store.

"Can you show me your special rolls?" I asked, not knowing what they looked like. He pointed to a rack full of hundreds of heavy looking pastries that looked nothing like rolls.

I looked at the list and said, "I need, let's see…" I looked at the list again. "Forty-eight of those things."

The man looked at me for a long moment and said, "We only sell dem by de dozen."

I laughed. He didn't.

After we got the math straightened out I carried a very heavy bag of special rolls back toward the Jeep. I chomped on one of the rolls on the way. It was an extra I ordered, which confused the man to no end when he started tossing in another dozen and I made him stop at one. He couldn't figure out how to charge me, so he let me go without paying for the extra roll. I thanked him and received a blank stare in return. I can't say the roll was special, but it was sweet and gooey in the middle.

As Captain Jay said, the hardware store was right across the street. I carried the bag of rolls with me and walked toward the hardware store. A scrawny local man with a scraggly grey beard and a torn T-shirt was washing a car in the parking lot and continuously mumbled, at nobody special, nonsensical vernacular. I made the mistake of making eye contact as I passed.

"Yo mutterscunk. Wha yo doin here? Yo not bawn here."

Did he just call me a mother skunk? I wondered.

I smiled and continued on my way. Behind me, about thirty seconds later, I heard a loud, "Wha yo doin here mutterscunt? D'own be lookin at me, mutterscunt."

I guess another unsuspecting person passed by and made the same mistake of glancing at the bearded crazy guy. And I don't think he was calling me a skunk.

What the hell does Captain Jay want with a black light, anyway? I thought.

I entered the hardware store and walked up to a guy at the counter. Silence.

I smiled and said, "Hi. Can you help me? I need a black light."

"In da back row but we d'own have black. De onliest we have is yellow, red and blue."

Funny. I smiled. He didn't.

"Okay. Thanks for your help," I said and left the store, avoiding the crazy man. I started the Willys and drove across the street to the department store for my own provisions. I grabbed the bag of rolls and then set it back. Who in hell would want these funny looking rolls. I placed the bag of rolls in the back of the Jeep and walked into the department store.

Chapter Seven

"Travel is fatal to prejudice, bigotry, and narrow-mindedness…"
Mark Twain

Captain Jay glared at me from his favorite chair. "I can't believe you couldn't find a black light," he said. I was glad to see he had his Elvis grin.

"They didn't have any. They didn't even know what a black light is. Why the hell do you need a black light?"

"No big deal. Where are the rolls?"

"Uh, they were stolen from the Jeep when I stopped across the street to get a few things I needed."

"Jesus, Rookie. What good are you, anyway?"

My other roommate, Chuck, laughed from where he sat on the sofa nursing a beer. Captain Jay's girlfriend of the month was visiting for the weekend. She was a nubile beauty from Tortola, the daughter of the prime minister. Also visiting was Chuck's brother, who had come down from Alaska with a real pet wolf. This thing was just over a year old and looked like a lanky adult German shepherd and had a personality from hell. Chuck and I kept our distance from the beast. Captain Jay didn't.

Later in the evening Captain Jay and his girlfriend sat together on the sofa. The wolf decided to jump up next to the nubile princess and lay its head on her lap. All was fine. After several minutes of peaceful conversation, the princess got up to check on the rice she was cooking for dinner, leaving Captain Jay and the wolf on the sofa. Captain Jay couldn't help himself. He slid over and started to rub the wolf's ears, which he didn't look too comfortable doing. I was quietly counting the seconds until Captain Jay lost his face.

"Hey, Rookie, you ever been divin'?"

"Uh, snorkeling, but I am pretty comfortable in the water," I answered, warily watching the wolf stare up at Captain Jay as though he was ready to pounce.

"What are you doing tomorrow? I have a resort dive in the mornin'. Wanna come along? You can help me get them in the water."

Grr. A slight growl from the wolf.

"Uh, sure."

Captain Jay started to get up to help in the kitchen. Bad idea.

There was a very loud, *Grrrr*. Not a normal grrr, but a deep, primordial growl that resonated throughout my whole body. Captain Jay laughed and tried to get up again. The wolf stood on all fours on the sofa—GRRRRRR! Captain Jay sat down with a sheepish Elvis grin. It must have been killing him to have a canine get the best of him in front of his friends.

We sat and stared. Chuck's brother tried to call his pet over to him. The wolf wasn't interested, and Chuck's brother didn't seem to be in a hurry to force the issue. All conversation stopped. Just below the sound of the tree frogs and an occasional low growl from the wolf, I could barely hear Jay's girlfriend humming a song in the kitchen.

We sat with uneasy smiles. I'm not sure, but I suspect we were all thinking the same thing—what is the quickest and safest way to escape Cujo? A few minutes later the nubile princess came back and sat down next to the wolf.

"You are all so quiet. What's up?"

The wolf wriggled next to her, never taking its eyes from Captain Jay.

Captain Jay stayed on the sofa the rest of the night. He may have even slept there. For the next several years, as long as I knew Captain Jay, I never again saw him as intimidated by a person or an animal as he was that week.

* * *

The next morning I went with Captain Jay to Caneel Bay to prepare
the boat for his dive, Captain Jay waving to every car he passed. We
drove through the employee's gate and parked next to a shack full of
dive gear.

"Why do you need a black light, anyway?" I asked, still wondering why anyone would need a black light.

"A friend of mine down-island is sending me some currency he
printed. I want to see how real it looks. Load those tanks from that
fresh water well onto that cart and take it down to the dock. I'll be
there in a while."

Counterfeiting? What's next? I thought.

As I left I asked, "Do you plan on spending the money?"

"Jesus, Rookie. You some kind of federal agent or somethin'?"
he answered and turned to walk toward a large maintenance building.

I pushed the cart with eight scuba tanks down the concrete path
toward the dock, where a Caneel Bay ferry was loading stylish passengers. At the end of the dock was Captain Jay's larger dive boat,
the *Jumbee Jay*. It was a fairly non-descript utilitarian fiberglass
mono-hull, custom built for diving. There was a large hinged dive
platform, or dive tray, as we sometimes called it, at the stern made
of metal tubing. The boat had an engine room below the main deck
and a small cabin below deck near the bow. Its wheel was in a small,
partially protected center console, but a spacious main deck with two
large ice chests in its center was the boat's main feature. Captain Jay's
uncle John had built it up in Florida and brought it down last year.

Gizmo, Captain Jay's first mate, was already on board. He had
grown up on a neighboring British island but spent a lot of time on St.
John working for Captain Jay.

"Hey, Gizmo. How's everything on Jost Van Dyke?" Gizmo's
strong physique and disarmingly easy humor brought a smile to everybody he was around.

"Okay, mon," replied the hulking West Indian. "My grandfad-
der was caught wit one of his marijuana crops on da nort side of da

mountain."

"Your grandfather? What happened?"

"They destroy da crop, but everyting okay, he has fo mo crops der deh d'own know about," he said with a big smile.

We loaded and secured the tanks while the paying guests started to arrive from their beach bungalows spread around Caneel Bay's seven world-class beaches. There were four women and two men, mostly in their thirties and forties, wearing beach clothes and swimming attire straight out of Vogue magazine, the Caribbean travel section. They had completed the obligatory shallow-water instruction on the beach earlier in the week and were now going out on their first open-water dive.

Captain Jay followed them down the dock and made the introductions as Gizmo and I helped them into the boat. Captain Jay asked Gizmo to drive while he talked to the guests. I stood next to Gizmo and watched St. John shrink as we headed south. It was a perfect day—most had been since my arrival to the islands. I was glad to be along for the ride. I could snorkel around the boat while Gizmo and Captain Jay took their paying customers down to see the reef sixty feet below.

As Gizmo drove the boat to our dive site about six miles from Caneel Bay, just off a small cay called Little St. James, Captain Jay reviewed the underwater rules with his guests. He had an easy style—a mix of just enough humor to put the nervous first-time divers at ease and enough authority to let them know that this was his boat and he was in charge.

We arrived to a sandy bottom about twenty feet deep just inside the shallowest part of the reef, which could easily be seen from the surface. Gizmo nosed the boat into the wind as I stood on the bow with the anchor in my hand and looked down through the diaphanous water and tossed the anchor out over the sandy bottom. When it reached the sand I signaled to Gizmo, who threw the boat in reverse. With adequate scope of about five feet of anchor line to one foot of water depth, I placed the line through one of the bow cleats and held on until I felt the anchor safely bite into the sand, then tied off the line to the cleat.

Captain Jay told everybody to suit up, which basically meant mask and snorkel, fins, a buoyancy compensator vest, which we called a BC, and weight belt. The Caribbean water, particularly at depths less than ninety feet, usually didn't call for wetsuits. All six passengers and Gizmo started putting on their gear. Captain Jay waited until everybody had their gear on before he donned his. But the two women hesitated. They were nervous.

"Ladies, I need for you to put your gear on so we can have some fun."

"But I'm scared," one of the ladies said meekly.

"Look, there is nothin' down there that is going to hurt you. Keep your hands against your chest and don't touch anything. As I have told you, fire coral is the only thing that can hurt you, and it can't swim or jump or crawl."

Still hesitant she said, "But all of this gear. It's confusing."

"Rookie, come over and put on the extra gear layin' next to mine. Look, Sugar Puddin', this guy has never been diving, and he's always confused. He'll show you how easy it is."

"What size shoe, Rookie?"

"Eleven," I said, and he threw some size twelve fins toward me.

"You don't need any weight as skinny as you are. See if this mask fits," Captain Jay said and tossed a mask to me.

"Now watch ladies. He is going to put the mask up to his face without using the strap and breathe in. If no air comes in it won't leak. Okay?"

"Don't we need to spit into the mask and rub it around?" asked one of the ladies.

Captain Jay smiled at the women and pointed to Gizmo and then to the tanks. "We'll do that when you are on the dive platform ready to go. Rookie, go over to the platform and put on your fins."

I did. I stood on the dive platform wearing fins, mask and snorkel, and must have looked like a real diver. Captain Jay checked everybody's gear. Gizmo checked the tanks to make sure the air was on by pressing the spring-loaded flap in the center of the regulator mouthpiece, listening for a strong hiss of air to escape.

Captain Jay handed everybody a BC and gave instructions how to fasten it.

"Okay, everybody, blow just a little air into the BC. When you get in the water I want you floatin' on the surface. When I know you're ready we will raise this little hose above our heads and press the air out of the BC with our other arm. Okay?"

The other divers seemed to be comfortable and had no problem with Captain Jay's instructions. The two hesitant ladies were shaking even though it wasn't cold. Even I was starting to get a little annoyed with them. But I wasn't in their shoes. I wasn't going diving, I didn't know how. I hadn't even attended the basic instruction course earlier on the beach.

Maybe they shouldn't have come. Or maybe Captain Jay should simply let them sit this one out, but that would not work. This was his boat, and his passengers would do whatever the captain demanded.

"Okay Gizmo, get a tank on the rookie," Captain Jay said and then turned to the group and added, "Okay, I want you to see how the tank and regulator go on. The mouthpiece you breathe through will be on the right. On the left is this hose with two gauges that show the amount of air you have and the other is to monitor depth," he said and held up the hose. "But you won't need to worry about those. We'll do that for you. Just follow me and remember the hand signals. Let's all see the hand signals again."

He went through each signal as a Simon Says routine. Everybody did their best, except me. I didn't pay attention. I wouldn't need them.

"Okay, how are we doin'? Any questions?"

Nobody had any.

"You two doin' all right?" Captain Jay asked the two ladies.

To me they looked more frightened now than when we started. Even I was getting nervous wearing all of the claustrophobic dive gear.

"Rookie, go ahead and put your mask on and put the regulator in your mouth."

I did. It was a strange feeling, standing on a dive platform that was gently rising up and down with the seas, fully geared up as though

I was going to dive, breathing compressed air in and out through a regulator and wearing a mask that slowly fogged up. When I inhaled, I could hear the hiss of air as it passed through the regulator and into my mouth with a high pitch that sounded like a question, then abruptly shut off by the sound of a small, spring-loaded, plastic trap door slamming shut. Upon exhaling, I could hear the steady sound of air going out around the inner trap door with a lower pitched sound, as though it was answering the question asked by the higher pitched intake. I assumed if I were under water this would be the bubbles.

I couldn't see through the fogged-up mask, but I swear I could hear his Elvis grin as Captain Jay placed his open hand against my chest and shoved.

"You see baby cakes, anybody can do it."

What the…?

I was all assholes and elbows going into the water and distinctly heard the entire group laughing. I remembered wondering if the ladies had finally reached a comfort level.

As anybody knows from their first plunge into water wearing SCUBA gear, there is a bit of a comfort curve, depending on how you entered. The normal way to get comfortable is to start in the shallow end of a pool or in a few feet of water on a calm beach. Mine was more drastic. In the few seconds and what seemed like minutes, I stopped rolling around in the sea of bubbles but still sank. Painful pressure built up in my ears. I swallowed hard, and it went away—until I sank another few feet.

I wished I had followed instructions and blown into the BC.

Figuring out which way was up, partly by the bubbles floating that direction, and partly by the noise of laughter and Captain Jay's loud voice somewhere above me, I was able to stop my descent. My vision was still blurred by the fog in my mask. I noticed, though, that by violently moving my head in all directions, which must have made the fish laugh, the little bit of salt water rolling around in my mask cleared the fog off the lens. The water in my mask was a nuisance, but at least I could see. I could also hear Captain Jay's muffled voice above me and the sound of compressed air going through my regulator upon inhaling and then the sound of bubbles scrambling to the surface upon exhaling.

I looked around. Wow. This was a different world. The gin-clear water allowed me to see forever in all directions. Fish were everywhere. It was like swimming in an aquarium. No guppies, but wrasses, damsel fish, and clown fish and many larger fish whose names I would need to learn. I started to feel pretty comfortable.

Nobody came to my rescue, so I swam down closer to the reef. I could easily see the anchor line and followed it up with my eyes to the hull of the boat. It was at least eighty feet from me but seemed closer. I heard splashes of the other divers as they entered the water and looked up to see them floating on the surface, not rolling around encased in bubbles as I had been. It amazed me how much I could hear underwater.

I swam along the reef for a while and then back to my starting point, occasionally moving out over the deeper sea grass and sand. Other than the pain from the tank valve digging into the back of my head while I tried to swim horizontally, everything was great. Braver now, I started experimenting with my newfound weightlessness, swimming in tight loops and circles. I sensed something close to me and stopped the underwater loops long enough to see Captain Jay and his flock of new divers swimming over the reef. He motioned for the flock to stop as he swam closer to me. He put his hand out and made a circle with his thumb and index finger and looked at me questioningly. I didn't need a lesson to learn that hand signal. I signaled back the same way and resumed the underwater somersaults in my new weightless playroom. Captain Jay shook his head and swam back to tend to the other divers. Including Captain Jay, who led the group, and Gizmo, who brought up the rear, all of the people from the boat were in the water, including the two hesitant women.

I have no idea what Captain Jay saw in me that made him think that I would survive this without drowning, if he saw anything. But one thing was certain—I was addicted to this new underwater world.

Chapter Eight

"When the end of the world comes, I want to be [on St. John] because it's always 20 years behind the times."
Mark Twain

Later that week I returned to our house after a day in St. Thomas. As I walked through the door carrying provisions, Chuck's brother passed by me. He looked a bit harried. Chuck followed his brother out the door, and I saw Captain Jay sitting in his favorite chair drinking a beer.

I looked at Captain Jay and said, "What's up?"

"Chuck's brother's dog, or wolf, ran away this morning. Chuck and his brother are going to drive toward Coral Bay looking for the damn thing, and they want us to drive around Cruz Bay to try to find it."

"Okay. Let me put these provisions away first." I wasn't sure how we would find a wolf on a tropical island if the wolf didn't want to be found, but I was willing to help.

We drove down to Cruz Bay, waving to everybody we passed. Captain Jay pulled into Mongoose Junction parking lot at the bottom of the hill.

"Why are we stopping here?"

"I want a beer," he said and looked at me as if waiting for another question. "You going to ask that damn wolf to get into the Jeep if we find it?"

I thought for a short moment and said, "Right. I could use a beer. I'm kind of hungry, too."

We finished our beer and appetizers of conch fritters, pronounced *conk*, and walked back out to the Jeep. A flock of bright green parrots were perched on overhead power lines and trees near the road. *Squawk, caw, caw, squawk.* I had never seen parrots in the wild.

I looked at Captain Jay. "You have parrots on the island?"

Squawk, squawk, caw, caw, caw. There must have been thirty or more.

"I've never seen one here."

A local man walked by, staring up at the cacophony of squawks. Captain Jay waved at him, "Hey, Egbert? Have you ever seen parrots here before?"

Egbert?

The slim local man with heavily creased long pants looked back at us and said, "Sometimes, mon. De come over from Puerto Rico, stay for a while and go to come back. Last time I saw dem was twelve or tirteen years ago."

Squawk, squawk, caw, squawk.

They were loud and harsh with no rhythm or melody in their calls.

We hopped into the Jeep and found a parking spot near the ferry dock. The boat was due in a few minutes, and it was always entertaining to watch who comes and goes. Sometimes, if you arrive to the park just before the top of the hour, when the boat leaves for St. Thomas, you can see some of the island gentlemen give their girlfriends a goodbye hug, saunter over to Mouie's bar for a shot of rum and an Old Milwaukee chaser, return to the dock twenty minutes later when the ferry from St. Thomas arrived and greet a different girlfriend with a hug and a kiss.

We sat down on a bench with a couple of cold Heinekens and chicken parts from Chicken Wing Joe's VW van, which was permanently parked across from the post office, on the north side of the park. A young couple we knew who were longtime residents stopped to say *okay*.

"Hey, have you guys seen the parrots?" the woman asked us.

"Yeah, we just left them. They are down by Mongoose."

"Wow, they're beautiful. They were out by our house in Chocolate Hole yesterday. We heard that they're from Puerto Rico."

"Yeah, that's what we heard, too," Captain Jay replied.

They moved on, and I heard a few more *okays* as they walked and greeted other people.

Captain Jay wanted to walk through Cruz Bay—so we did. We were stopped by just about everybody we passed, with the exception of tourists, but most of them looked on with interest as Captain Jay held court every few feet.

Most of the buildings in Cruz Bay were old, hip-roofed wooden structures with corrugated galvanized roofing. No frills—no air conditioning, no fancy doors or windows, just open windows and wooden shutters. There were a few seventies-style modern concrete buildings, mostly government buildings—modern concrete minimalist structures that looked as though they belonged in Siberia, or in prison camps—designed by morons and paid for by fools.

We found ourselves next to a construction project behind a row of small shops on the main street. Carpenters were working late and building a series of wood decks in and around several large trees on a partially cleared jungle-covered lot in the middle of Cruz Bay.

Captain Jay asked, "Hey, guys. What're you buildin'?"

One of the shirtless, long-haired carpenters looked up from the tool chest he was filling after a long day's work. With his best West Indian accent he said, "Captain Jay, everyting okay? We buildin' a new bar, mon. De owner she want to call it de Backyard."

"I guess we could always use another bar," Captain Jay said with a laugh.

"When we're finished here we're going across the street to build a two-story building for Chicken Wing Joe," the carpenter said while taking off the leather bags belted around his beer belly. "Seems he has been saving every nickel he has made selling chicken wings and plans to build a real restaurant," he said, pointing across the street at an empty lot with a few tall trees and hibiscus bushes.

We walked down the street and nodded an *okay* to everybody we passed until we found our way to Fred's, a local bar restaurant and very limited grocery store. It was really just an outdoor concrete patio with a simple concrete structure behind in the back. The bar had a few folding tables and plastic chairs occupying the unfinished concrete floor. There was a kitchen hidden somewhere in the back, and next to the concrete patio was a small general store. The reason I knew there was a kitchen is because I ate my first Thanksgiving dinner there. Most places on the island closed down during hurricane season and didn't reopen until after Thanksgiving. Fred's was the exception. He was always here. No reason not to sell a beer or two. The menu choices on that first Thanksgiving were fish heads, complete with eyeball, a West Indian favorite, or goat stew. I couldn't eat fish eyeballs so I chose the goat, hoping it didn't come with eyeballs. It was boney and didn't taste like chicken. It tasted like goat.

We went into the bar and ordered a couple of beers. Sitting at the bar were three men the captain knew, all continentals.

The one closest to the door saw us enter and nodded to Captain Jay. "Hey Captain Jay, have you seen the parrots? Great to see parrots on the island, uh?"

We sat down. Two of the guys seemed interested in something Captain Jay was saying. The third guy looked me directly in the eye with a piercing stare and stuttered his way through an introduction.

"H-hi. Are y-you new t-to the i-island?"

I guessed he was drunk and didn't say anything, not really wanting to get into a conversation. He kept stammering. The more I tried to ignore him the more he stammered. I finally muscled my way through an uncomfortable conversation, careful not to make eye contact. Finally, Captain Jay said, "Let's go."

I smiled, more with relief than politeness. I was fairly sure the drunkard was looking for a fight.

Jay looked at the guy and said, "Hey, Tommy. Play dive tomorrow. Wanna come?"

"N-no, I g-got oth-other things t-to do. But th-thanks anyw-way."

"Okay."

We walked out into the street.

"Who was the guy talking to me? He was really drunk. Couldn't even talk right."

Captain Jay laughed. "He wasn't drunk, he stutters. Good guy. He doesn't like rude people, though. And he's a tough guy. Golden Glove boxin' champ and state wrestlin' champ back in the US. You weren't rude to him, were you?"

I looked behind us to see if he was following. Sure that he wasn't, I asked Captain Jay, "What is a play dive?"

"I forgot to tell you, we're goin' divin' tomorrow with some friends of mine from St. Thomas. They're all owners of dive shops, or were once. We go divin' together about once a month, and nobody has to babysit anybody. It's playtime for us. You ever been spearfishin'?"

My second dive and I'm going spearfishing? It sounded easy enough. I saw plenty of fish the first time that I probably could have speared. They swam right next to me and were a lot bigger than the perch and blue gill I grew up catching in Illinois.

With a lot of bravado, I said, "Great. Can't wait. What do we spearfish with?"

"I have everythin' you will need. We'll leave around seven. Let's get one more beer."

It was Friday evening in Cruz Bay, and there were a lot of people milling around—a few tourists, a lot of continentals, and even more St. Johnians; almost everyone with either a Heineken or an Old Milwaukee in their hands.

"Hey, Captain Jay, everyting okay?" we heard behind us. It was the voice of a large local guy I had met several times.

Captain Jay turned around with a big grin and shouted, "Irie!"

The big West Indian was walking hand in hand with a tall white lady who looked like a fashion model. I had seen her before, but we had never spoken to each other. She always seemed a bit aloof to me.

"Okay, Captain?" the man said, then nodded politely at me before turning back to Jay with a big grin.

"You betcha, mon. Looks like you're okay, too," Jay said, smiling at the tall lady.

She gave him a demure smile and didn't acknowledge my presence.

"I jus' checkin'," the local man said with a laugh. "Where are your girlfriends tonight?"

"They're all tired. I'm giving them a break while I show my rookie friend here the island."

They laughed and continued to walk up the street, stopping to join in with a group of locals huddled together laughing at something one of them had just said.

We walked past them. "Was that his wife?" I asked Captain Jay.

Captain Jay smiled. "No, the locals never bring their wives to the bars, only their mistresses."

"Do the wives know about this?"

"Yeah, it's all cool with them. They get a break from their husbands, who tend to talk a lot and loudly."

I had noticed that. Days earlier I'd walked to the ferry and passed a local couple arguing. The lady was mad but seemed to be keeping her cool. The guy just kept getting louder. As I passed them I heard the lady say, "You jus' bein' wrong and strong."

At the end of the block was another group of local guys whom we knew pretty well.

"Hey guys, what's goin' on?" Captain Jay asked and leaned into the group, putting his arms around the shoulders of the two closest.

"We jus' be limin', mon," Slim, one of the locals replied.

Captain Jay smiled and said, "I've got a new joke."

They all started laughing. "No, mon. No. Your jokes, dey jus be too funny. Hurts us to laugh."

"Why don't sharks eat you black guys?" Captain Jay started.

I couldn't believe he said that.

They laughed harder. So did the captain, who answered, "Because they think you're whale turds."

I stood back waiting for the fight that never came. They laughed even harder.

One of them stopped long enough to say, "Okay, I gots one fo you. How long it take fo a white woman to take a crap?" he said and waited for the laughter to die down.

Captain Jay said, "Okay, how long?"

"Nine months."

I laughed nervously and looked at the local guys, then to Captain Jay. Everybody laughed and slapped shoulders or knocked fists.

We returned to the Jeep and headed out of town to the house. The popular place to be on Fridays was Grunkies, which was recently taken over by a lesbian couple. They changed the name to The Eat Out, but everybody called it The Out. It was on our way home, and Captain Jay pulled the Jeep into the parking lot it shared with the recently built Mongoose Junction. We started to walk into the bar, which was nothing more than a big pavilion with picnic tables spread around on a concrete slab and a bar and kitchen in one corner. A small stage had been built at the far end, and two nights a week there was live music. The street had a public phone, and I used the opportunity to call my cousin in the US. I had not reported in for several weeks. Captain Jay went into the pavilion while I dialed my cousin's number.

"Hi Mike, it's me. I thought I should check in so you guys up there would know that I am still among the living." I went on to talk about the things I had been doing and about the island.

"What is that noise?" he interrupted.

I paused for a moment and then laughed. "Tree frogs."

We finished our conversation, and I walked to the bar to find Captain Jay, passing a few continentals on the way and pleased to get an acknowledgment from all of them. The more seasoned continentals, those who had been here quite a while, were not particularly friendly. They were polite, and I would have an occasional conversation with some but, for the most part, they kept to themselves and seemed most comfortable with other long-term residents and the St. Johnians. It was as if they had seen enough of us rookies come and go and had no interest in befriending short-termers. One of these characters I saw around town frequently was a very large barrel-chested man probably in his fifties. He had a military crew cut, beady eyes, and a fairly friendly smile, but you wouldn't mess with him—no way. I never heard him speak much but when he did it was in a quiet, gruff voice that was never excited or animated and everybody he talked to listened intently.

I entered the open-air bar and saw Captain Jay at the bar talking to one of the owners, who was tending the bar. It was fairly early. The live music hadn't started, but the place was filling up with locals and tourists and the typical array of island characters. Two couples sat together at a table not far from the bar and were enjoying dinner and a quiet conversation. One of the men was the barrel-chested big guy I had seen around the island. I skirted by their table and sat with Captain Jay at the bar.

More people came in, including an unkempt-looking tall, skinny white guy who was probably in his late twenties. He walked slowly past the big guy's table, staring at him. The big guy didn't seem bothered. The skinny kid was on a mission. He sat at the next table, which was empty, and, with angry eyes, continued to stare at the big guy, who seemed unimpressed. Another man, who was standing across the bar with a group of people and who must have known the skinny kid, walked over and said something I couldn't hear. The kid didn't respond or even look at the newcomer. He just angrily stared at the big guy. His buddy shrugged and walked back to his group.

Most people in the bar, including Captain Jay, were busy laughing and talking and were paying no attention to the angry skinny kid. I kept watching. The kid got up and walked the three or four feet to the big guy's picnic table and said something that the big guy responded to. I couldn't hear what the kid said, but it was clear the big guy told the kid in his quiet, gruff voice to leave. Instead, the kid sat down on the right side of the big guy.

I was sure that was a big mistake.

The big guy didn't even look at the kid as he rambled on about something. The other people at the table did. After about five seconds a big right arm with a big rigid hand flashed as fast as lightning and karate chopped the kid in the throat. If I had blinked I would have missed it. The big guy hardly moved and didn't even watch as the kid coughed and choked his way out of the bar, stumbling into the street. A few people saw the exchange but didn't seem bothered by it. More people witnessed the kid stagger out to the road, but nobody followed him. The big guy continued laughing and conversing with his friends as though nothing had happened.

I thought things like this only happened in the movies.

After a while the two couples paid their bill and got up to leave. Captain Jay turned around and acknowledged the big guy as he was leaving, "Play dive tomorrow Charlie, wanna come?"

Damn, I didn't want to be on the same boat with Charlie.

Charlie smiled at Captain Jay with his beady eyes. "No thanks, I have house guests," he replied in his godfather-like voice.

I thanked my lucky stars.

Chapter Nine

"Courage is resistance to fear, mastery of fear—not absence of fear." Mark Twain

The next morning Captain Jay and I drove to Caneel to get his big boat. We parked the Jeep and walked down the path to the dock and ran into the couple we saw in the park a few days ago who operated the snorkel concession at the resort and were on their way to work.

"Okay."

"Okay."

"Captain Jay, you going out today?"

"Yeah, gonna do a play dive. What kind of fish you want?"

"No lobster?" asked the woman.

Captain Jay laughed and said, "Too deep today for bugs. Big fish only."

I wondered what that meant.

The man laughed. "Okay, any fish would be good. My parents are visiting. They would like anything fresh. Hey, have you heard those fucking parrots lately? All they do is caw, caw, squawk and squawk. Can't wait for them to fly back wherever the hell they came from. Everybody's ready to shoot them."

I laughed all of the way down the path to the dock. Gizmo was on the boat, and we took the dive boat four miles across Pillsbury Sound to Red Hook. It was a great day. Calm seas, sunny, temperature was already in the mid-seventies and would only climb into the low eighties by noon, and I was going on my second dive.

We slowed as we motored into the bay at Red Hook. A ferryboat had just left the dock heading for St. John. There were many live-aboard sailboats anchored in the bay. Pelicans lined up like kamikaze divers and plunged into the sea, beak first, to grab whatever fish they had spotted from their lofty glide pattern above the bay.

We tied along the dock at Johnny Harm's Marina, which was full of large sport fishing boats being prepared for the blue marlin tournaments coming up in a few weeks. On the dock were four men carrying dive bags and spearguns. Captain Jay had told me on the way over not to tell any of them that this was only my second dive. Otherwise, they would all feel responsible for me in the water and not have any fun.

Introductions were made all around. They were a friendly but rough looking group, looking more like Delta force members than a bunch of guys on a play dive.

"Where we going today, Captain Jay?" one of the divers asked.

"Calm seas, I thought we'd go to the Banks," Captain Jay replied as we motored out of the bay and headed north.

"Great. I haven't been there yet this year. Better take our bang sticks along. There are bound to be plenty of teeth."

Bang sticks. Teeth. What are they talking about?

Captain Jay pulled out a nautical chart to show me where we were going. It was about twenty miles north and called the Barracuda Banks. I read the depths. The Banks were on the southern edge of the Puerto Rico Trench, which plunged to over twenty-nine thousand feet in depth. They were a blip on the chart in an expansive and deep sea. All around the Banks and for a few miles south the depth ranged from one hundred fifty to two hundred feet deep. A little north of the Banks was the Trench. Where we were going was just a ninety-foot deep dot on the chart in the middle of an ocean.

I was scared to death. Captain Jay noticed and grinned as he watched me register the depths on the chart.

"How many bang sticks do we have?" somebody asked.

One of the divers pulled out a short pole with an object on the end that looked like it could hold a shotgun shell. Another diver pulled out two longer poles that were thinner and had stainless steel cylindrical cartridges on the end with cotter pins stuck through them.

"That bang stick won't do any good. We'll be too deep. The powder in that twelve gauge shell will get wet. Then all you're going to do is smack the shark upside his head and piss him off."

What shark?

"I got these things up in Miami last month. They're the newest and bestest. They're powerheads."

He pulled the cotter pin out and unscrewed the round stainless cartridge. It was hollow and looked like the barrel of a handgun, but in two pieces. He pulled a long assault rifle shell from his bag and loaded it into one of the stainless parts, screwed them back together and replaced the cotter pin, which acted as the safety.

"I painted the primer and the shell casing with finger nail polish. That keeps the shells waterproof."

He loaded the other one and placed a few more waterproof shells in a bag he tied to his weight belt.

"Captain Jay, you get one and I'll take the other. If any of you guys have sharks trying to steal your fish give us a holler."

Captain Jay's shoulders bounced up and down as he laughed, seemingly seeing recognition on my face as to what *teeth* meant.

"How are you going to anchor over the bank?" I asked. It seemed like a logical question that maybe they hadn't thought of, one that would force the captain to head for shallower water and away from the teeth.

Nobody looked up from their preparation.

Captain Jay said, "Tell him Gizmo."

"I gonna drive de boat over top of you while you spear dem fishes," he said with a big smile.

Captain Jay pointed to the gear I would be using and told me to check it out. Along with the fins, mask and snorkel, there was a wet suit and a tank with the regulator already attached, and a weight belt with two square lead weights attached.

Captain Jay looked at me and whispered, "You need the weight because of the wetsuit."

Next to the tank were a speargun and a mesh bag. The speargun seemed understandable enough. It was a metal pole about three feet long with a handle and trigger at one end and a spear about the same length that rested on top in a groove and pushed back into a slot in the handle just above the trigger. The butt of the spear was attached to the front of the gun by very thin nylon rope that was double wrapped along the bottom of the shaft, making it about six feet long. The business end of the gun had two surgical rubber bands attached, each with a wishbone-shaped rigid piece of metal in the middle. The rubber bands were hanging limp at the moment, but to load the gun you stretched the bands back to catch two grooves on the top of the handle with the rigid wishbones. Once you pulled the trigger these bands gave the spear all of the propulsion it would need to reach the maximum length of the spear, line and gun combined. Theoretically, the spear could reach a target almost a dozen feet away from the shooter—theoretically.

We were a half an hour or so from the dive site and miles from land. Behind us I could still see the north side of Jost Van Dyke with St. Thomas in the distance. The seas were big and getting bigger by the mile. We motored past a lone pelican that bobbed in the water next to a couple of coconuts that had found their way to the middle of the ocean. Other than the neck and long beak it was hard to tell the difference between the pelican and the coconuts.

Captain Jay saw them and, with a laugh, said, "Looks like he found some buddies."

The other divers bantered and drank beer that had been stowed in a five-foot-long cooler on one side of the deck. Though they were, or had been, competitors, they shared the camaraderie of being the best divers in the area. They seemed to enjoy each other's company. I enjoyed being around them. Their easy humor gave me comfort.

Captain Jay hollered back from the wheel, "Everybody is going to carry their own bag today. We don't have any rookies to give that job to."

I looked around and saw a few chuckles. Nobody looked in my direction.

It was clear that Captain Jay was not going to cut me any slack but was helping me understand what I needed to do without exposing me. I now knew what the mesh bag was for and started to understand what I was supposed to do once we got into the water—I somehow needed to learn how to shoot the spear into a fish, remove the fish from the spear, place it in the mesh bag, and then swim around with a bag full of bloody fish while looking for more fish to spear; all of this without being eaten by a shark.

I wondered if I should bail on this dive. I could fake sickness or an injury.

Captain Jay and Gizmo watched for the blip on the fathometer that would indicate when we were over the bank. The seas were much bigger. Not choppy, but big, rolling swells coming from the Atlantic. I felt queasy while everybody else seemed fine—laughing, joking, and putting on their gear, getting ready to murder some fish. I followed suit, not because I was eager to dive, particularly after what I had just learned about the depth and the teeth, but because I was seasick and needed to get in the water to stabilize.

Because of my previous impromptu lesson I knew how to put on all of the gear, except the wetsuit, which I put on backward. Only Captain Jay seemed to notice and corrected me with eye movement and hand signals. I recovered and got all of my gear on and walked out to the dive platform carrying my flippers, the speargun and the mesh bag. I sat down on the deck with my feet on the platform and grabbed the speargun to load up the rubber bands. They were hard to pull back.

"Hey, no loaded guns on the boat," the diver farthest from me said.

"Uh, I was just checking the bands to see if they were old." I couldn't think of anything else to say.

"They're not old. I changed them a few months ago," Captain Jay shouted while wriggling into his wetsuit.

"Okay. We're here," Captain Jay shouted. Gizmo throttled back the engines.

I started to get seriously nauseous and stepped to the stern. Two other divers joined me. I put on my flippers and mask, put the regulator in my mouth, grabbed my speargun and bag, walked cautiously like a frog to the end of the bouncing platform and stepped into the blue.

A little water leaked into my mask, so I cleared it and sank about fifteen or twenty feet below the surface, clearing the pressure in my ears as I descended. I kicked my flippers gently to keep me in place while figuring how to pull the rubber bands on the speargun back underwater. I continuously looked around and below. The water clarity made for an incredible view. The visibility was forever. It needed to be—that's all there was, just blue water stretching forever in all directions. The loneliness I felt in that moment was deafening. Far below I could see the dark shape of Barracuda Bank. I tied the mesh bag to my weight belt, flipped head first and kicked downward. I felt a lot better. Every few feet I needed to pinch my nose and blow to equalize the pressure in my ears. I still hadn't figured out how to pull the stiff rubber bands back. There was simply no resistance under water. So I just slowly swam downward.

I finally heard other divers splash into the sea. Bolstered with confidence that other divers were just above me, I swam toward the reef, which looked awfully small. Except for the top of the reef, I couldn't see the bottom anywhere, just eerie, deep-blue water. As I swam down I noticed shiny fish spiraling up toward me. The closer they got, the larger and shinier they got. I thought they must have been tarpon.

Within seconds I was in the middle of these large shiny fish, and they weren't tarpon. They were silky sharks, all about six to seven feet long. I knew the kind of shark because I'd spent several hours at the Cruz Bay library learning all I could about the sea since my first push into it.

There were at least eight that I could see. They were shiny because of their smooth, silvery skin. In moments I was surrounded by seemingly non-aggressive sharks.

Above me, not only did I hear a loud *BANG,* I felt the concussion in my chest. I looked up and to my left just in time to see a six-foot silky spiraling back the way it had come, but not under its own power. Its head was at a strange sideways angle, and it was definitely dead. I guessed one of the sharks had become too aggressive. The rest of them scattered to the edge of our vision. They never bothered us again.

I was to see more sharks during the dive—a few Caribbean reef sharks, two small tigers, which keep their tiger stripes until they get much larger, and a thresher shark, with an upper caudal tail almost as long as the entire shark. They all kept their distance.

I arrived safely at the reef, which was comprised of large coral heads the size of Volkswagens, with all kinds of nooks and crannies for fish to hide. I heard a sharp noise to my right and looked over to see Captain Jay's spear halfway through a large tiger grouper. The fish was thrashing against the spear so hard I could feel the vibrations in my chest.

Captain Jay motioned for me to come over and help him. He held the mesh bag toward me as I swam to him. I held my speargun under my right armpit, took his bag and held it open as best I could. Jay held the fish and the spear at the same time. The spear gun hung from the line attached to the spear. The stainless steel spear tip had two spring loaded barbs on either side, which, if fully penetrated to the other side of the fish, sprung open and locked the fish on the spear as it thrashed. To remove the spear, the barbs could be squeezed against the spear shaft and kept in place with a small washer that slid up the spear and around the barbs, allowing the diver to slide the spear out of the fish. This is exactly what Captain Jay did. He held the spear in one hand and the fish by the gills in the other. As I kept the bag open he placed the still very much alive fish into it. He looked directly at me and managed a bubbly "Okay?" through his mouthpiece. I didn't know what he was asking, so I nodded my head yes and he let go of the fish, which immediately swam back out of the bag and limped out into the blue, where it would become lunch for a larger fish.

A bubbly "You fuckin' Rookie" emerged from around Captain Jay's mouthpiece.

I got it now. I was supposed to be ready to close the bag as quickly as possible so the fish couldn't escape.

Captain Jay looked sufficiently pissed as he started to reload his speargun. I was wondering if this wouldn't be a good time to swim back up to find Gizmo and the safety of the boat. I watched how Captain Jay placed the butt of the gun in his gut and grabbed the rubber bands one by one and pulled them back to place the wishbones in their respective grooves.

When Captain Jay didn't shoot me I handed his bag back and loaded my own gun just as I saw Jay do it. Captain Jay smiled, shook his head and swam off to find another fish.

I had read somewhere about how buddy diving was critical for diver safety, but there was no buddy diving on this trip. It was a free-for-all. I would occasionally see bubbles from other tanks float up over distant coral heads, and I could hear the spears as they left the guns, but the reef was a lot larger than it looked from above, with thousands of holes for fish to hide in. It was truly an amazing place and an easy place to lose track of a partner.

I eventually shot my first fish, a twenty-pound dog snapper that was staring at me with its two menacing canine teeth from the back of a huge hole in the coral. I even managed to bag it successfully. There were big fish everywhere. I frequently looked behind me to make sure a shark wasn't going to sneak up and take a bite out of my ass while my head and upper body were buried under a coral head. I saw more shark tails than heads. It was as if the shark had already seen the clumsy human and, having no idea what this rather large, ugly animal was or why it hadn't skirted away like normal prey, probably thought it might be an equal adversary. They preferred wounded fish that couldn't bite back. But the more thrashing fish we speared, the braver, or hungrier they became. Toward the end of the dive more sharks swam leisurely through our group, fortunately without incident.

Besides the sharks and the thousands of reef fish swimming in and out of the coral heads, schools of fry would swim by overhead, darkening parts of the reef like a cloud over fields of wheat. Swimming through them in search of a meal, in sets of three, were yellow tail snapper and amber jacks. Barracuda were everywhere, loitering solo or in random groups, waiting for any of our speared fish to escape.

I was able to bag two more fish, a tiger grouper and a black grouper, which was the largest and gave me the most trouble. We had been under about thirty-five minutes, and I still had about one thousand pounds of air. The plan was to regroup at the top of the reef after thirty minutes of diving. Captain Jay had given me a large titanium dive watch to wear so I could keep track of time, and I struggled with my bloody bag of fish toward the rendezvous area. I kept my speargun loaded as a precaution against sharks, not that I wanted a three-hundred-pound shark on the end of my gun, but it gave me comfort to hold something between me and sharp teeth. I looked back at the bag and saw a milky-green trail. It made no sense to me at the time. Later I learned that the color red loses its reflective powers before all others under water, as the sunlight dissipates, and becomes green. I had been looking at a blood trail.

I made the rendezvous safely and waited for the other divers to arrive, which they did in moments, all with bags full of fish and milky-green trails. Barracuda were trailing all of us, like stray dogs following tourists, hoping for a scrap of food. We ascended slowly, and I could hear engine noise above us. We surfaced to see the boat bouncing up and down in the large swells, the dive platform impossibly attainable. I wondered how this was going to work.

Gizmo grabbed the bags and guns as the dive platform rose and then smashed on the surface in rhythm with the large swells. Captain Jay removed his weight belt and tank and handed them, one at a time, to Gizmo through the bucking seas. Then, with perfect timing, using the downward motion of the boat as it dropped from the crest of a swell, he placed both palms on the edge of the dive platform and propelled upward, spinning around and landing firmly on his ass as the next swell took the platform a few feet out of the water. You wouldn't have found this dive on any tourist brochure.

Each of us repeated the maneuver until we were safely on board. Once situated on the boat, we opened the cooler and headed to St. Thomas, sharing fish stories the entire trip. In this case, it was impossible to exaggerate. Captain Jay broke the news that I was a rookie, and that this was only my second dive. The other guys didn't seem too surprised. I suspect a couple of them noticed before we entered the water. Nobody bitched. They even happily shared Captain Jay's name for me—Rookie. I guess I passed the test... this one anyway.

All of the fish we speared would find their way to the dinner table. What we couldn't eat we offered to locals, who accepted with big smiles and sometimes a *God bless you.*

Chapter Ten

"Sanity and happiness are an impossible combination."
Mark Twain

As time passed for me on the island, every day seemed like the last, with no mystery about the next one. Tourists came and went. To the locals I would say *okay* at least fifty times a day. There was more diving and more socializing in Cruz Bay. Our carpenter friends finished the Back Yard Bar, which quickly became a popular hangout on the island. More homes were built, and an army of new island residents, mostly carpenters, seemed to pop up from nowhere to help fill the labor void on the island, which was significant. The busiest place on the island was still the ferry dock at seven a.m. and four p.m. The majority of the labor force still came from St. Thomas.

Chicken Wing Joe had finished his two-story, non-descript, concrete building across from the Back Yard. He abandoned his VW van and moved all of his chicken parts to the lower floor. Rumor was that he was going to open a Chinese restaurant on the second floor. We needed another restaurant. Other than Fred's and Ric's Hilltop and another rumor of a restaurant opening soon in Mongoose Junction, there wasn't much on the island.

The Hilltop was not actually on the top of the hill. It was halfway up, which was a good thing, particularly if walking, because this hill was really steep. Eric, the owner of Hilltop, was the first local to greet Lawrence Rockefeller when he sailed into Caneel Bay in the early fifties, which, at the time, was a small cottage rental business set up on an abandoned sugar cane plantation. Eric was the cook and manager. After Rockefeller bought the bay and the business Eric moved to Cruz Bay and opened Ric's. He did it all: woke early each morning to take his boat out to catch the yellowtail snapper, his specialty, prepared and cooked the fish, waited tables, served the food, worked the cash register and cleaned up afterward. He was Mr. Quality Control. Some nights calypso music from a steel drum was masterfully played by Tiny, who, as you could guess, was as big as a refrigerator. He also sold records from his orange VW van near the Cruz Bay Park on weekends, sometimes competing with Big Lou Sewer, who set up a record store in a brown VW van parked on the opposite side of the park.

We looked forward to the possibility of two new restaurants. The only other restaurant on this side of the island was at Caneel Bay, and it had a dress code. T-shirts, shorts and flip-flops, the unofficial uniform for all continentals on the island, were not allowed at night. It was coat and tie territory. We all had long pants, mostly to wear on the occasional trip to the US during the cold months, but none of us had a sport coat. Finally, somebody brought a sport coat down from the US, and we simply passed it around as needed.

"Hey, I was invited to Caneel tomorrow night. Who has the jacket?"

"I think Tommy was the last one to use it. Call him."

And so it went until somebody lost the damn thing.

* * *

I graduated from being Jay and Chuck's roommate when I received a call from the US one night from my friend who was having his house finished and expanded. But he had fired the contractor for cutting down a palm tree.

"Hey, Condon, how are you doing?" I answered after he said my name.

"Good. I need to finish my house so I can visit for a week or so next winter. Can you do it?"

I had no construction experience. I came from a bridge-building family in the Midwest, but other than a few minutes sitting on my grandfather's lap while he operated one of his cranes, I had never spent any time learning the business.

I laughed. "I don't know how to build a house. Maybe I should practice with a dog house."

"Dammit, you know I don't have a dog. Look, how hard can it be? Just hire some of the local carpenters and watch over them. Call me when you need money. The house is only livable for two people. I want to add on to it. You can stay in the house when I am not there and in the new section after you finish."

I thought for a minute. I did need to start making some money, and having my own place would be good. Captain Jay was always charming any girl I brought to the house right out of my grasp. If he didn't, Chuck did.

"Maybe," I responded, hesitantly. "I don't have a vehicle. How am I going to pick up materials and workers?"

"Find a cheap truck and I'll send money."

As close friends and mentors, Condon and his wife, Joan, meant a lot to me. They immediately bolstered my confidence by trusting me to do something for them that I had no experience with. If they thought I could build their house, then I would build their house.

I was almost afraid to ask the next question. "How much do I get paid?"

"I was thinking five-hundred a month."

Being the stupid rookie, I replied, "Okay."

"Great. What is that noise in the background, anyway?"

"What noise?"

* * *

Later that night I heard the phone ring and Captain Jay's voice as he answered. He said a few things I couldn't make out and hung up. He came to my room, opened the door and said, "Come on, Rookie. We have to go save a boat."

A tropical storm was passing a couple of hundred miles to the south, and the weather was pretty bad. We drove to Caneel and Captain Jay's boat. On the way he had explained that Mary McQuin had called him using WAH ship-to-shore radio. Before cell phones, not only did we have more peace and quiet in restaurants and movie theaters, but if you needed to make a call from a boat to a land line, you would call the regional marine radio operator, in this case WAH on St. Thomas, and the operator would patch you into a land line.

"McQuin is off-island buyin' supplies for their restaurant at Mongoose. His wife, Mary, is on board by herself, and she's draggin' anchor," Captain Jay explained.

We used *Rumpled Foreskin* to get out to the boat, which was not an easy task. The winds were strong and the seas were big. If we went too fast the wind would catch the underside of our bow as we crested each wave and threaten to turn us over. We untied the dive boat from its mooring, replaced it with the dinghy and struggled through the rough seas to Hawksnest Bay, where the McQuin's Swan 38 sailboat was anchored. She was only about fifty feet from hitting the rocks at the mouth of the bay. Captain Jay pulled alongside and as close as he could.

"Rookie, you're gonna to have to jump," he shouted over the wind and crashing waves.

"I am?"

"Next swell I'm gonna turn hard to port and gun it. Stand on the side and hold onto our roof. The Swan will be at the bottom of the swell first. When the stern swings toward her and you're higher than the Swan, jump. You'll make it."

"I will?"

He did what he said he would do and I made it to the Swan, landing hard on the deck. Mary had already started the engine, and we motored forward into the seas to pick up her anchor and move the boat farther into the bay. This went without a hitch. Captain Jay carried her second anchor out and dropped it the same distance from the Swan and about one hundred feet from the other anchor, which would ensure that the boat wouldn't drag again.

"You should be good for the night. The storm has moved to the west and won't be turning north. Do you want us to take you to shore anyway?" asked Captain Jay.

"No, I'll stay with the boat. If the wind picks up any more, I'll call, but I should be fine. Thanks."

This was the second rescue I had gone on with Captain Jay in as many weeks. The first one had also been a late-night call, but from shore. A local man was waiting for his wife and daughter to arrive from St. Thomas. They were late. There was no storm that time.

Captain Jay and I had gone into Cruz Bay to meet the husband and get more information. Jay had his boat tied along the Creek for the night. The Creek was a second, smaller bay adjacent to Cruz Bay and the home of the National Park Service headquarters and the Bulkhead, the unofficial name for the concrete wall in the Creek where barges off-loaded containers of building materials or sand and gravel. It was called the Creek because it was where a major watershed dumped into the bay from the top of the closest mountaintop. The seasonal rain runoff had carved a ravine, or a gut, as they were called on the island, through the volcanic rock as gravity pulled the water down to the sea. There were many guts on the island. They resembled dry creek beds in the dry season and made great hiking trails. During the rainy season they filled with hundreds of tons of gushing water.

We parked on the Bulkhead next to the boat. The husband was waiting.

He hurriedly explained, "Charlie Kline used my boat today to go into Charlotte Amalie. He was to pick up my wife and daughter, who had been visiting the US. They were going to meet Charlie at the waterfront instead of going all the way out to Red Hook. They called about three hours ago and said they were on their way."

Captain Jay looked puzzled. "Seas are calm, not much wind. They should have been here over two hours ago. Okay, Rookie, let's go."

We retraced the typical St. Thomas waterfront to St. John route in reverse. With the help of the powerful spotlight Captain Jay had installed on his boat and his knowledge of local currents, we found the boat drifting well past Cow and Calf, a popular dive spot on the southeast side of St. Thomas. Cow and Calf were two small rocky islands that jutted up out of the ocean, becoming hazards to passing boats in bad weather. The light shone on Charlie, who was climbing into the boat wearing the black Speedo we had all seen him in so many times while swimming and walking the beaches close to Cruz Bay.

"What the hell is he doing in the water?" I asked Captain Jay.

"Who knows, but I'll bet the sharks swam away when they saw his big shape."

Charlie and his passengers were seasoned island residents and didn't seem too concerned about their predicament, but were glad to see us. Who knows how far they may have drifted before daylight and another chance of rescue.

We moved them to our boat and towed the smaller vessel back to the Creek. Charlie Kline, the big guy with the beady eyes and no stranger to trouble, explained that the boat's battery quit as they were passing the rocks, and the current was going to take them dangerously close. Charlie went overboard with a line tied to the bow and tried swimming the boat on a different path so they could safely drift past the rocks. He wasn't making headway and yelled back at the mother and daughter in the boat to find anything they could hold up in the wind that might act as a sail. They opened one of their suitcases and pulled out bed sheets they had bought in the US. They each held onto an end of a sheet, placing it where it would catch the most wind. Charlie continued to swim. They somehow skirted the rocks and were drifting past them when we showed up. Everybody laughed as he told the story, and we motored back to St. John.

In both boat-saving instances Captain Jay asked for and expected nothing in return. And nothing was offered except a sincere "thank you." It was as though the entire island knew that it could rely on Captain Jay when needed.

* * *

Some weeks later, settled into my new house-sitting job and trying to figure out how I was going to finish building the house with absolutely no previous experience pounding nails, Captain Jay came by in his baby-blue Jeep.

"Hey, Rookie, we're goin' over to Red Hook for gas."

"What's wrong with the gas station here?" I asked him.

There was one gas station on the island, but it occasionally ran out of gas. It had been recently taken over by a local man after the three continentals who built it went broke. You'd think that a single gas station on an island with a few hundred cars would be a gold mine. But this was a small, friendly island. Everybody knew everybody. Each of the partners had been giving gas away to their friends without the other's knowledge. They were constantly running out of fuel and, by giving their profits away, closed down after a year.

"We're gonna do some surfin' on the way over," Captain Jay informed me as I climbed into his Jeep.

"I've never surfed. There weren't many big waves in the Midwest."

Jay grinned and said nothing.

Gizmo and Scott, the new divemaster Captain Jay had hired from one of his competitors on St. Thomas, were on the boat, along with about twenty, empty, five-gallon jerry jugs.

"Okay," I said and nodded at them.

"Okay, okay," came back at me in unison.

We headed north toward Carval Rock, a nasty looking, two-acre rock outcropping with nearly vertical jagged sides that reached a hundred feet above the ocean. When the seas were high, huge swells rolled in from the Atlantic, crashing against the rock's north side. For hundreds of thousands of years the rock deflected everything the sea could throw at it. Even when calm, the underwater currents were notoriously wicked. But, when conditions were perfect, the imposing mass of rock could be one of the best and most active dive spots around. Active meant lots of animals.

This day it was rough, and there seemed to be a strong current running south.

Captain Jay told Gizmo, "Take us around to the north side. We'll drop in, and you come around the south to pick us up."

"Okay, mon."

"Rookie, put your scuba gear on."

"I thought we were going to surf."

"We are," Captain Jay said with a laugh. "Under there." He pointed to the rock.

Another way to get killed, I thought.

Carval had a water-carved passage that ran more than one hundred feet through the rock underwater north to south. It was a cavernous tunnel about fifty feet high and just as wide. Perfect for extremely strong currents to shoot through the passage north to south, and twelve hours later, south to north. It was called *the cut* and now was as strong as the current would get all day.

The three of us had our gear on. No BC and no wet suit, this was going to be a very quick dive. Captain Jay barked orders as we stood on the platform. "Okay, we go in together but don't get too close. Try to steer to the middle."

"Steer what?" I asked, having no idea what I was in for.

Captain Jay stepped off the platform holding his mask in place as he entered the water. Scott and I followed. There was no swimming. As soon as we sank close to the cut the current shot us into it at an amazing speed. I kicked hard, trying to stay away from the jagged rock walls the best I could. Hitting one at the speed the current took us would hurt. I heard a muffled metal clank against rock and somebody shouting through a regulator. I looked up in time to see Captain Jay bounce off the wall about fifteen feet ahead of me.

I was horizontal and moving forward like a rocket. Captain Jay, now vertical and recovering from his crash, was in my path. I knew what was coming—he didn't. His back was to me. I held out my arms and tried to hit him somewhere that wouldn't do too much damage, but I didn't have much control. I smashed into the back of his head and bounced up over the top of him. I tried to look back, but that was impossible without my mask coming off. I could turn my head far enough to see wide-eyed Scott fighting his own battle trying not to smash into the other side of the passage.

Almost as soon as we started it was over. We were shot out of the other side like cannon balls and then immediately slowed as we surfaced. Scott and I both held an arm up as we surfaced so we didn't accidentally crash into the hull of the boat that we knew was bouncing in the waves above us, moving with the southern current about the same speed as us. There was no way we could turn around and swim against the current to see what had happened to Captain Jay. We surfaced and swam to the platform and hung on to the bouncing aluminum frame as best we could while scanning the sea behind us for the captain.

Gizmo looked at me and asked, "Where's Jay?"

As soon as he asked, a maskless head popped up about thirty feet from us with an Elvis grin. Captain Jay had survived—kind of. He swam toward us with a one-armed dog paddle. After handing Gizmo our gear, Scott and I climbed onto the dive platform and reached back to grab Captain Jay's gear—a tank with regulator, a weight belt, one fin and no mask. We helped Captain Jay into the boat. His right shoulder was a bloody mess, his right knee was no better and he complained about a sore neck.

"Which one of you ran into me?" he asked while turning his head in an effort to lessen his neck pain.

I changed the subject as quickly as I could and asked, "Do we need to get you to the clinic?"

"No, we have a first-aid kit on board. I'll patch the cuts up," Jay said and slapped me on the back. "Good clean fun, uh, Rookie? Nobody got an eye poked out or anythin'."

I looked at his shoulder and knee, both looking like the top of a tomato pizza, and said, "Right."

* * *

We drove the boat to Red Hook and filled the jerry jugs at Johnny Harm's Marina, riding low in the water all the way back to Cruz Bay. We unloaded most of the jerry jugs onto the Cruz Bay dock and left them there. Their owners knew we would be back sometime in the afternoon. The jugs would be there when we arrived, that night or the next day. Nobody who lived on the island bothered other people's things. Sometimes, very rarely, a passing boat from somewhere down-island sailed into the bay during the night and stole whatever they could carry from unoccupied boats and homes around the village. But they were usually caught, not by the authorities but by a collection of islanders who had a variety of special talents and tools—pilots, ex-mercenaries, fast boats, and locals with families on other islands who were a phone call away with valuable information about new boats sailing by or entering their harbors.

We drove Captain Jay's boat back to Caneel with the remaining half-dozen jerry jugs. Captain Jay told me that we were going to drive them out to Coral Bay, so we loaded them into the Jeep and headed out on the scenic north shore road to Coral Bay.

We drove past Trunk and Cinnamon Bay, where I had stayed a couple of nights more than a year earlier. The drive was spectacular—canopies of overlapping palm fronds blocking out the sun as we drove beneath them, lush jungle with an occasional donkey or two standing on the roadside and huge dark brown adobe-looking mounds in the crooks of trees, which were termite nests and the reason why the island never experienced forest fires. The termites consumed all available tinder. All around us on either side of the road were jungle scenes that reminded me of photos in the *National Geographic* magazines from my youth.

We drove uphill to the center of the island and intersected Centerline Road, which would take us back down the mountain into Coral Bay. We arrived in Coral Bay and dropped off the jerry jugs at the Sputnik Bar, where a collection of old timers drank Vita Malt and played dominoes.

"Young Captain Jay, wha brings you to dis part of de island, me son?" asked a wiry, good-natured old man with a big smile.

"Mr. Benjamin," replied Captain Jay respectfully, "We're deliverin' some gasoline. The station is out again. Hey, you guys seen Dante lately?"

"Yeah, mon. He be back on-island fo a few weeks. But wit him yo never know, he always be travelin wit his boat somewhere. He convinced dat der gonna be a revolution soon. You should see de tings he got round his house."

"We're going to drive out there to see him. How's the road?"

"It good, mon. Der be no rain lately. Tis passable."

We waved goodbye and said our *okays* and drove to where the paved road stopped, and a rocky narrow road continued. This part of the island was wind-blown and arid. Besides donkeys and mongoose that stood out in the sparse vegetation, there were hundreds of plants that resembled the agave plant in Mexico that tequila is made from. They were called century plants. Their thick, succulent, three-foot green leaves stuck out from the base and were distinctive enough by themselves, but when the plant was in bloom, which happened every ten years, which makes their name confusing, they were in their glory. Those in bloom had up to eight-foot tall, dried, scraggly stalks with stubby horizontal branches every foot or so. Many islanders, including me, cut out the stalks and used them as Christmas trees. It was a pathetic sight, a dried out, scraggly century plant bloom with a few ornaments, stuck into the sand with brightly wrapped Christmas packages spread out at its base. But it was all we had.

Jay and I arrived at a simple wooden structure with a corrugated metal roof, completely open to the west and north but with walls with small windows facing south and east, the direction from which prevailing winds and storms came. We parked the Jeep, and from a distance Captain Jay hollered *inside*, the traditional way to announce your arrival when visiting the open homes in the Caribbean. Dante was a warm, funny guy, the kind of guy you liked immediately. He was a Viet Nam vet who had seen way too much action. He kept stores of dried food, water, medicine and a ton of untraceable weapons, which he sometimes sold. That was why Captain Jay was there. He wanted to use his boat for long-line sword fishing and needed something powerful and handy enough to dispatch unwanted hooked sharks. There were few things as nasty as a pissed off shark pulled into a boat when the long line was cranked in.

When he had explained this to me earlier I asked him, "Why don't you just cut the shark loose when it is close to the boat?"

"Because that might be the one that bites me in the ass when my head and shoulders are inside a coral head workin' on snarin' a lobster," he replied.

Dante proudly showed us all sorts of weapons and survival gear stored in waterproof bags and hidden in nooks and crannies around his property. Captain Jay settled on a Ruger mini M-14. Before we left, Dante insisted on showing us the pride of his arsenal. He grabbed a flat-nosed shovel and led us to the middle of the rocky public road that passed by his house. After scraping away a few rocks and several inches of sandy gravel we heard a metal on metal clank. Dante opened the lid of a waterproof, heavy metal box and looked at us with a big smile. Inside was a grenade launcher with fresh grenades placed on either side of the launcher in molded foam housing.

What the hell is he going to do with that? I thought. If I hadn't thought so before, I was now convinced that Dante took his paranoia a bit too far.

Captain Jay looked as surprised as I did. He looked at Dante and said, "Cool, Dante." Jay looked around and asked, "Why is it buried out here?"

"It's illegal as hell. If any dick-face government asshole comes searching while I'm on one of my down-island trips, I don't want the prick running off with it. Who the hell would ever think to look here?"

We thanked Dante, returned to the Jeep and started back to Cruz Bay with Captain Jay's new assault rifle onboard.

We passed a series of salt ponds on our way through the bottom land of Coral Bay. The ponds, found throughout the Caribbean, were an integral part of buffering pollutants from running into the sea from the steep slopes, but we found ourselves holding our breath to keep from breathing in the strong sulfur smell of the shallow, brackish water. After passing the ponds we drove past a local man walking on the road toward town. Captain Jay stopped the Jeep and backed up.

"Rupert," Captain Jay shouted, "You need a ride?"

"Tanks."

Rupert climbed into the Jeep and we were introduced.

"What you doin wit dis weapon, mon?"

"It's to shoot niggers," Jay said, and they both laughed out loud.

I turned my head toward Rupert to gauge his reaction. The laugh was genuine, further convincing me that Jay was crazy.

Rupert was a well-traveled Viet Nam vet who didn't carry the baggage associated with most combat vets. He looked like a young Harry Belafonte and was equally charming. But what was most interesting was that, on an island of extraordinarily self-reliant individuals, he was the single most self-sufficient person I had ever been around. He and I became close friends over the next few years.

Chapter Eleven

"All you need in life is ignorance and confidence; then
success is sure."
Mark Twain

I remember something my father told me when I was a child: "There's a first time for everything." Building a house was definitely a first for me, and I took my new construction responsibilities seriously. The fact that I had never built anything before was completely lost on me, but not on the half a dozen workers I had hired. They were seasoned masons and carpenters, all older than me by five to twenty-five years. I was their boss and they looked to me for leadership.

Under normal circumstances, I could have handed the crew architectural drawings and faked my ignorance by standing back and letting them do whatever the drawings instructed. But there were no architectural drawings for this house. I had to wing it. Fortunately, I had a sense of humor and they had a lot of patience, which allowed me some time to get my act together as a builder.

I started with books. I ferried to St. Thomas to a bookstore and bought the ubiquitous, at least in the sixties and seventies, orange and black *Audel's* 'how to' carpentry, plumbing and electric books. I scanned each one thoroughly enough to know what type of information was found in each chapter. There wasn't enough time to become an expert. I simply needed a crash course in basic construction.

A lot of help came from an experienced builder, Dick Bramble, who had moved to the island after WWII, where he flew troop-carrying gliders in Burma. I had met him months earlier at the bar at Gallows Point while he and a few other 'Big War' vets, who also lived on the island, were sharing some lighter moments of the war. I never heard them, or any other WWII vet, talk about the blood and guts, only the funny stories. Instead of having the attitude of a competitor who just lost out on the job, Dick congratulated me and was glad to offer advice whenever I asked.

For several months we'd heard rumors about a wealthy developer from California who was planning to build a big resort on St. John. Nobody had met him, and no plans of the resort were available to view. We had a lot of fun with rumors like this on the island. With no US newspapers or TV news shows available, there was little known about what was going on with real world drama, so it was necessary to create our own. Dick surprised me one evening when he told me about several brand new Jeeps and Ford trucks being sold by a legal firm on St. Thomas. It seemed that this wealthy developer did, in fact, bring the equipment down but never showed up to claim them at Customs. He had disappeared.

The law firm representing him was owed a lot of money and finagled the vehicles from Customs, intending to sell them in lieu of fees. Word got around quickly. They were selling them cheap. Dick had picked up a Jeep truck and showed it off to me the next day. I called the law firm and met the representing attorney in a parking lot where the few remaining vehicles were parked. I agreed to buy a beige Ford F250 truck. I asked Condon to wire money and had the truck on the island the next week. It was the newest, shiniest truck on the island at the time, other than Dick's Jeep.

Armed with my new truck and construction library on the passenger floorboard, I was ready for business. Our job was to finish the lower level of the house and build a new addition.

All construction on the island then was done by hand—excavating, mixing concrete and moving materials around the site. This wasn't because we wanted to, but because we had to. Every builder on the island had to. There was no equipment on the island that allowed us to do it any other way. When the hard volcanic rock that made up the island was in the way of construction, which was normally the case, you either pounded through it with a sledge hammer, blow by blow, or you redesigned the house. Redesigning was time-consuming and difficult. Most construction material came from St. Thomas, or the States, and the only way to get it to the island was by the one barge that transported materials to and from St. John. In this case, it was a seventy-five-foot WWII landing craft LCM, Landing Craft Marine, made famous as the grey, metal barges that took troops from ships to shore at Normandy and throughout the Pacific theater. One truck with its bed full of construction materials could fit on the LCM.

The volcanic rock was called *blue bits*, but was more affectionately known as "blue bitch." Down-islanders, particularly the guys from St. Lucia, were the best at breaking blue bitch. They had it down to a science. There was little top soil on the island. When you dug through what little there was and found blue bitch, it tended to be the tip of the iceberg, the mother lode of rock reaching through the earth's crust and into the upper mantle. But the rock had small hairline cracks throughout that the St. Lucians capitalized on. They lit fires around and on top of the rock and let them burn all night. In the morning they threw water on the hot rock that they hauled up from the sea, not wanting to waste valuable potable water from the cistern. The cool water opened the cracks a little, just enough to allow their barrage of sledge hammers to eventually break the rock. Dynamite wasn't available at the time. It would arrive a few years later with the impending construction boom.

As construction started to flow I tried to keep the materials coming to the job. Frequently, though, the crew found problems for me to solve, the result of no architectural drawings and several redesigns when we couldn't move the blue bitch. I listened to the problem, gave them something to do to keep them busy, walked to my truck and, without letting them see me, quickly researched through my how-to books until I found the section I needed to learn. I became a good speed reader. After learning what I could, I walked back to the crew and made a few general suggestions about the pending problem. Usually, after a few minutes of discussion, the crew would come up with a solution, never knowing that it had been suggested from a construction 101 textbook lying on the front seat of the truck and still opened to the pertinent page.

Succeeding or simply surviving when in over your head, like being thrown alone into the ocean for the first time with full dive gear, or spear-fishing for the first time in the dangerous shark-infested waters of Barracuda Bank, demands that you understand exactly what you need to know to survive for that moment, saving the broader picture for later. I had Captain Jay to thank for that lesson.

I liked my new job and spent a lot of time learning the craft. When the St. John crew refused to work weekends, I found two men from Tortola to work Saturdays and Sundays. I wasn't trying to break any records for length of time to build a house, I just wanted to see what the damn thing looked like finished. It was my first one.

On an island fraught with a host of logistical and weather problems, building a small home could easily take a couple of years to complete. We finished our work in six weeks.

The only real problem we ran into was a redesign that we couldn't accomplish with the materials we had on site and weren't available at the small lumberyard on the island. I had to travel to St. Thomas to purchase the material from a larger lumberyard and hope I could get it back to the job so the work wasn't held up too long.

I contacted Captain Rick, who owned the LCM and used a concrete ramp at road level near the post office to load and off-load his barge. My truck fit onto the barge only after we pulled the side mirrors in. I asked Captain Rick if he could take his barge to Red Hook alone and drive the truck to the lumber yard to retrieve the material we needed. I had other things I needed to do. That was fine with him, and he told me that he would be back by two that afternoon.

I tried to keep my crew busy the rest of the day and returned to the Bulkhead around two o'clock. There was no LCM. I looked out over Pillsbury Sound to see if I could see the LCM crossing. No LCM. I walked down to the ferry dock. The two o'clock ferry had arrived from St. Thomas at two-twenty and my buddy Rupert Morris hopped off.

"Hey, Rupert."

"Okay, mon."

"Did you see Captain Rick's barge in Red Hook?" I asked Rupert, glancing over his shoulder at Pillsbury Sound again.

"Yeah, it der. Had a truck filled with lumber. Look to be your truck, too. The captain was nowhere around, dough."

Damn.

"You should check the Slip Away. The captain he likes his drink, me son." He laughed.

"Okay, thanks, Rupert. Captain Jay and I are going to dive this weekend. You coming?"

"Sure ting."

I caught the three o'clock boat to Red Hook. Sure enough, there was the LCM with my truck and materials backed onto the barge, but no captain. I walked up a steep hill across the street from the ferry dock to the infamous Slip Away Bar. More pirates, movie stars and locals have rubbed elbows in this place than just about any other Caribbean dive. And it *was* a dive. This was the place we all visited when we missed the last ferry and were too early for the next. After a few drinks we usually stumbled and rolled down the steep hill to the boat.

I walked into the dark, stale-beer-smelling bar. Captain Rick sat poorly balanced on a stool at the bar, his head on his chest. I looked at the bartender, who had a sheepish smile. This was normal for him and Captain Rick. It was new to me.

The bartender asked, "That your truck on the barge?"

"Yep."

"His bill is sixty dollars."

"That's a lot of drinks."

"Normal amount for Captain Rick. I'll help you get him down the hill."

I paid the bill and we each grabbed an arm. I thanked the bartender and led Rick to the helm. I returned to shore to untie the barge and heard the engine start up. Rick gunned it. The lines went taut and the heavy wood pelican poles holding the LCM in place creaked and leaned seaward.

"Hey, Captain. Wait a minute. Let me untie us."

He grumbled something and his head slumped. The barge re-laxed and settled back toward shore. I untied it and returned to the helm to tell Rick we were clear to leave the harbor. I ran interfer-ence for any approaching boat as we left, a little faster than necessary. There was a close call with the ferry coming in from St. John, but the ferryboat captain, who was familiar with the often wayward path that the LCM took in and out of the harbor, laughed as we waved to each other.

Captain Rick and I spent the next thirty minutes weaving s-curves all of the way back to the island. By the time we got to the Bulkhead, Captain Rick was sober enough, just barely, to run the barge up onto the concrete ramp. I drove my truck off without looking back.

Condon was so impressed with the short time it took to finish the house, and probably more impressed that it was under budget, that he talked to me about an inn he wanted to build in Cruz Bay in the near future. I was interested, but in the meantime needed to visit my underwater friends whom I'd neglected far too long.

***

I drove through Cruz Bay and stopped to talk to Robert, a carpenter I'd met months earlier while he and his buddies were building the Back Yard. One of his co-workers had died unexpectedly of a con-genital heart condition. It was sad, but death on the island is always taken in stride. Unless you were a local, most of your friends were not childhood friends and not family. When death came, we made the best of it and moved on.

Burial at sea was the choice for many continentals, as it was in this case. I was asked if my truck could be used to haul the casket from the church to the boat. No problem. It was still the shiniest truck on the island. I was told to drop the truck off at the church the next day an hour before the services, which I did. I expected to leave the truck and return for it later in the day. I didn't know the dead carpenter well and thought it out of place to attend the funeral. I backed the truck into the churchyard and got out.

"Hey, we need some help in here," Robert shouted at me from inside the church.

I walked in to see the Italian doctor who gave me a ride my first night on the island, Robert and one more guy standing over a plywood box with holes drilled in the sides. I walked up to the box to find that it was what I was afraid it was—an occupied coffin. I never gave much thought to a burial at sea, being from the Midwest. I had no idea how it was done. In the movies the body was wrapped in a sheet and placed on a plank that was tilted up so that the body could slide into the ocean. But this was no movie.

The body was not dressed up in a suit, just a T-shirt and shorts. No shoes. There were three and four-inch diameter pipes and a few rocks on the floor next to us.

"Hand me one of the shorter ones, please." The doctor looked at me and pointed to the pipes. It was heavier than I would have thought. I helped him place it in the box and work it up the right arm. Robert and the other guy did the same to the other. We repeated this with the legs, which was much more difficult. Robert placed a few rocks in the coffin before we helped him secure the lid. Except for the screw gun it was all done quietly. They thanked me, and I solemnly walked out of the church, never having expected that I would have been preparing a body for burial at sea.

Enough of this, it was time to get in the water.

* * *

A week later I drove to Caneel and met Captain Jay, Rupert Morris and the big guy Charlie Kline, at the resort. I walked through the resort lobby, boarded the boat and expected to hear that we were going to dive down to two hundred feet and wrestle whales with our bare hands.

Captain Jay and Charlie were deep into a strained discussion and paid no attention to me when I boarded. Captain Jay still owed Charlie some money for the dive business and I assumed, as with all small businesses, Captain Jay was in a hard stretch. Rupert was already on board, and we talked about a recent night at the Out. I asked about Gizmo, and Rupert told me he was on Yost visiting family. Captain Jay announced that we were ready to depart. Rupert and I each untied a line and jumped back into the boat. Captain Jay stood with Charlie and drove the boat toward St. Thomas, and we eventually settled into a bay next to Coral World, a tiny theme park with pet dolphins and a geodesic dome.

I asked about tanks, which I didn't see anywhere onboard. Captain Jay leaned back while maneuvering the boat to a good anchoring spot and said, "We are going to get some conch today. No tanks. No guns."

I had seen live conch in the sea grasses and a lot more empty shells on most of the beaches on every island I visited. I had eaten conch fritters, and one night Rupert made conch ceviche for us after a dive that yielded no dinner except for the conch Rupert brought up from the bottom as we prepared to return to the island empty-handed. To me, it didn't seem sporting to grab a big, slow snail that has no chance to hide or to eat you. I had no interest in hunting them, but I was along for the ride and would make the best of it.

Rupert put his mask and snorkel over the top of his head and walked to the dive platform. I did the same. We sat down to put on our flippers, and I looked down into the clear water. I could make out a few patches of sand but mostly dark patches that I assumed were sea grasses. We positioned our masks on our faces, placed the snorkels in our mouths, slid into the water and hung out on the surface while peering down to the sea grass. I noticed neither Charlie nor Captain Jay had put on their gear. I had assumed they had business to discuss, but in reality neither one was much of a free diver. I wasn't either—until this day.

I watched Rupert take a couple of deep breaths and jackknife toward the bottom, pinching his nose and clearing the building pressure in his ears every ten feet or so. I could see conchs sitting on the grass. From the surface they looked like small snails. When Rupert reached the grass he looked like a midget. He was pretty deep. I saw him pick a conch up and turn it over. He discarded the first one and grabbed another one about ten feet away. Not fully understanding why, I took a couple of deep breaths and jackknifed into the depths, clearing the pressure as I went.

I kicked my way down, but after thirty feet or so I noticed my body wanted to sink naturally, and I relaxed. I didn't know it at the time, but relaxing helped conserve my stored oxygen. Almost to the bottom I felt a strong urge to take a breath, but I had to make it. My pride was at stake. I looked over and saw Rupert kicking strongly up to the surface carrying a conch in each hand. I was close to the bottom and aimed my body toward a conch to the right of me. I needed to breathe. I grabbed the conch, which now looked huge, and kicked toward the surface as hard as I could.

It was a torturous ascent. The crystal-clear water made the surface seem deceptively close. I swam as quickly as I could, my lungs bursting. I finally broke the surface like a trained Sea World dolphin and took a deep breath. I'd forgotten to spit the snorkel out of my mouth and sucked in a half cup of sea water, exacerbating my situation and sending me coughing and hacking all the way to the boat.

Rupert was there and hung on to the platform ready for his next dive. His two conchs lay on the deck next to the cooler, one of them trying to scrape across the fiberglass deck with its large, single blade claw. I tossed my conch next to them. It was a lot smaller than it looked underwater. Captain Jay, deep in discussion with Charlie, seemed to barely notice that I'd thrown a conch onto the deck. He walked over to my conch, picked it up and smiled when a crab-like claw reached out from the interior of the shell.

"Jesus, Rookie," he said and threw the conch back into the sea.

I frowned and looked at Rupert, still hanging onto the dive platform next to me. He laughed as he placed his snorkel in his mouth and disappeared under the water.

Captain Jay looked at me before turning back to Charlie and said, "It's a fuckin' hermit crab. We're lookin' for conch."

I found out later that the claw was from a hermit crab temporarily residing in the abandoned conch shell. Terrestrial hermit crabs crawl around houses close to the ocean eating coffee grounds and orange peels left out for them by a lot of islanders. Their look-alike cousins, aquatic hermit crabs, spend their time in the ocean freeloading homes in anything from conch shells to beer cans.

I put my snorkel in my mouth and ducked my head underwater to watch Rupert, trying to understand why this was more effortless for him. After one strong kick he simply glided to the bottom, slowly but with no effort. He picked up two conchs and started his ascent, kicking strongly but smoothly, his arms at his sides carrying the conch. Bubbles shed off his body were seemingly going downward but, in reality, were just moving upward slower than Rupert. His body seemed to grow exponentially as he neared the surface.

I followed Rupert's example and felt more relaxed, though it took a little longer to reach bottom. I grabbed the first conch I saw and turned it over, just as I had seen Rupert do on the first dive. It was a real conch. I carried it with me and looked for a second. I proudly returned to the boat and threw my two conchs on the deck. Nobody noticed. Captain Jay and Charlie talked and stared at each other like two circling tomcats. Rupert was already underwater again.

Rupert and I spent the next thirty or forty minutes swimming from the surface to the bottom and back to the surface like mosquito larvae in small, clear mud puddles. The learning curve for me shrank, and I began to keep up with Rupert. I knew, as I ascended the last time, that this was my sport. We climbed into the boat, and I glanced at the fathometer—sixty-five feet. I hadn't thought to ask about the depth earlier. If I had, I probably wouldn't have made it.

We put all of the conchs into one of the mesh dive-bags.

"What do you do with these things?" I asked Rupert.

"We clean dem at Captain Jay's."

I shrugged and sat on the cooler as we motored back to Caneel Bay. I thought about what I'd learned that day, realizing that this sport would be a big part of my future. Diving with a tank was fun and necessary in many locations, but it couldn't hold a stick to the less constrictive free diving, as long as you had the skill to go deep. Success-ful, deep free-diving was all about one's ability to be comfortable and relaxed regardless of how deep or much time underwater or how big the fish that swim next to you are. I also discovered that when you're down at the bottom and have a strong urge to return to the surface for a breath, if you swallow, the urge dissipates.

Rupert and I drove with the conchs to Captain Jay's house. Cap-tain Jay and Charlie followed in the baby-blue Jeep. Rupert and I were charged with preparing the conch for dinner. I grabbed one and tried to pull the conch out by gripping its claw. It didn't budge.

"Okay, how do you clean them?" I asked Rupert.

Rupert pulled out a machete from Jay's storage shed and grabbed a conch shell. He rotated the shell until the opening with the claw was on the opposite side. The top of a conch has several sets of round-ed spiked rings on its narrow end. Rupert counted three rings down and carefully hit the shell with the machete with just enough force to break the shell where the body of the conch had attached itself. Rupert grabbed the claw and easily pulled the meat out of the shell.

I looked at Rupert and said, "But now there is a hole in the shell. What if I wanted a complete shell with no hole?"

"You can freeze it for a day or two and pull out the meat when it taws, but it don't taste the same. Or you can boil dem, but de stink up da house."

I tried my hand with the machete. It took a few failed smacks before I figured it out. The meat was covered with a sticky STP-like substance that was hard to wash off of your hands afterward.

It took a half hour or so, but we finished and created a fairly large pile of conch meat. Almost finished, I told Rupert about several crushed conch shells I'd seen in the sea grass. "What causes that?"

Rupert smiled and said, "Mostly tiger sharks, deh jus crush dem and eat the meat."

Conch—the easiest underwater food to catch, and the hardest to clean. Now I'd have to look over my shoulder for tiger sharks when I dove for conch.

Chapter Twelve

"I can last two months on a good compliment."
Mark Twain

Condon called to let me know that he was going to visit for a couple of weeks and that he had just purchased land in town on the one-way loop, next to the Catholic church, across the street from the Frazier house. He told me he had a half-assed pencil sketch for an inn he wanted me to build and that he was also negotiating to purchase the little sub-standard lot on the corner that had a small, semi-livable shack. If successful, the shack was to be my office and home when he was on-island. I guessed that he'd changed his mind about me living in the house that I had completed for him, and was still living in, which was too bad. I loved it. It was wide open to the elements and, other than a few days in August and September, cooled by the trade winds, which kept the island at a comfortable average temperature of seventy-seven degrees. Nobody on the island at that time had air-conditioning systems, the power supply being too erratic and prone to blackouts. And there were just as many brown-outs when the voltage into your house dropped to eighty or ninety volts, which was deadly to appliances and electrical devices. Unfortunately, an open house also gave comfort to the mosquitoes and the lizards, birds, bats, rats, mongoose and an occasional goat.

The rats weren't the ugly sewer rats you would see in urban America; they were big, cute mice with large eyes and long tails with a bushy end, and they were strictly nocturnal. They hadn't always been nocturnal, though. A few hundred years earlier, ships from Europe sailed to the islands to pick up sugar and rum from plantations. They brought with them the old European bricks still visible mixed with the indigenous stone used to build many of the old commercial buildings in St. Thomas and Mongoose Junction on St. John. These bricks were used as ballast for the otherwise empty ships, aside from the stowaways—rats.

It didn't take long for the rats to populate the islands, and they had only one natural enemy—snakes. But there were too many rats for the snakes to eat. The sugarcane plantation owners, searching for a solution to the growing rat problem heard from British sailors about a vicious little rat-eating animal that lived in India. Soon mongooses were imported to the Caribbean from India.

For a while it was a free-for-all—rats, snakes and mongooses sharing the same habitat at the same time. The rats, at the bottom of the triangular food-chain, understood the drill sooner than the other two species. They declared that they would become nocturnal animals, knowing that the stubborn mongooses would continue to go to sleep at sundown, no matter what. The snakes would still be a menace; they hunted day and night. That left the snakes and the mongooses to deal with each other during the day, perfect for mongooses, who needed a new food source now that their favorite rat delicacy was not available, so they ate the snakes—all of them. In short order, the island became active mongoose habitat all day long and rat habitat all night long, with no snakes.

Besides the bugs, the lizards, birds, bats, rats, mongooses and an occasional goat that would wander in, there were many other intrinsic problems that accompanied the wide-open homes of the Caribbean. During the frequent, long-term power outages there were no fans to blow away the mosquitoes, no ice available to cool warm beer and no electric lights to read by. To this day I have books that I brought back to the US from the island with the remnants of bugs squashed between pages as I read by candlelight. Some have so many squashed bugs on the pages they look like historic bug collections.

I enjoyed my last few weeks at the Condon house before being kicked over to the one-room shack, which I still needed to renovate before moving in. The Condon house was nick-named "The Telephone Booth" because it was a twenty-foot square, two-story house with a four-foot-wide cantilevered deck around the second level. Tall palms and other tropical canopy gave the house almost total privacy. The only house that had a view inside any part of our house was above us, a concrete monstrosity built teaspoon-by-teaspoon by a retired bureaucrat from South Carolina. It took him years to build it, and most of the aggregate in the poured concrete walls consisted of empty rum bottles, which we found out after a heavy rain caused the wall just above our driveway to collapse. Whole and broken empty rum bottles and concrete mortar fell onto two dilapidated Mini Mokes that were permanently parked in Condon's driveway awaiting repairs that never happened.

We'd built a redwood hot tub on the deck on the side of the house that faced the monstrosity, but with so many palm fronds in the way, a person would struggle to see anybody in the tub from its concrete pool deck, which was closest to the hot tub.

This was exactly what Charlie Kline did. Captain Jay had used the house for a couple of days while I was traveling down-island. The sperm count in the tub tended to get a little high whenever Captain Jay and his girlfriends borrowed it. It needed to be drained and cleaned.

Charlie was visiting my neighbors and spotted me through the palm fronds, or maybe he was looking for me.

"Hey, you know what you're doing around here now," he yelled down in his graveled voice. A strange thing to say since it was the first time he had initiated a conversation with me.

I looked up through the palm fronds that were waving in the breeze, making it difficult to get eye contact, but he did.

"Hi, Charlie. Come on down," I shouted.

I had no idea why Charlie sought me out, but my curiosity was piqued, and after I saw what he could do to a windpipe I didn't want to get on his bad side.

A few minutes later I saw Charlie between the gaps in the fence at the entry to the deck that led to the house. He could have opened the gate and come in, but he was too old school.

"Inside?"

I smiled at the irony of his politeness and said, "Come on in."

Charlie opened the gate and said with his gruff voice, "You're supposed to answer with 'Outside.' That way I know it's okay to walk into your house."

"Sorry. Outside."

He smiled and sat in a chair at a table just inside one of the wide openings on the west side of the house.

I offered him a beer and sat opposite him. We had a clear view of Moravian Point, which I was to later call Goat Hill, in the foreground and St. Thomas in the distant background. Charlie sat with his military crewcut and massive chest, sipped his beer and said nothing.

Since my first encounter with him I had asked around about the big man. Most locals and longtime residents would look at me and smile. It seemed that everybody who knew him genuinely liked him and weren't willing to tell me much about him. They probably didn't know much. Some did, and I found out that he was a real piece of work and somewhat of a mystery.

He'd come to the island in the sixties and started the island's first dive operation. He took on a partner to help out because he would leave the island sometimes for months at a time. When anybody would ask him where he was going and when he was coming back he would look at them with a smile and say, "As the wind blows."

Charlie had lied about his age and entered the Marine Corps at seventeen. He stormed many Pacific beaches during WWII and was shot several times by a Japanese sniper during a beach invasion late in the war. He survived his wounds and after the war became one of the very few certified SCUBA divers and an instructor in SCUBA's infancy.

He made his living underwater in legitimate and illegitimate ways. He tested shark repellents for the Navy. He was a stunt man for movies and advertisements that required anything underwater. After I got to know him he once showed me a *Life Magazine* pictorial advertisement from the fifties for some kind of whiskey or scotch that had two guys wearing SCUBA gear jumping out of a plane with parachutes and landing in the ocean, stripping the parachute gear and diving down to a treasure chest full of whiskey. The last frame was a smiling Charlie with a dive mask sitting on the bottom of the ocean holding a bottle of whiskey.

The people who did talk to me about Charlie and knew him the best told me he was a CIA contractor. I laughed at first. How often does one meet a real CIA operative? He certainly had the history, admittedly having had a strong presence in Cuba before and after Castro seized power. One story, later confirmed to me by Charlie, was that he was part of an abandoned assassination attempt on Castro that involved a poisoned ink pen.

Another story told to me was that sometime in the late 1940s, gold bars were smuggled out of India, which at the time was still under the protection of the British Navy. The smugglers used a small freighter to take the gold by sea to the nearest foreign port. The backup plan was to hide the gold in the linings of vests designed to sink with the wearer. If they were pursued by the authorities they would put the vests on the local crew and throw them overboard, ridding themselves of witnesses and marking their location the best they could using dead reckoning navigation. Evidently, the backup plan was needed, and after sufficient time had passed so as not to raise suspicion, Charlie was hired to recover the gold bar vests, which he did.

A few years later Charlie and I became close. We even lived together on Goat Hill for a while, during which time I met many of his old Cold-War friends who visited. They were real enough. Eventually, I gingerly asked him about some of these stories. Sometimes he told me a little about them, confirming they were true. Other times he would just look at me with a beady-eyed smile and say, "Don't believe everything you hear."

I wasn't about to ask him about any of those things on this day. I didn't know him well enough, and I valued my windpipe.

"So, you know your way around the islands now. You've proven that," he finally said after we both had almost finished our beers.

I smiled uncomfortably. He was not the type of guy who would kiss ass.

"I guess so."

He got right to the point. "What if you were to go down-island, say to Grenada, and open up a small business?"

"Why would I want to do that? I like it here."

"But what if somebody gave you maybe fifty thousand dollars to set up a business there?" he pressed, but in a polite jovial way.

With the little bit I had heard about Charlie to that point, I started to vaguely understand what he was getting at. Grenada had been in the news in the Caribbean lately. A Marxist, Maurice Bishop, had overthrown the elected government of Eric Gairy and started to get cozy with Cuba.

"So what kind of business would I start?"

"Any type of tourist or construction business. You know what you're doing."

"And what would I be doing while not running my business?"

"Well, you just watch things," he replied, completely relaxed. It was as though he had had this kind of discussion every day.

"What kind of things?"

Charlie took another sip. "Activity. Planes, ships, troops."

"And who do I report this to?" I asked. This was intriguing, but surreal. I was certainly not in the Midwest anymore.

"We'll have somebody there," he replied with a smile.

I thought about this and offered him another Heineken.

Was this a compliment for this guy to have faith in my ability to be a spy? Or does the CIA recruit only naive dummies?

"What happens if I get caught watching things?"

Charlie hesitated, smiled and said, "We never heard of you."

I don't know if he was serious or if he thought I would take the bait. There was no way I would do this. There were a dozen guys on the island he could have recruited. Maybe he did. People came and went so often I would never have known. My concern was how to gracefully decline.

Captain Jay arrived and saved me from the rest of this conversation, if there was to be any. Somehow I don't think Charlie cared one way or another how I answered.

There was no *inside* with Captain Jay. He just bolted through the gate like he owned the place, helped himself to a beer and asked, "What are you two hoodlums up to?"

Charlie rose from the chair he sat in and said, "We were just talking about the weather."

Captain Jay laughed. I wondered how many times he'd been recruited.

"As the wind blows," Charlie said and walked out to continue his visit with the neighbors to the north. His mission to recruit me had failed.

"Come on, Rookie, we're gonna drive out to the East End and visit McQuin."

"Isn't it about time you called somebody *else* Rookie?"

"I do, but you're the original Rookie. Kind of like Rookie the First."

"And you've never been a rookie?"

"Not like you," he said and laughed as he walked through the gate to his Jeep.

We drove into town to see who was around before heading up Centerline Road and to the other side of the island. Passing Chicken Wing Joe's building I noticed that not only was he selling a lot of chicken wings downstairs, the Chinese restaurant upstairs was packed.

Captain Jay stopped to talk to a lady who worked in a small shop across the street from the Chinese restaurant. Captain Jay's newest distraction was setting up a retail shop in town to rent snorkel equipment and sell T-shirts. The woman he stopped to talk with was in charge of painting and adding nautical-looking shelves inside.

While I waited, Chicken Wing Joe walked by the Jeep. He saw me and said hello.

I nodded and said, "Hey Joe, looks like you're doing well with the new restaurant."

"It busy, very busy." He smiled and walked away.

We drove up Centerline and passed through the only place on the island where the road flattened out for just enough length to maybe put a Jeep into fourth gear. We didn't try. We just watched the pigs on either side of the road as we passed.

An industrious local man, Iva Moses, who dabbled in farming, trucking and anything his land could accommodate, including fence-less pig farming, owned the land on either side of the road and a plethora of half-finished buildings and one almost finished building that housed a laundromat. His master plan was to build the island's first major shopping center on his land, and he was doing it—block by block, a rate that I figured would take a hundred years. He was helpful and friendly but hard to get to know because he never quit working long enough to talk. Children ran around his property, but if they were his, I had no idea how he had enough time to make them.

We drove down the backside of the mountain and arrived at sea level again. I looked out into the ocean and saw squall lines of rain moving toward us from the southeast and hoped we got to cover before they hit. We had to stop to wait for about thirty goats to cross the road, bleating loudly. The government had built small, three-sided, light-blue concrete block structures that resembled bus stops and placed them strategically around Coral Bay and the east end of the island for school children to take shelter from passing rain squalls while waiting for the school bus. They were constantly commandeered by goats, especially during heavy rains. These goats seemed to sense the rain and were crowding into a bus stop to our left.

This part of the island was arid, and unlike other parts of the island where homes are mostly hidden from view by the thick vegetation, here you could easily see a mix of exposed local homes in various stages of construction.

Locals built their homes over time—long time. Most locals had land but lacked money and time to build a home. A few pockets of locally-owned land on the island had not yet been sold and filled with vacation homes. These were large parcels of land that were often divided into smaller parts as families grew, forming enclaves of locally-owned square or rectangular masonry homes with small aluminum jalousie windows. These were not tourist homes; they were homes of necessity. Large windows with sweeping views and modern baths and kitchens were not important. Affordable, simple shelter was the priority.

We drove through Coral Bay and on to the east end of the island, passing Dante's house.

"Oh, shit. Do you notice something different?" I asked Captain Jay.

He cocked his head, looked around and said, "The road is paved. They paved the damn road. Dante has been gone for months. He's gonna be pissed when he gets back."

We both laughed, and I said, "He'll probably blow the whole road up looking for his precious grenade launcher."

We drove to the end of the road to Tim and Mary McQuin's property. They'd lived here for over ten years before anybody beyond the immediate neighborhood knew that Tim existed. Mary taught school while Tim hibernated out here doing who knows what. Then one day Tim drove into Cruz Bay and opened a restaurant. He grew up on the east coast of Florida where in high school he ran a world-class hundred-yard dash. But, instead of pursuing a college track career, he studied political science and ended up as a legislative assistant in Washington, DC, where he met Mary. At the same time, he was being groomed by an elite branch of the military. During a vacation to visit family in Florida he ended up in a bar fight at a popular night club chain and broke a few arms and legs—not his own. His political and military connections kept him out of prison, but he and Mary quietly disappeared to a life in the Caribbean.

There was no reason to shout *inside* when we exited the Jeep in the driveway and walked toward the house because the inside of the McQuin house was already outside, and vice versa. Tim had carried rounded beach rocks the size of grapefruits from the rocky beach one hundred and fifty feet below their house to use as the floor in the circular home design. The only wall in the entire house was a half-round stone wall on the east side of the house, where all cabinets and appliances were located. There were no rooms other than a bathroom. Hammocks hung from posts that held up the round roof, which was a combination of corrugated metal, wood and canvas. It would have been mosquito heaven if it wasn't for the strong winds that buffeted the site continuously.

Mary was in town managing the restaurant. Tim brought three Heinekens out to greet us.

"How's the movie goin'?" Jay asked Tim as we leaned against the Jeep. Tim and Captain Jay, both being native Floridians, had the same quasi-southern accents.

A movie to be called *Four Seasons* was being filmed out at Hawksnest Beach. Alan Alda, a frequent guest at Caneel Bay was responsible for bringing the movie set to the island. Tim's restaurant had been hired to cater food for the movie set. I had gone to Hawksnest to visit with Tim, thinking it would be fun to watch a movie being filmed, but I found it extraordinarily boring.

Tim laughed and told us that Rowboat Wayne and a local, Henry Smith, rowed through the set while they were filming, holding up a white sheet with the words, "YOU ARE INFRINGING ON OUR ANCESTRAL FISHING GROUNDS. WE DEMAND COMPENSATION," painted in large, red letters.

"I didn't know those guys fished," I said.

Jay added, "I didn't know they could write."

Tim replied, "They don't fish, and it's illegal in national park waters."

"And were they compensated?" I asked with a laugh.

"The crew was using *Sandavore* as the movie boat. Lance's boat."

We nodded. Lance was from the Canary Islands and was charming but dangerous, and his classic wooden sailboat was precious to him.

"They had the boat rigged to some palm trees on shore, so it was leaning over like it might have been in a strong storm. Anyway, Lance took his dinghy out and threatened to kick Wayne and Herman's asses—or worse. They took the sign down and rowed out of the bay."

We spent the rest of the afternoon *limin'*, as the locals would say. Rupert stopped by. He had a knack for always knowing where to find anyone on the island when he wanted to. I casually disclosed that I was going to start building an inn next to the Catholic church.

Tim said, "I didn't know you were a builder."

"I'm not. I'm just the only guy Condon knows who is usually sober enough to see it through."

On our way over the island to Cruz Bay, Captain Jay said, "Hey, Rookie, can you help me tomorrow with a dive?"

"What happened to Scott?"

"Scott's fine. He's takin' the other boat. I had hired a new guy to help out and invited him over for a beer. He pulled out some cocaine. I fired his ass, after kickin' it first."

That seemed strange. Captain Jay frequently smoked pot through a bong that was a permanent fixture on his living room coffee table, no matter who was in the house.

"Did you light up your bong before he pulled out his drugs?" I laughed.

"Yeah, but that's beside the point. It's only pot," he responded incredulously.

"Maybe you're being a bit hypocritical?"

I could tell I had passed some kind of warped line in the sand.

"Don't call me a hypocrite, asshole. He was doin' drugs."

I'd not been diving as much with Captain Jay lately, and it would be good to go out on a dive with him, even if it was with his resort guests. I'd been busy trying to learn more about construction, reading everything I could find and visiting Dick's building sites when I could. But the other reason I had not been diving as much with Captain Jay was because I had spent a lot more time free diving, something that didn't interest him.

As much as I liked free diving, I also missed tank diving with Captain Jay. "Yeah, I can help," I told him.

Chapter Thirteen

*"Do not argue with an idiot. He will drag you down to his
level and beat you with experience."*
Mark Twain

The next day I walked through the lobby of Caneel Bay with my
speargun and yum-yum yellow fins in my mesh bag on my way to
meet Captain Jay at his boat, which I knew would be tied along the
dock, full of dive gear and ready for guests from the resort who had
signed up for a two-tank dive that would take up four hours or more
of the day. In my rush I bumped into the resort manager, who was
hurrying to a set of stairs that led to his office.

"Hi Dave," I said.

Dave Brewer smiled and asked me how I was doing, not ignor-
ing my speargun or Speedo swim trunks, which had the attention of
everybody else in the lobby.

"I'm helping Captain Jay with a dive."

The last time I'd seen Dave was at Captain Jay's last birthday
party, which I am sure he didn't want me to remind him of.

Dave put his hand on my shoulder and said, "Captain Jay told
me that you're going to renovate the shack next to the church. I wanted to tell you that we have a couple of warehouses full of things you
might be able to use. When you get back from your dive I'll take you
there, if you have time."

"Thanks, Dave. I'll look you up later today when we return. I
really appreciate this," I said and turned to walk to the boat.

I was the last to arrive. I had hoped to be the first so I could hide my speargun, which I planned to use to spear dinner after helping Jay get his paying guests into the water. Whatever direction they swam, I'd go the opposite and return with a bag full of fish, which I'd stuff into the cooler before helping Jay's guests back onto the boat. I introduced myself to a young Texas couple on their honeymoon, an older man with his daughter, who looked to be in her twenties and a couple in their forties who wore matching wetsuits with useless dive knives strapped to their legs. That made me smile.

I jumped down onto the deck and, as discretely as possible, slipped the speargun behind the cooler, climbed back onto the dock and untied the boat as Captain Jay put the boat in gear and moved into the bay. I stood next to Captain Jay and asked, "Where to today?"

"Carval Rock. We should get there at slack tide."

I lowered my voice and said, "You sure? That's a tough dive. Are these people certified?"

Captain Jay smiled and said, "Absolutely, pool certified in the US and ready to star in *Sea Hunt*."

"Pool certified, uh? I could tell by the knives." We both smiled, knowing that getting certified in a swimming pool with the required open water dive in a gravel pit meant nothing. They may as well have been beginners. The first big fish they saw or the first time they lost sight of the other divers, they'd be pissing their wetsuits.

I stepped back to make small talk with Captain Jay's paying customers while he drove the boat to Carval Rock. I tweaked the matching couple a bit by telling them that I was glad they had the knives. We would likely see big green moray, and if they bit any of us we would need a knife to cut their heads off—the eel's head.

The man and his daughter looked at my speargun I had placed behind the cooler and asked, "What is that for?"

Captain Jay heard the question, turned around and said, "It's a speargun a friend found washed up on a beach on the other side of the island. We're takin' it later to St. Thomas to a friend who owns a dive shop."

Jay didn't want his guests to report to the resort management that the dive instructors were murdering fish on their dives.

"Looks new to me," the man said and picked it up.

I grabbed the gun from him and said, "I spent a lot of time cleaning it for our friend, who'll likely sell it for a pretty good price."

The man seemed satisfied with the answer and walked back to sit next to his daughter.

Ten minutes later we approached Carval Rock. The seas were fairly calm, but that could change quickly. Captain Jay maneuvered the boat to where we could drop the bow anchor safely in the sand. I let out enough scope to pull the line tight to set the bow anchor. We wanted to be as close to the rock as possible. I let out more scope while Captain Jay rigged a stern anchor. His anchor ready and lying on the deck near the dive platform, he walked back to the helm and put the boat in reverse. When satisfied that the bow anchor bit into the sandy bottom, he walked back to the dive platform and dropped the stern anchor. I pulled on the bow line until both the stern anchor and the bow anchor bit into the sand. Captain Jay tied off the stern anchor as I secured the bow anchor. The boat was going to stay in a straight line regardless of changes in the wind or current.

Captain Jay went through his perfunctory humorous dive monologue that helped the divers prepare and relax. I moved tanks toward the stern. Jay's pep talk over, we both helped the divers with their tanks, many of which were now equipped with the new regulator and buoyancy compensator combo, which was a BC attached to the tank and supplied with air by a simple push on the regulator.

Captain Jay asked me to get into the water to keep everybody together while he put divers in and put his gear on. On the way out to the dive site I thought I would free dive, but now that I had a tank on I chose to scuba. I was going to have to pull myself back up onto the boat and frog-walk with flippers across the deck to get my gun after Captain Jay and his flock swam away to visit the reef where thousands of small aquarium fish made their homes. While the divers were wowed by the small fish I would be hunting in deeper water for much larger fish—fish that would become dinner.

The visibility was great—a hundred feet or better. The current was slack. I watched Captain Jay move his flock around the rock counterclockwise, thinking that the current would be with them as they rounded the back side of the rock to return to the boat. I swam toward deeper water in the same general direction, confident I could return to the boat to hide my fish well before the flock returned.

Current is tricky and probably the single most dangerous challenge while diving in the Caribbean, unless you attempt to pet tiger sharks, which would be immeasurably more dangerous.

When I reached the area where the coral and rock met sandy bottom I realized that the current had picked up noticeably.

I scrubbed any plans for a fish dinner and swam back toward the boat. We mistimed the current, which turned much quicker than we had planned, and all of us were going to have to swim against it to get back to the boat. It would get stronger and more difficult to swim against in the next ten minutes and unmanageable after that. The alternative of making it back to the boat soon was to fight to the surface and float to the British Virgin Islands, BVI, hoping a passing boat would see us and come to our rescue.

I kicked hard and realized that I was making little headway. Fortunately, I always wore gloves, those cheap white cotton gloves with little black rubber dots for a better grip. I grabbed coral and rocks, anything for better purchase while fighting the current. Kicking hard and grabbing rocks and coral with one hand, the other hand holding onto the speargun and the mesh bag, I made progress. I looked to my right and saw Captain Jay fighting with one of the divers with matching suits. It wasn't a fight really; it was more a panicked diver grabbing Captain Jay for safety, putting them both in a dangerous situation.

I couldn't help. I had no choice but to try to get to the boat—somebody had to. When I glanced back I saw the diver shoot up toward the surface. Captain Jay had been swimming around punching everybody's BC button, filling the BCs with air, taking the divers to the surface. This is something a certified diver should have known to do themselves in an emergency.

The current was almost to the unmanageable stage. I crawled my way past the boat to the stern anchor and lifted it up out of the sand in order to release its grip on the bottom. With the current now at my back I could hold onto the anchor and, with the current's assistance, moon walk toward the boat. I dropped the anchor in a clear area below the boat and kicked like hell up and onto the dive platform where I stripped my gear and pulled up the stern anchor. I tied old BCs Jay kept on the boat to some of the full tanks and threw them into the water, knowing that the current would take them in the direction of the divers and might provide Captain Jay with additional air in case he couldn't get everybody to the surface. I started the engine and was ready to pull up the bow anchor when I heard a loud cough behind me. Captain Jay was hoisting himself up onto the dive platform.

"How the hell...?"

"Come on Rookie, we have to go pick them up," Captain Jay said with a cough. He then stripped his gear and took the wheel while I pulled up the bow anchor.

Captain Jay could drive a big boat like a race car. He rammed the boat into forward, and we lurched toward our target, a bobbing head and mask about fifty yards in front of us. Captain Jay bolted past the head, turned the wheel slightly and threw the boat into reverse, a move that caused the ocean to ride up onto the deck, almost knocking me off my feet. I hopped to the dive platform and grabbed the diver by the collar of the BC and yanked him onto the boat. It was the honeymoon husband. He was fine.

The next two divers we retrieved were the father and daughter, who were a little rattled but okay. Not far from us in the water were the matching wetsuits. We bolted past them and put the boat in reverse again, knocking all of the divers on the boat off balance. I pulled the closest diver onto the boat. It was the husband. He was fine, and I asked him to move back while I hauled his wife up. She had lost her mask. Her face was white with purple lips. I was sure she was dead.

I pulled her up onto the deck, and we all prepared to perform CPR, which I hoped somebody on the boat knew how to do—I didn't. Her eyes fluttered open and she spit salt water as her husband and I lifted her into a sitting position.

The newly-wedded wife was still missing. I stepped next to Captain Jay and whispered, "Did you get her to the surface?"

"No."

Captain Jay wore his in-charge exterior, but I could tell he was concerned. He took the boat farther east with the current when I heard something.

"Wait," I shouted. I strained to hear it again. "Cut the engine."

Captain Jay cut the engine, and we heard a faint "Help." We looked in the ocean and saw nothing. I happened to glance back at Carval Rock. Clinging like a tree frog onto a jagged section of rock just above the water line and being pummeled by the crashing seas was the young, just-married girl from Texas. Her tank, one fin and mask were gone.

Getting her into the boat would be difficult. Jay backed the boat up as close as he dared while I tried to coax her off the rock. She wouldn't budge. The waves continued to slam against her, each one pressing her harder into the sharp edges of the rock. Jay had to move the boat away from the rock to keep from crashing into it, then let the seas carry us close again, repeating the process several times.

To get her off the rock I was going to have to do what I didn't want to do—get in the water and swim to her. I looked to Captain Jay and he nodded.

I donned my fins and jumped in. Captain Jay moved the boat a safer distance from the rock. With the husband shouting encouragements to his wife, I swam as close to the rock as possible and shouted to her to let go. A wave smashed me against the rock just to her left. I would be hamburger if I didn't get her away from the rock soon. The seas had picked up, and I saw the boat bobbing higher with each passing wave. A large wave picked me up and threw me into the poor girl. She lost her grip and we both fell back into the sea. I used this to my advantage and pulled her toward the boat. Captain Jay saw the opening and jammed the boat into reverse to get as close as he could without letting the next wave push him onto the rock. Her husband and the two other men heaved her up into the boat, leaving me to fend for myself.

Thanks a lot, I thought as I kicked up onto the dive platform.

Captain Jay throttled hard to the lee side of Lovango Cay, a few hundred yards away. I threw the anchor in the shallow, calm water. Nobody talked much during the five minutes it took to get there. The honeymoon girl had bad cuts on the insides of her arms and legs, all the way up to the insides of her thighs. She was going to need some medical attention. Her poor husband wasn't going to get laid the rest of his honeymoon, and then some.

Captain Jay turned around and lit into the divers, shocking all of us.

"You're all certified divers and you all screwed up. What do you do in an emergency like that?" he stammered. "You could have all died today."

I didn't think it was quite that bad. A passing boat would probably have located them before they floated to the BVI. The girl on the rocks might have died, though.

The husband with the matching wetsuit spoke up and said, "Aren't you being a little hard?"

I looked at him and wondered how he would take the wrath of Captain Jay, which I knew would come any second.

Captain Jay turned to the man, and I thought he was going to throw him overboard. He took a step toward the man and stopped.

"Hard? You don't know hard. You need to be better prepared or don't come divin' with me. And don't think that your pool certification makes you an expert. You should have listened to me before the dive."

I asked if anybody wanted a drink from the cooler.

Captain Jay snorted, turned back to the wheel and said, "Get the anchor, Rookie." He didn't say another word until we pulled alongside the dock at the resort. He had called ahead and told the front desk a diver would need medical assistance.

After the guests disembarked I looked at Captain Jay and said, "Maybe we shouldn't have taken those people to Carval. You know how dangerous it can get."

Captain Jay glared at me, stepped onto the dock and said, "You don't know what the fuck you're talkin' about."

What, no *Rookie* this time?
We both knew that he'd just exposed a chink in his armor.

Chapter Fourteen

"It's not the size of the dog in the fight, it's the size of the fight in the dog."
Mark Twain

I stopped to see the resort manager who, true to his word, drove me to a warehouse stashed away in a far corner of the resort. Walking through it I could see the history of the resort from the days even before Rockefeller owned it—old cast iron Hunter ceiling fans, worn rattan furniture, sections of wooden bars taken from one or more of the few resort restaurants, doors, windows and many more antiquities stored in partially organized rows within the large metal building.

In a corner half covered with some old screen doors were solid mahogany shutters. At a full two inches thick, they were definitely made locally and had heavy iron strap hinges, the kind hardware stores don't sell anymore, and locked with large iron throw bolts. I could use the shutters as windows and create Dutch doors for my new shack.

"How much do you want for the shutters?" I asked Dave.

Dave looked a little surprised. I realized he was probably not going to ask for anything.

He smiled and said, "You can have whatever you want for fifty dollars."

Later that day I brought my truck to the warehouse and loaded it with my new mahogany shutters, a few pieces of old rattan furniture and an old desk.

The shack, which many years later became a famous fish restaurant that remains open to this day, ended up being my home for the next year. It started as a homely, five-hundred-square-foot simple structure with a five-hundred-gallon metal tank as the cistern, a fallen concrete porch deck and stairs barely hanging onto the back of the shack by rusted and bent rebar. The main structure, located a few feet off the one-way loop, consisted of concrete piers that held up a concrete slab with a wood-framed shack with a metal roof. The rest of the property was an empty lot, bordered by the road and the Catholic church. It was also the unofficial cockfighting grounds for Cruz Bay.

Across the street and above a stone retaining wall that held the steep slope on the other side from falling onto the road, roosters were tethered to trees in the thick bush. Their owners kept them far enough apart so they couldn't injure each other when not fighting. Why the mongooses didn't get them had always perplexed me. Chickens ran wild throughout the village. Hens were followed by freshly hatched clutches of chicks in single file. The clutch would usually start eight or nine strong, and each day that number would be reduced by one, victim to the hungry mongooses, until there were two or three remaining chicks. This seemed to be the magic number of chicks a mother hen could protect.

On Friday nights, the owners of the cocks brought them to our property, which was cleared and flat, to fight. I never saw them fight to the death, like they do in so many other parts of the world. After a few hours of fighting the healthy and mostly injured roosters were tied up across the street in the bush for a week of retirement. Crowing roosters could be heard constantly all over the island. The locals told me there were three crows of the rooster—the first at three in the morning, the second at five and the third at seven. I never found this to be true, or maybe the roosters across the street from me, the fighting roosters, suffered brain damage and didn't know what time to crow. The fighting roosters crowed erratically, twenty-four hours a day, some sounding like cats burping.

The cockfights slacked off and eventually moved elsewhere when I brought my crew in to fix up the shack. The crew replaced the concrete porch with a metal-covered wood deck that wrapped around to the front of the shack. They painted the interior and exterior, adjusted the window and door openings to accommodate the mahogany shutters and poured a few concrete steps to get up to the road.

Tommy Lowell, the stutterer whom I had met at Fred's a year earlier, came onboard to help with the renovation. I had run into him in Red Hook before starting the renovation. We happened to line up in front of the ferryboat kiosk at the same time to buy tickets.

"Hi, Tommy, you been provisioning?"

"N-no. I h-had to check on my p-permits for a h-house I'm g-going to b-build."

This conversation would take a while.

I had gotten to know Tommy a lot better since our first encounter. He was a good guy. Usually, anybody who had lived on an island for a few years had cultivated at least some enemies. There were simply too many strong personalities living in the same space. Not Tommy. Everybody liked him. And I knew I was going to listen to every stuttering sentence, as long as it took. He demanded it with his eyes and body language. He also demanded that you not swear while talking to him. If you did, he called you on it. If you did it again, you had to apologize. If you didn't apologize, you would find yourself on your ass wishing you had. He did not stand for rude behavior and was talented enough to put just about anybody on their ass.

"It's a pain in the ass that we always have to come to St. Thomas for permits. Why can't they place an inspector on the island? Did you get the permit?"

Tommy, distracted, looked over my shoulder as he answered, "N-no."

A blond-haired lady we knew from the island was in a heated discussion with one of the loudmouthed taxi drivers who were always in Red Hook competing for riders, constantly badgering ferryboat passengers as they disembarked. The lady, Sherry, worked as an accountant at the resort, and because she had a black belt in one of the martial art disciplines, held her own fairly well when confronted.

"Listen, Tommy, I'm going to start a renovation on the shack next to the inn I'm going to build. I would love it if you could help out."

He continued to look over my shoulder as the commotion surrounding Sherry increased. Two other taxi drivers joined the discussion, obviously on the side of their fellow driver. I was next in line to buy a ticket and stepped up to pay. As I waited for change from my five-dollar bill I looked back to Tommy. He wasn't there. He'd walked to where Sherry and the taxi drivers were now arguing. She could handle herself physically but was in over her head this time. I saw one of the drivers shove Sherry. I heard Tommy say something to the taxi drivers as he neared them. I couldn't make out what he said, but I know that there was no stuttering when he said it.

"Dis ain't yo business, mutterscunt," one of the drivers shouted at Tommy.

I grabbed my change and decided I'd better join Tommy, if nothing else, just to hope that these guys would back off if they saw a third person they would have to confront.

A whole lot happened in the eight or ten steps it took me to get there.

Tommy was called a mutterscunt again. He stepped into the middle of the group, very close to three taxi drivers, took the sunglasses he wore off and held them out for a moment before letting them drop. When the glasses hit the ground Tommy struck, fast as lightning. He punched the tallest in the throat causing him to drop down holding his throat with both hands. Before the other two could react, Tommy punched the driver whose back was to me. I don't know on what part of the head or face the punch landed, but the driver staggered back and fell at my feet. He was in no hurry to get up. The third driver, recovered from watching his buddies go down, threw a wild punch that Tommy easily side-stepped. He grabbed the driver's left arm and brought it up behind the driver's back at a severe angle, incapacitating him, then drove him forward into the concrete wall of the restroom a few feet away. The driver fell onto his ass and held a broken nose with both hands.

The few onlookers on their way to the boat kept their eyes on the violent scene and kept walking to the boat.

I looked at Tommy and said, "You all right?"

"Yeah, n-no p-roblem," he replied, calm and stuttering again. "B-better than th-they are," he said, watching the three drivers stumble and crawl away not daring to say anything or make eye contact with Tommy.

"Thanks, Tommy," Sherry said, and meant it. She and her black belt might have been able to take one of them, but not all three. And if she wasn't so strong-minded the fight wouldn't have taken place anyway. But the taxi drivers were wrong and needed a lesson.

We all sat next to each other on the ferry.

"So, Tommy, can you help out with the shack renovation?"

"I can p-probably help with th-the shack until I g-get p-permits for the h-house I'm b-building."

"Great." I sat back on the bench and said, "Hey, Tommy, what was with the sunglasses, anyway?"

Tommy looked at me and smiled. He said, "I knew th-that they would w-watch the g-glasses fall inst-stead of watching m-me. I h-hit th-them when th-they weren't l-looking."

Chapter Fifteen

"Apparently there is nothing that cannot happen today."
Mark Twain

We finished renovating the shack and I moved in. Every Sunday morning I listened to church music. I wasn't sure, but I thought Catholics didn't sing much in church. They did here—loud and out of tune. My only other neighbors were a few remaining roosters in the bush across the street to the south and, next to them, Lindy Frasier. He later became somewhat of an island fixture, but these were his early years.

He was a tall, skinny West Indian, probably in his mid-twenties, who lived alone in the house inherited from his grandparents. The property was elevated above the road by about six feet and retained with a long stone wall immediately adjacent to the road. Lindy was troubled, to say the least. Most people thought he was developmentally disabled, or as they would say—retarded. I was sure he wasn't. He walked around his property rolling and smoking joints using banana leaves. I would sometimes hear disjointed, but passable, electric piano music banged out from somewhere deep in the darkness of his shuttered home.

Occasionally, he came over to visit me, always smoking an unraveling banana leaf joint. After each puff he licked the banana leaf and rerolled what was left of the joint, ready for the next puff. We stood on the street outside my shack as he mumbled.

I always met him on the street because he stunk—badly. He had different levels of coherency. I would sometimes hear "Mr. Arlan" in the middle of his mumblings and an occasional question like, "Who has de title to dis property now?" I know that anybody who knew Lindy in later years as he walked the streets, stinking and mumbling incoherently, would find this hard to believe, but before all of the medications and homelessness, Lindy and I actually held several coherent discussions.

Back then, Lindy's favorite pastime was to stand on the stone wall and masturbate. And he was hung like a donkey. Unsuspecting tourists walked off the ferry and climbed into the omnipresent open-air surrey buses on their way to Trunk Bay. The road that left the dock was one-way, and all traffic, including the taxis, would have to pass my shack on the left and Lindy's wall on the right. With their heads about the level of Lindy's knees, Lindy would mumble and masturbate a penis the size of a small baseball bat. I could hear tourists' shrieks from inside my shack. On busy days surrey buses stacked up, stopping traffic for several minutes next to Lindy's wall. Lindy's smile was bigger and the shrieks louder and longer on those days.

This went on for quite some time. During the construction of the inn, the construction crews used to signal the beginning of the Lindy show by loudly applauding. A few were pissed off, but I think they were just intimidated by Lindy's size.

The police finally put a stop to it by picking Lindy up and taking him to jail on St. Thomas, where he didn't need to be. They didn't know what else to do. I talked to a health service official I knew on St. Thomas, and she had Lindy admitted to the hospital for treatment. But with no mental health facility in the islands the hospital could only keep him for fourteen days at a stretch.

Needless to say, he spent many stretches in the St. Thomas Hospital being fed a number of drugs that were supposed to keep him off of the wall. The result, after a couple of years, was an unwashed and homeless Lindy mumbling and roaming the streets of Cruz Bay.

He always recognized me though. Inevitably, whenever I walked through Cruz Bay with new customers hoping to sell them one of my houses, a smelly Lindy would approach our group with a "Mumble, mumble. Okay, Mr. Arlan, me son? Mumble, mumble." This always brought a smile to my face as I watched my clients back away holding their noses with looks of horror. I was never sure if these confrontations ever cost me a sale, but if they did, it was the way it should have been. Lindy was part of the experience they were buying into. If they couldn't deal with it, they should have looked elsewhere for their second home.

* * *

Permit applications for the new inn were submitted. While waiting for them to be issued, I dove and hung out with Captain Jay.

One day I was to meet Captain Jay at his new retail shop. Before ducking into the little shop, I looked over at Chicken Wing Joe's restaurant. The chicken wing outlet downstairs was busy, but I noticed a "Closed" sign in the window of his Chinese restaurant upstairs. I walked over to talk to Joe, who was behind the counter of the chicken wing outlet wrapping an order in aluminum foil.

"Hi, Joe. What's going on with your restaurant upstairs?"

"It too busy, too busy. I close down," he said and returned hurriedly to his work.

I walked away shaking my head and returned to Captain Jay's shop. He looked at me when I entered the shop and said, "Hey, Rookie, let's go to McQuin's bar. I made some money today."

He stood at the cash register and told the girl working the shop she could leave. She smiled and out the door she went. Captain Jay opened the cash register and grabbed all of the money.

"Come on, we're ready to go. I must have made two hundred dollars today. That'll buy a lot of drinks," he said, his Elvis grin shining.

I frowned, "That's all profit?"

"Yeah, look," he said, flashing the handful of bills at me.

I shrugged, and we walked toward Mongoose Junction.

McQuin's restaurant was entirely open to the elements, just like his house. It was dominated by a large rectangular bar built in the middle of a larger main dining deck that straddled a creek bed where rain water runoff flowed to the bay. The deck's perimeter had built-in tables that could seat four green director chairs. Covering the entire area was an exposed wood and metal roof perched about twenty feet above the dining deck that reached the roof of the second floor of Mongoose Junction, which was leased by a strange German man who sold strange European furniture and hired even stranger Europeans to manage the shop.

I occasionally visited the furniture store to look at the weird knick-knacks made of heavy wire and twisted steel bars. I don't think the store ever sold much of anything, and it shut its doors after a couple of years. It was currently empty, but I heard someone checking out a loud PA system in the darkened space.

Captain Jay and I sat at the bar on either side of Father Henry, the island's Catholic priest. You would never know he was a priest though; he only dressed the part while in church. He had a lot of island experience, having preached on a few Pacific islands before landing on St. John. Captain Jay loved to tweak this guy's religion, or anybody's religion. Jay didn't understand the philosophies behind religion and could not discuss the merits of one versus another, but he would bring up bazaar sex acts or tell homosexual priest jokes to Father Henry, anything to get a rise. Father Henry was cool, though. He took it all in stride and even told a few priest jokes in return.

Tim McQuin came out of the kitchen and saw us and joined our group from the other side of the bar.

"What's going on upstairs?" I asked him.

"Somebody wants to open a disco," he said, rolling his eyes. "They moved a huge sound system in earlier today."

Captain Jay paid no attention, busy making eyes at a skinny tourist with black, scraggly hair who sat with her boyfriend, or husband, across the bar.

I leaned in front of Father Henry to look at Captain Jay and said, "She's not only ugly but her boyfriend is with her. What are you going to do?"

Jay didn't notice or listen.

I looked at Tim and said, "Hey, Tim, Captain Jay is buying. He thinks he made a boatload of money today. Let's go to the Backyard for some beers. You can relax there."

"Sounds good. I have to feed Blue and do a little paperwork up in my office first. Mary can close tonight and pick me up later, wherever we end up."

"No problem. It's going to take that long for Captain Jay to get over the heartbreak of not scoring with his new girlfriend across the bar," I said, pointing.

She and Captain Jay were in a deep stare. Her boyfriend or husband seemed angry.

McQuin left to feed his dog, Blue. He'd brought down the stocky black rottweiler from the States as a puppy. Though these dogs are everywhere these days and have worn out their welcome in most places, at that time few people had ever heard of one of these giant, ominous-looking animals. Blue was big and never seemed to be very happy. He was so committed to Tim and Mary that he would throw a threatening glare at anybody who came close to either one of them, never wagging his stubby tail. I think he truly wished all other humans were dead. Though used to my presence, I usually declined invitations to visit with Tim in the restaurant office, where Blue hung out during the day.

Between stares at the skinny tourist, Captain Jay told more off-color stories to Father Henry. After a while she left the bar with her boyfriend behind her. I thought that was the end of it. I was wrong.

Father Henry asked me about the inn I was going build next to the church. While we talked, the skinny tourist reappeared sans boyfriend and stood behind Captain Jay.

She leaned in close between Captain Jay and Father Henry and, very clearly, and somewhat loudly, said to Captain Jay, "I want to suck your dick."

Father Henry, who had raised his glass of beer to his mouth to take a drink, I think to avoid being addressed by the lady, spit his beer across the bar. All eyes within hearing distance, including Mary

McQuin's, looked over in shock. The skinny tourist left the bar with Captain Jay in pursuit.

I guess Father Henry was finally tweaked by Captain Jay. I could hardly stop laughing—until the music started.

As if on cue, somebody upstairs decided it was time to check the sound system and started playing a painfully loud disco song that visibly moved the bottles and glasses on the bar top and the surrounding tables. The whole structure vibrated along with the bass line to Rod Stewart's "Do You Think I'm Sexy?"

Captain Jay was somewhere chasing the skinny tourist. Tim McQuin came around the corner in time to see hundreds, no, thousands of two to three-inch dead palmetto bugs falling out of the exposed ceiling rafters above the bar, where they had three years to accumulate. Dead bugs fell into our drinks, our hair, in the food… everywhere, and they continued to rain down on us as the loud, vibrating bass knocked them from their lofty graves.

Most of us laughed. Some didn't. Most swatted dead bugs as they left the area as quickly as possible. As Father Henry and I left I looked at him and shouted, "Didn't the Bible refer to *frogs* that rained from the sky?"

Father Henry smiled, shook his head and walked to his Jeep.

Many left and didn't return. Between the loud music and the falling bugs they had had enough. Others waited, hoping the palmetto storm would stop so the bar could be cleaned up and they could continue drinking. I walked around to the back of the restaurant to use the restroom and found Rupert Morris peeping through the hole in the restroom door that the builder had drilled for a lockset but never installed.

"Rupert. What are you doing?"

Without moving his eye from the hole, he shushed me and said, "Captain Jay is in there with some ugly white lady getting a blow job."

I walked back to the bar area. The music stopped a few minutes after the last of the dead palmetto bugs fell. The restaurant employees and owners swept bugs off the tables and floor. I pitched in.

"Looks like the disco might be bad for business," I told Tim, who didn't seem happy.

We cleaned up the bar and things returned to normal, at least island normal. Tim, Rupert and I were at the bar when a red-faced Captain Jay returned. He knew Rupert had spied on him and his ten-minute girlfriend through the hole in the restroom door and that now the entire bar knew. We quietly stared as he sat down, flashing an embarrassed Elvis grin.

Mary handed him a white Russian and said, "It's penicillin. Drink it."

Captain Jay grinned and turned a little redder.

Tim, Captain Jay and I left for another bar, where Tim and Captain Jay decided to try to spend all of Jay's *profits* by attempting to out-drink each other. After a couple of hours I wasn't sure who was ahead. I lacked the ability to keep pace with the professionals and was ready to go home.

At one time during the night the skinny tourist and her boyfriend came in. It was a popular bar.

"Hey, buddy," Captain Jay shouted across the bar when he saw them. "Hey, buddy, you got any pictures of your wife—naked?"

She giggled. Her boyfriend looked pissed, but he didn't look like the type who wanted a fight. He tried to ignore Jay who then said, "You want some?"

Captain Jay laughed. Everybody in the bar laughed. The guy stormed out. The woman followed, smiling at Captain Jay.

"Ah, don't stare sugar plum, you weren't that good."

The smile disappeared as she left the bar.

I thought about how ugly this could get if we didn't leave soon.

An hour later Mary came into the bar to retrieve Tim. She shook her head and said, "Tim, we need to go. We have a long drive."

"But we're having fun, and I have to protect Captain Jay from pissed off husbands," he slurred.

"Yeah, and pissed off ugly tourists, too," Captain Jay piped in.

Mary looked at me. I shrugged. "Hey, guys, let's change bars," I said, trying to help out.

"Fuck you, Rookie," Captain Jay snarled.

Tommy No-Legs was on the other side of the bar in his wheel-chair happily drinking a beer with some locals we knew from Coral Bay.

Captain Jay looked over. "Hey Tommy No-Legs, let's go kick the shit out of some niggers."

I was astounded and gave Tommy No-Legs and the locals on the other side of the bar an apologetic shrug. Tommy smiled and waved it off. The locals laughed. They knew Captain Jay too well. No harm done.

"Mary, get your truck, and I'll meet you out front with these guys," I told her, trying to figure out how I was going to get them out to McQuin's truck.

I sat down next to them and conjured up the best fabrication I could think of.

"Hey, guys, I just walked outside, and there was some idiot out there with a southern accent saying that 'anybody from the State of Florida is a chicken-shit weenie cause Florida ain't the South,' and that 'anybody who says they are from Florida is a liar and a sissy, cause nobody's from Florida. It's full of Yankee weenies from the north.'"

"Who said that?" Tim slurred.

"Same guy out there who was also screaming that 'anybody who owns a rottweiler is a pussy.'"

Jay and Tim looked at me with slack jaws and red eyes.

"No shit, that's what he said. Go out there and see for your-selves," I pointed toward the exit.

Captain Jay stood up and said to Tim, "Let's go beat the shit out of that pussy outside."

Good. They were both up and moving. I was sure they would forget about my made-up raving idiot by the time I got them into the truck.

Mary was outside when I led the staggering zombies into the street. McQuin's truck was a small Japanese pickup. I lowered the tailgate so my new passengers would not have to try to climb over the sides into the truck. They drunkenly held on to each other and staggered to the lowered tailgate. A little nudge and I had them sitting, kind of, on the tailgate. The springs protested as the back of the little truck sank about a foot.

"Hey, Rookie, where's the son-of-a-bitch who called us weenies?"

"Gee, I don't know. I don't see him anymore."

I went to the passenger door to get in the cab. Blue had already laid claim to the front seat. I said, "Hi, Blue," without patting his head and hopped over the side of the truck into behind the cab. "Let's go. Slowly," I said to Mary.

Mary drove around the square toward Mooie's bar near the dock. As we passed the bar Captain Jay shouted, "You fucking niggers."

The bar was full of locals.

I looked through the window at Mary who spun around to look at me. She mashed the gas pedal, trying to get us away from the bar, hurling Captain Jay and Tim off the tailgate and onto the road, about five feet from the entrance to the bar.

They're dead, I thought.

Mary slammed on the brakes and put the truck in reverse, stopping short of the two rolling idiots who were slobbering and laughing and grabbing onto each other in the middle of the road. I got out of the truck and tried to help Captain Jay up. Mary was doing the same with Tim. Blue barked. I looked into the bar expecting to see a small army of St. Johnian taxi drivers grouping together and preparing to pounce. But most of them were laughing. There were only a few frowns in the crowd. Most in the bar knew Jay and Tim. I heard laughing from inside the bar, and then somebody said, "Dem be two crazy white boys. Best leave dem to crawl around in de road."

More laughs from deep in the bar.

I got Captain Jay on his feet. He continued to laugh and shout obscenities in every direction and wouldn't sit down on the tailgate. When I lowered my shoulder to pick him up into the truck he took a wild swing at me. I ducked and felt his fist brush the top of my head. That was a first, though I'd felt tension between us lately.

He didn't try again, either because he forgot that he wanted to punch me or simply lacked the energy. I hoisted him up and into the bed of the truck.

Mary somehow got Tim into the truck. She scrambled into the driver's seat while I hopped in the back next to Tim and Jay. Mary gunned it, and a barking rottweiler, a sober driver, a partially sober rookie and two completely drunken idiots exited, leaving the good people of Mooie's Bar behind.

Chapter Sixteen

"Find a job you enjoy doing, and you will never have to work a day in your life."
Mark Twain

We received permits for the inn, and I busied myself finding construction crews to build it. Once the crews were in place, we would build a ninety-thousand-gallon cistern that would collect rainwater from the roofs, providing potable water for the inn, which would be placed on top of the cistern and built of wood—mostly termite-resistant, pressure-treated southern yellow pine. There would be enough open space for a laundry on the church side of the cistern at ground level, a few feet from the jalousie windows on the church's east side. Cleanliness next to godliness.

Most cisterns in the Caribbean are poured concrete structures made water-tight by an interior plastering process. Once the walls of a home, or in this case, the inn, were raised, metal was commonly used as the roofing material. Other materials, such as thatch or tile, are much less efficient for collecting rain. Much of the liquid absorbs into the more porous material or evaporates before it can drain into the gutters that carry the water to downspouts that lead directly to the cistern.

Cisterns are a great idea and should be required everywhere in the world. They are mandatory on the island and enforced by building codes. There are no lakes or perennial streams in the Virgin Islands, and drilling wells through the blue bitch rock is cost-prohibitive. The codes require ten gallons of cistern capacity for every square foot of roof area. If the building is two or more stories, the requirement is fifteen gallons of cistern capacity for every square foot of roof area. This means that the typical one-story tourist house covered by fifteen hundred square feet of roof would require a fifteen-thousand-gallon-capacity cistern. With a lot of rain and parsimonious use of water, this formula usually provides the occupants of the house enough water to at least continue to flush the toilets, even during the dry season—unless the house is filled with tourists, particularly tourists and teenage daughters, when no formula works.

Most of the forty-four plus or minus inches of annual rainfall comes when the tourists don't—May through November. Tourist season unfortunately coincides with the dry season, when all of the lush roadside bushes shrink and turn brown, exposing the layers of trash thrown out the windows of locals' cars or just plain dumped in the closest ditch on the way to a landfill.

Most people across the US have never experienced a water outage, not a limited outage but totally nonexistent. No water to flush toilets, no showers, and, unless you thought ahead to store water in bottles and jugs, no tooth brushing.

It usually takes no more than one or two waterless events to learn how not to abuse the privilege of potable water. The water-saving methods learned over a few years living on the island become so entrenched into your psyche that they stay with you for a lifetime. I still cannot take a shower longer than three minutes. I never run tap water while brushing my teeth or shaving. And no matter where I have lived since my Caribbean life I am on constant guard for the sound of water leaks in pipes and toilets throughout the house.

To help water-guzzling tourists learn to respect the fact that things were not always perfect in paradise, just about every restaurant and rental house on the island had been appointed with bath art that read, "Here in the land of sun and fun, we seldom flush for number one." Or, "If it's yellow let it mellow, if it's brown flush it down." Not exactly classic art, but it always produced a smile and had limited effect.

The island had a one million-gallon, rusted, round, steel water tank that would occasionally be filled during the dry season by an even rustier and noisy water barge from Puerto Rico. It cruised into Cruz Bay late at night every few weeks during the dry season and kept everybody awake while its loud pump transferred murky, barely potable water into the big tank. The next day the two competing water truck operators, Pimpy and Paris, took turns filling their two-thousand-gallon-capacity trucks from the rusty tank for island-wide deliveries to those homes out of water. There was never enough to go around, and the supply lasted only a few days.

My plan was to build a ninety-thousand-gallon cistern, the largest private cistern on the island to date. I hired two brothers who had recently arrived from Quebec and claimed to be concrete experts to help oversee the operation. They were pretty good, if you could understand their French accents. Between us we concocted a plan to mix and pour so much concrete, having no idea if it would work.

There was not enough room on the construction site to accommodate all of the material we needed so we had to set up a delivery system that required us to hire the one backhoe and two dump trucks on the island. To help mix the concrete I rented three, gas-powered, twelve-cubic-foot concrete mixers from three different builders on St. Thomas. We stacked hundreds of bags of cement near the mixers and Pimpy parked his water truck off the road as close to the mixers as possible. We had a backhoe and two dump trucks to ferry sand and gravel to the site from the Bulkhead, where it had been off-loaded earlier in the week. I also had one of the laborers flag traffic as best as he could on the one-way loop that bordered the land and was used by all taxis and vehicles that had picked up tourists and goods from the ferry dock.

Sounded simple. Too bad it wasn't. We didn't know how long it would take to hand-mix and place our ninety-yards of concrete. Complicating the effort was one crazy island tradition. If you kept your crew past the normal 3:30 quitting time, you had to supply them with beer before they went back to work and we were nowhere near finished at 3:30. The mutiny started slowly, but by 4:30 it had picked up enough steam to shut down the operation. I acquiesced and sent for four cases of cold Heineken. It wasn't enough. Another problem was that many of the West Indians who manned the mixers couldn't count how many shovels full of sand and gravel they loaded into the mixers, causing inconsistencies in the wet concrete mix. I found one man to count for each mixer crew, which improved the quality. The police chief came by several times to tell me about complaining taxi drivers being held up by the construction. There was nothing I could do about that. I told the chief he could have the leftover bags of cement. Even covered with a tarp they would likely harden after the first blowing rain came through, and I didn't have room to store them in the shack. He went away happy. Taxi drivers continued to honk their horns.

Almost dark and the fifteen-man crew had been at it for twelve hours, and we weren't finished. The beer ran out and they threatened to quit again. I promised more beer and they staggered back to their posts. We lined up as many headlights as we could angle toward the work area and finished an hour after dark. The Canadians didn't like to wear the bulky concrete boots and opted to wear tennis shoes all day. I had to take them both to the clinic to be treated for concrete burns. One of them ended up in the St. Thomas hospital for a couple of days.

In the end, fifteen men had spent fourteen hours and placed ninety yards of concrete, mixed by hand using shovels, gas mixers, a backhoe, two dump trucks, a water truck and eight cases of Heineken. It must have been some kind of record. A few days later, when the plywood forms were stripped, I spotted more than a few glints of green glass from Heineken bottles that had fallen into the mix during the last hours of placing concrete.

***

The next day, as the crew started to form up the walls so we could pour more concrete, two men in suits approached. They were sweating. They deserved to be sweating. Who in hell would wear a suit on St. John? They walked up to me, I guess assuming that I was in charge because I was the one giving instructions to everybody, although I was the youngest person on the property.

The men in suits wore serious looks and presented me with two things—identification cards with the letters "FBI" prominently emblazoned on the cards and a bill of sale with my name on it.

Uh-oh.

I smiled and confirmed that the name on the receipt was mine. I don't know if they tried to be assholes or if they really were assholes as they started questioning me about my shiny beige truck that I had bought from the law firm representing the missing California developer.

I had little information to offer. When it became obvious that I had no association with the California man and was obviously too naive to be considered a pirate, at least by their terms, they relaxed a little.

It turned out the California developer was laundering drug money, and the whole island development plan was a scam. Imagine that. He was simply buying land and equipment with cash and selling what he could to clean his money. This was just before the DEA and the IRS started working closely together to close down the more unprofessional launderers, which this guy seemed to be. I asked if they had caught him, and they told me they had lost track in Nicaragua, where I assumed he was safe from the FBI, as long as he had enough money to pay the Sandinistas.

I was able to keep the truck.

Chapter Seventeen

*"Good judgment is the result of experience and
experience the result of bad judgment."*
Mark Twain

I made my weekly run to deposit unusable construction materials at
the local landfill, which happened to be the favorite playground for
Iva's pigs. I had done this many times. My father, visiting me for the
first time from the US, hadn't. He was a rookie.

"I'm glad you told me to stay in the truck. There's no way I'm
getting out. How could I? What the hell is going on? These pigs are
rocking the truck," my father said, eyes wide open.

I rolled down the window on my side of the truck and climbed
into the bed, which was full of pressure-treated sawdust and pieces
of wood too small to be used for anything useful. Some of the inn's
sawdust made it to the weekend cricket fields, where I was invited
once to learn the game, which I soon realized required an eternity to
understand.

My father had flown a single engine plane from central Illinois
to St. Thomas, just to see if it would make it. I guess there was little
mystery how I could deal with Captain Jay's nonsense without too
much panic. I grew up as the son of a daredevil. But he was out of
his element, particularly with forty or fifty pigs nudging the truck,
bouncing it around as they vied for first position to snatch rancid food
scraps.

"Sorry, piggies, no food scraps in this truck," I told the pigs as I started to offload the construction scraps.

They were medium-sized pigs, ranging anywhere from sixty pounds to about twice that size, and they were aggressive. Who could blame them? Iva left them to roam to search for their food. The landfill was well within their range and provided them with a never-ending supply of fresh, high-quality tourist trash.

I continued to throw trash from the bed of my truck, much of it landing on the pigs that had completely surrounded the truck and wouldn't move. I lowered the tailgate and swept the last of the debris onto the pigs then climbed back through my open window, started the truck and drove on top of the compacted garbage hill to the road. More pigs were on the way in. My father was silent all the way back to town. Once we arrived he simply shook his head and said, "I don't know about you."

I shrugged. I guessed it could have been alarming to have a drove of pigs attack the truck you happened to be in, but it was part of the drill on St. John.

* * *

The cistern of the inn had been completed, and framing of the three units on top of them was nearing completion. I learned a lot about construction but even more about how to fire people. It became a weekly ritual. I sat down with the person I was firing and explained why they were no longer needed, gave them a check and said good luck. Most took it in stride. Some even welcomed it, wanting to get back to work on their sailboats.

The framing crew had been on the job several weeks. They were four guys from somewhere on the East Coast and had arrived on the island several months earlier. I was no expert, but after a couple of weeks it became starkly clear that they weren't either. They made little progress and I was frustrated.

My go-to guy on the job was one of the rock-breaking St. Lucians whom I kept busy as a laborer since we had finished the Condon house a year earlier. He was a giant, soft-spoken man with a perpetual smile who always had a crowbar draped over his shoulder and could drink a Heineken in a couple of gulps. His name was John Johnson. Everybody called him Jonesy. He and I were tight, but I don't think he cared much for the new framing crew from the States. He told me several times that I should get rid of them.

One morning I asked the much older lead carpenter why they weren't making progress. They seemed to be confused about how to frame a hip roof, particularly the compound cuts needed for the hip rafters. He seemed pissed that I had confronted him. I was sure he didn't like the fact that I was far younger than he was, that I was his boss and, most critical, I dared to question his capabilities.

"You don't know what the fuck you're talking about," he spat, inches from my face.

If there's one thing that I don't like, it's an asshole spitting in my face.

In measured Clint Eastwood style, I said, "Get your tools and your crew and leave." I even said it with a smile.

He looked shocked and went over to gather his crew. I walked back to my office. Jonesy approached me and said, "Wha yo do to dem white boys?"

"I just fired the pricks."

He grinned and said, "I never like dem boys."

The fired crew were gathering their tools and shouting obscenities, louder and nastier by the minute.

The head carpenter shouted, "You son-of-a-bitch. You know nothing about construction. You should be the one getting fired, you bastard. We're going to kick your ass, you fucking punk."

He was right, I didn't know much about construction, but I knew the cost of incompetent jerks and how disruptive they could be. I learned that in my youth, playing on various sports teams. I also knew that it was the jerks that needed to be confronted, no matter the outcome.

I walked back to the middle of the construction site where the crew had been gathering their things. The leader picked up a three-foot two-by-four and shook it at me.

I knew this wasn't going to end well for me, but I was committed.

He shook the board at me, spewing nasty names. I held my ground, saying nothing while his crew stood looking like they would rush me at any moment.

It didn't happen.

"You're an asshole. You have no right to fire us," he said, waving the two-by-four.

He and his crew could have easily kicked my ass or worse. Instead, the crew loaded their tools into their truck. The leader wasn't finished and said, "I should kick your ass."

I waited for the pain. It didn't come. He turned toward the truck, the two-by-four still in hand. He climbed in the back of the truck as it drove away shouting, "Asshole! You don't know anything about construction."

I shrugged and turned around to head back to my office. There was Jonesy, five feet behind me with a big smile and the crowbar resting in both hands.

"Did you see what just happened?" I asked.

Jonesy smiled and nodded.

"Were you standing there the whole time?"

"I never like dem white boys," he answered and casually swung the crowbar onto his shoulder.

I guess I know why they didn't kick my ass.

Slim, a local guy who was known more for his calypso singing and who'd told me many times that the crew I had working on the inn didn't know what they were doing, brought a crew the day after he learned that I'd fired them to finish the job. They were good and a lot easier to work with. They didn't care that I knew little about construction; they wouldn't have listened to anything I had to say anyway.

Slim finished his first week on the job and came to me for his check.

"Okay, Slim. What name do I put on the check?"

"Ahh, mon. It's Slim. Everybody know me, mon," he said with his big smile and booming voice.

"Everybody but the bank, Slim," I answered.

"Okay. My last name is Thomas."

"I think the bank is going to need your full name."

He sighed, reached to his back pocket and handed his driver's license to me.

The name on the license was *Berthwaite Thomas.* I wrote his name on the check, looked up and said, "Yeah, Slim is better, between you and me."

Slim took the check and said, "Tanks, mon," as he walked out.

Chapter Eighteen

"It takes a long time to lose my temper, but once lost I could not find it with a dog."
Mark Twain

Captain Jay's most recent money-making scheme was fishing for yellowtail snapper, which he did at night, then selling the yellowtail from the back of his Jeep in Cruz Bay the next day. It seemed to be a legitimate business, and Jay claimed it was profitable. He asked me to go along next trip, and I agreed. In the morning we caught the bait. Beaching the boat in a shallow bay on Peter Island, Captain Jay pulled out a round seine net and waded down the beach, tossing it out like giant pizza dough, then pulling it back by the thin, weighted rope threaded around the net that caused it to constrict when pulled, trapping anything too slow to escape. Most times the net came up empty. Sometimes it came up with a few fish too big to be used as bait. When successful, it came back full of one-inch fry—exactly what yellowtail snapper love to eat. In thirty minutes we had a cooler full of fry and were ready to go fishing, after spending the afternoon diving for an early lobster dinner.

Around ten that night, Captain Jay, Gizmo and I motored to the south side of the island to an area that I knew from previous dives. Below us was a fairly long, steep bank that always had schools of fry swimming its length with yellowtail, barracuda and amberjack swimming in and out of the schools, feeding.

We cut the engine and drifted with the current, which kept us parallel with the bank. Gizmo opened the cooler of mostly dead fry and used a coffee can to dump a gallon or so of the bait into the water around the boat. Captain Jay pulled three balls of fishing line with hooks tied to them from the soffit. We each unwound several feet of line, put a fry on our hooks and threw them overboard, holding onto the ball. Within minutes we had all caught a one to two-pound yellowtail. Gizmo continued to throw fry into the water until we had filled half a cooler with yellowtail. The fishing was not my preferred method. It was too easy. But this wasn't about sport—it was about making money for Captain Jay, who seemed to always be short of it. We kept throwing our baited hooks into the sea and, within minutes, sometimes seconds, pulled up yellowtail—but they got bigger.

"Hey, I just pulled up a fat five-pounder," I shouted, proud of myself until I looked over and saw that Gizmo had an even bigger fish. The fish we were catching were larger than the species should have been.

Gizmo threw another coffee can of fry into the water.

"Captain Jay don't you think it's time to stop feeding these things? Look how fat they're getting," I said, stating the obvious.

Captain Jay laughed and said, "Keep fishin', Rookie. I sell them by the pound."

"Yeah, but once we clean them they're just going to be skinny fish carcasses again."

Captain Jay looked at me with incredulity and said, "We don't clean them. We sell them whole." He threw his baited hook into the sea and mumbled, "Jesus, Rookie."

We were back to the dock by midnight with a cooler full of fat yellowtail snapper.

The next day I went to the ferry dock to pick up some construction materials sent over from St. Thomas. I drove past Captain Jay, who was holding court with several West Indian women and sitting next to a big open cooler that was crossways on the back of the baby-blue Jeep and full of melting crushed ice and what was left of his yellowtail catch.

I stuck my left arm out the window and waved it downward, stopped my truck in the middle of the road and said, "Looks like you've sold most of the fish."

"I've made some money, but I've given a lot of the fish away to the locals. They love yellowtail."

A short, heavy local lady walked by and, with a big smile said, "Okay, Mr. Arlan. Okay Captain Jay. What you got der?"

"Here, Miss Gwennie, have some fish." He pulled out three yellowtail, put them into a plastic bag and handed the bag to her.

"Tanks, Captain Jay, you be such a nice boy."

I rolled my eyes.

"Mr. Arlan, me son. Da nex time you go divin' you make sure to bring back dem an*gel* fish fo me."

I acknowledged her request with a laugh and Miss Gwennie waddled away on her fireplug legs.

"Who the hell would eat an angel fish?" Jay asked with a wince.

"She does. Every time she sees me with my speargun she hollers at me from her house, 'Mr. Arlan, me son. You be sure to get dem angel fish.' They stink up the boat so much I wait until the last dive to shoot one or two. They're so damn easy to shoot, the way they swim together in twos and threes. The last time out I was able to engineer a three-in-one shot."

"I can't believe you would shoot those smelly fish, even for Miss Gwennie," Captain Jay said.

"That's the bad thing. I threw them in my bag with the rest of my fish. By the time I got back to shore, all of the fish smelled like stinky angel fish. I ended up giving them all to Miss Gwennie."

I left Captain Jay to his fish and went back to the inn. About two hours later I received two calls in quick succession. The first was from Gizmo.

"Mr. Arlan. Da police jus took Captain Jay away in handcuffs. Trew him in da back of de car, too."

"Gizmo, we know the police. They are our friends. They wouldn't do anything like that to Captain Jay. Hell, he just gave them both a bag of fish."

"No. Did is a new fella. From St. Thomas. He mean, mon."

I hung up ready to go the police station when the phone rang again.

"Arlan, me son. Dis is Alex. Jay is here at the station. You need to get here, fast."

"Hi Alex, I just saw you in Cruz Bay, I thought you weren't working today."

"I off duty. De startin to rotate in officers from St. Thomas. I saw wha happened to Captain Jay and came to call you."

The police station was a simple, blue, one-room concrete building across from the ballpark. No jail, just a counter with a desk behind it and a bench. Captain Jay sat on the bench, hands cuffed in front of him, and he was crying. Not from fear, but from pure anger. He seethed and stared at the new police officer. I was glad he was cuffed.

Alex was out of uniform and standing behind the counter.

"Okay," I said to Alex.

"Okay."

At the desk sat a stern looking police officer whom I had never seen, working on a written report.

Captain Jay intermittently sobbed and screamed, "He slapped me. He fuckin' slapped me. He put handcuffs on me and then slapped me. The fuckin' pussy. Can you believe it? He slapped me." His face was red and his eyes were watery.

It was hard to say if the redness and the tears were from a slap or not. It would have to have been a pretty hard slap. I could tell that Alex was not happy about seeing his friend in handcuffs, but he remained silent. Gizmo walked through the door.

"Tell him, Gizmo. Tell him he slapped me. Sittin' in the back of his car with handcuffs on, and the little pussy slapped me."

Gizmo affirmed what Captain Jay said with a nod.

"Excuse me, officer…?" I politely addressed the uniformed guy behind the desk.

"Pearson," he stated, not looking up from his paperwork.

"Yeah, whatever. Are you charging Captain Jay with something?"

"Sellin' fish witout a vendor's license."

"Are you kidding?" I said, looking at Alex, who shrugged.

"The little pussy slapped me in the face," Jay screamed.

We've heard that, I thought.

I continued, "Listen, he was giving most of the fish away. He's been doing this for a while. Hell, everybody sells things down by the dock. This is St. John. It's not like we have a lot of stores around."

"You his attorney?"

"No, but what are you going to do, drag him back to St. Thomas—for selling a few fish?"

"I'm going to teach da people of dis island dat der are laws. And dat the police from St. Thomas are goin to enforce dem."

I rolled my eyes and smiled. Great, Elliot Ness has arrived to save St. John from itself.

I looked at Alex and asked him, "Alex, can I use the phone?"

"He cannot use dis phone," growled Pearson.

"He fuckin' slapped me. He can't do that. I was handcuffed. The pussy," Captain Jay cried, again.

Alex grabbed the phone off the desk and placed it in front of me at the counter. Officer Pearson looked like he was going to pull his gun and shoot us.

"Who you call*in*?" Officer Pearson asked.

"A friend, asshole."

Pearson stood, and I said, "The new attorney general, Alan Hendrickson."

I had met the new attorney general a few weeks ago. He was from the US and was dating a good friend of mine on the island. They had invited me to dinner. He seemed to be a good guy. Our friend, Linda, and I had discussed the lack of autonomy on St. John. He realized the frustration of being the *little brother* island and seemed to have some sympathy. Or maybe he wanted to ensure that he would get laid later that night. To impress Linda, I suppose, he made sure to tell me that I could call on him at any time for help and handed me his card, which I luckily remembered and had brought with me after Gizmo's call.

I was about to see if the new attorney general was going to be good to his word. I hoped he and Linda were still dating.

Pearson wheeled around as I dialed the number of the attorney general's office.

"The son of a bitch slapped me," echoed Captain Jay again from the corner.

A secretary answered. I introduced myself and asked to speak to her boss.

Alan came on the phone, and I told him what was going on. Pearson fumed. I checked to see if his hand was going for his sidearm. Captain Jay hollered in the background.

"Yeah, that was him. He's still handcuffed," I told Alan.

Alan asked me to hand the phone to the officer, which I did. Whatever was said I don't know. It was pretty much a one-sided conversation with Pearson doing the listening.

"Yes, sir," he finally said, handing the phone back to me.

Alan said, "The officer is going to let Captain Jay go. You guys come over to talk to me about this next week."

"Thanks, Alan. I'll tell Linda you've been a big help."

Officer Pearson, steaming, walked past me to take the cuffs off Captain Jay.

"Um," I cleared my throat trying to get Officer Pearson's attention.

"I think you should get back in your patrol car and let Alex unlock the handcuffs when you are far away from here."

Pearson looked at Captain Jay, who licked his lips like a lion about to bite into a fresh kill. Without saying a thing, Pearson threw the key to Alex and left.

We never did go to the attorney general's office to discuss Jay's predicament. The next week, the attorney general was off-island, and the following week the headlines in the St. Thomas paper read, "Police officer placed on leave after shooting through waterfront crowds at a rental car filled with tourists."

Officer Pearson had stopped a car full of aging tourists for rolling through a stop sign on the crowded St. Thomas waterfront. It didn't seem to matter that the stop sign was hidden by a police van that was to be used as a headquarters for the upcoming carnival. Pearson was on foot and ran a half a block to step in front of the tourist car, holding up traffic. The driver could not understand why a policeman stepped in front of the car, and it was further reported that the tourists were not sure that the police officer was real. They had heard about robbers dressed as police officers on islands in the Caribbean.

Confused, the tourists drove on, leaving Officer Pearson standing on the side of the road waving for all traffic to stop. Some did and some didn't. Pearson took out his service revolver and shot at the fleeing tourist car, hitting the left rear tire.

The permanent police headquarters was a few blocks farther up the road, and the frightened tourists pulled into the parking lot and ran into the station to report that a crazy guy dressed like a police officer was shooting into the waterfront crowd.

Pearson was eventually fired, and we heard that he had moved to New York City.

Several months later Captain Jay and I were at McQuin's restaurant when Tim came down from his office with the day's paper from St. Thomas. Stuffed on the third page was a story about an ex-St. Thomas police officer who was arrested for armed bank robbery in Queens. His name was Pearson.

Chapter Nineteen

"The Doors Open at 7, trouble begins at 8."
Mark Twain

Time passed, and the normally abnormal island life went on, but not without changes—small but critical additions that would pave the way for bigger changes. New people moved to the island to try their hands at life in this pirate's paradise. Few were normal. It was as though someone turned on the whacko spigot, allowing more unusual characters from the US to flow onto the island to live with the whack-os that already lived there. With island life becoming easier—fewer power outages, more restaurants, more stores with available staples, the promise of cable TV so we might receive current news from the world microwaved from St. Thomas and even a new barge that could hold several trucks in one trip—maybe they would stay.

One newcomer, who called himself Michael Angelo, walked around Cruz Bay all day long, playing a triangle. Not one coherent sentence ever left his head. Rumor was that he was the ex-drummer for the group that recorded that ridiculous song, "In-A-Gadda-Da-Vida." He made about as much sense as the title to the Iron Butterfly song.

Two recently retired female porn stars from New York City moved down together and kept the island interesting for a while. The island even had a new, and meaner, criminal. Ramsted Cashew came to the island from Dominica, by way of St. Thomas, and was fond of entering the wide-open homes when people were sleeping and taking what he could carry, scaring the hell out of anybody who woke up. Nobody knew where he lived or where he took the goods he stole, and he was elusive.

He tried many times, unsuccessfully, to molest ladies on the beach, particularly if they were alone. He had tried this once to our friend Sherry, the black-belt, and she responded to his overture by black-belting the shit out of him. He was caught several times for burglary but never showed up in court. Bench warrants were issued but never served. It's not like he was a clever criminal; he just happened to live in a place with a less than clever criminal justice system and a mostly apathetic population.

As more people arrived to live on the island, there was a demand for a higher degree of professionalism with all things. "May I help you" started to replace the blank stare when you entered a store. Fancier signage replaced many of the hand-painted and sometimes hand-scribbled signs that hung above entrances to shops and bars. There were more brand name products to be found in the stores. Even the quality of construction increased, thanks to the hoard of new carpenters who had moved to the island.

There was also a more ominous change. Some of the old-timers started to disengage from the village, not pleased with all of the newcomers and the commotion in town. The island was outgrowing them.

Drugs were always present on any island, but other than pot smokers, there hadn't been much of a drug culture on St. John. That began to change when cocaine became the new chic drug throughout the developed world and began to trickle down to the islands.

The DEA flexed its muscles in the early eighties by cooperating with the IRS to find out how suspected drug dealers obtained their assets. The few dealers on St. John weren't selling drugs on the island but either lived on profits they had made elsewhere or were actively involved in transporting drugs from Mexico, Jamaica or Belize, into the US. When they got wind of the DEA and IRS strategy many moved down-island and out of reach—for a while.

I ran into Rupert one day in Cruz Bay, and he introduced me to some guys who had moved to the island within the past year. We sat at a roadside table and ordered a round of beers. Captain Jay drove by and shouted, "Hey you," causing all four of us to look at him.

"No, you two gay guys," Captain Jay said and nodded to the side of the table where Rupert and I sat.

We laughed. The two newcomers didn't. One of them looked at me and, in a low voice, said, "Who is that asshole?"

I couldn't think of a time when somebody didn't know who Captain Jay was.

Captain Jay couldn't hear the question and paid no attention to the new guys. He asked, "You gay boys want to go fishing tomorrow?"

Both Rupert and I had to decline for different reasons.

"Okay then, go fuck yourselves," Jay said with a laugh and drove on.

The newcomers watched with pained looks.

"You guys don't know Captain Jay?" I asked.

"No, is he always an asshole?"

I shook my head in disbelief. Had the island changed that much?

***

Construction on the inn was winding down, and I was looking for other things to do. I'd been approached by the new owners of Gallows Point to help them develop a resort. It was tempting. Maybe I could get more than five hundred a month. I told them I would think about it and see them the next time they came to the island.

My construction mentor, Dick Bramble, stopped his Jeep next to the inn when he spotted me climbing down from the roof.

"How's the truck holding up?" he asked.

"Probably as well as your Jeep. Hey, did the FBI come to see you?"

Dick smiled and said, "Yeah. Hop in. I want to show you some land I'm thinking about buying."

We drove up Centerline Road a couple of miles from the village and turned down a rocky jungle path near the top of the mountain. On the right of the path was steep downhill terrain. Not a sheer cliff, but steep enough so that large trees could not take root. On the left was a gentle upward slope with large canopy trees and a mostly shaded understory that turned out to be easy to walk through.

Dick angled his Jeep off the road as far as he could on the uphill side. The ass-end partially blocked the road, but it was unlikely that anybody would be using it. Leaving the keys in the ignition, just in case someone needed to move it, Dick climbed out of the Jeep and pulled a hand-drawn map from his pocket.

"I think the property is a little farther where the land flattens out completely," Dick said over his shoulder as we walked through the tall trees.

A few minutes later the natural sounds of birds and trees rustling in the trade winds were interrupted by several loud crashing sounds. We both stopped and looked behind us.

I said, "Jesus, Dick, are there elephants up here?"

We both laughed and listened for a moment. All was quiet.

Dick said, "It could have been a boulder that lost its purchase on the mountain side. I had one go through a house I was building once. Luckily, nobody was in it. I had to reframe the entire living room and kitchen."

He shrugged, and we continued through the bush to where we thought the property was and climbed a rock outcropping where the mountain dropped off on the west and south side, exposing stunning views.

I said, "Wow. This is the best view I have ever seen. Look. You can see homes on St. Croix. That's forty miles from here. And look how clear Puerto Rico is. That's at least eighty miles away."

We both took in the view for a moment.

"You should buy this," I said.

"I don't know. Who the hell would want to be way up here in the middle of nowhere?"

"I would. I think a whole lot of other people would, too. The island is changing, Dick. New people with different priorities are moving here, or trying to anyway. The days of needing to be walking distance to the dock are gone."

"I guess I'm getting old. Hate to see the place change so much."

"Buy it," I said.

"Maybe," he grunted, and we climbed down the rocks.

We retraced our steps back to his Jeep. But there was no Jeep.

"Dick, didn't you park around here?"

"I thought so," he said, looking as perplexed as I.

"You think somebody took it?"

Leaving the key in your vehicle was common, but nobody would ever steal a car. They'd just move it if it was in the way. I didn't hear any other car drive up the rocky trail while we were looking at the land.

"Na. Who'd steal a car on St. John?"

I walked across the path and noticed a swath of mountain scrub missing and small trees broken or bent over on the downhill side.

Dick noticed at the same time. We walked to the edge of the road. About fifty feet down the slope, caught up in the brush, was Dick's new Jeep truck, upside down and pretty beat up.

"There's our elephant," I said.

"I guess I didn't set the brake," he said and shrugged.

We both laughed and started to walk down the path to Centerline Road where we knew we could get a ride to Cruz Bay pretty quickly.

* * *

Captain Jay's uncle John was on-island to talk to Jay about building new boats. John was a successful, small-time boat builder in Florida. Captain Jay wanted a larger, diesel-engine dive boat. He had convinced Uncle John to come to the island, where he could rustle up orders for other boats from local fishermen, maybe getting enough orders so that Jay could get his boat at a heavy discount.

I'd been at a rare Saturday meeting with an attorney on St. Thomas. When the ferry docked I walked directly to the Backyard Bar, where I knew I would find Jay and his uncle. The popular bar wasn't crowded yet, and I sat next to Jay and Uncle John at the bar. They'd already had a few beers and were in deep discussion about the boats. Uncle John talked about the cost-efficiency of building in threes, which was small enough for him to manage, while using the same mold and identical diesel engines.

"Yeah, I could probably come out all right building three, as long as we can sell the others fairly quickly," he said, looking at Captain Jay questioningly.

"I know we can sell one to Victor. He wants a larger boat for his fish traps. I want my boat. Just build the third one anyway. We'll sell it," Captain Jay told his uncle.

The discussion went on as the evening crowd wandered in with *okay's* flying freely.

Rupert held court across the bar with recent female transplants to the island that he had yet to conquer and was using his best Harry Belafonte smile and Rupert charm to try to change that.

The two ex-porn stars came in and sat on the stools next to Uncle John. They always got smiles from the men—none of the women.

Maynard, a wiry boat captain from the US, sat close to us on my left. He liked knives and had spent a fair amount of time in a US prison for taking his passion a little too seriously. You always had to keep your eye on him. He sat in bars, talking to no one in particular, his shifty eyes constantly scanning the crowd, waiting for the first sign of trouble so he could jump in with his knife. He was a scary guy but, fortunately, made up for it by being small.

Beatles music played through the bar's speakers, and most of the patrons were a few beers into the night. The continentals and tourists sang along or swayed to the music, which wasn't calypso or reggae enough to get the locals involved.

Captain Jay and Uncle John continued talking about the new boats. Maybe he was getting bored with the conversation and wanted to stir up some trouble, or maybe he really didn't like the Hawaiian shirt that I wore, but Captain Jay turned to me with a grin, then grabbed my Hawaiian shirt by the collar and tore it open to the last button.

"That gay boy shirt is just plain ugly," he said and turned back toward John.

My Hawaiian shirt was one of two collared shirts I owned. I had bought it at a used clothing store in Tallahassee before coming to the island the first time. I only wore it when I had meetings on St. Thomas. I thought it looked good.

"You son of a bitch," I said and gave Jay a hard shove. He was off balance because he had immediately turned on his seat to see if the ex-porn stars had watched him tear my shirt. He fell into Uncle John, who fell into the first porn star, who fell into the second porn star. Had she not been sitting on the last stool in the row, more would have gone down.

Four people and four stools and four drinks were on the floor. I laughed, but I was pissed off and drunk enough to not think about the possible repercussions of the shove. Other people in the bar hesitated for a moment but carried on. The bartender wasn't happy.

Captain Jay lay on the floor, surprised but laughing. Uncle John picked up the stool he had been sitting on and pulled it up to the bar. The ex-porn stars were pissed; their drinks had spilled all over the fronts of their skimpy halter tops. I would have thought they would have liked showing off their ample assets. Guess not. Maybe the indignity of landing on their ass in front of the crowd made them a little mad.

Captain Jay got to his feet and pushed me and my stool over, grabbing the right side of my open shirt as I fell, ripping it so that it now hung on one shoulder, then righted his stool and sat down. I did the same. A couple of beers later Captain Jay looked over at me with his Elvis smile.

"Take that shirt off, gay boy," he said with a laugh and shoved me off of my stool. I broke the fall by placing my hand against one of the trees the bar had been built around and recovered to grab his T-shirt by the v-neck and jerk hard downward. The shirt tore, but my forward momentum as I stood to finish the job sent Captain Jay and his stool flying backward into Uncle John, and Uncle John into the two ex-porn-stars. People, drinks, and stools were down—again.

Uncle John was the first up. He looked at me with a bewildered smile and said, "You're a tiger."

I looked at Captain Jay, expecting to get pummeled any moment.

Captain Jay staggered up and shoved me hard. He wasn't going to let me push him over twice in front of the crowd. I grabbed what was left of Jay's shirt as I fell, and he went down hard on top of me. We rolled on the ground trying to get to our feet when a shot of whiskey was tossed in my face.

Anything but whiskey.

I hated the smell of whisky and almost threw up. Vodka was thrown into Jay's face.

The porn stars had their fill. After their second less than graceful forced fall they each ordered a shot of whatever they were drinking and then threw them in our faces and stormed out of the bar. The other bar patrons, fully engaged with our brawl, laughed.

From the ground I noticed that nobody in the crowded bar rushed to take the porn stars' stools, opting instead to stand off to the side, away from us. It also seemed that some of the people who had been on our side of the bar earlier either stood or sat on the other side of the bar.

We settled back at the bar and ordered another drink. Uncle John was still with us but showing signs that he might too move to the safer side of the bar.

Two drinks later, just as it appeared that things were settling down, Captain Jay said, "You think you're tough don't you, Rookie?"

"Fuck you."

This time he grabbed me by my shoulders and threw me against the tree that had saved my fall earlier. I bounced off and landed next to it on a little bridge that had been built over a fake pond. While on my back, Captain Jay jumped on me, straddling my chest. I was stuck. I glanced over at the crowded side of the bar and saw the weasel Maynard scoot over to a closer bar stool with a deranged look in his eyes, his right hand resting on his waistband.

Shit.

My head exploded as Captain Jay grabbed my ears and pounded it on the wooden bridge, similar to the way he pounded Stu Black's head on the bottom of the dinghy.

I had two choices to try to stop him from spilling my brains onto the bridge. One was to ram my knee into his testicles. But that might raise the stakes and make it a real fight, which I was sure to lose. The other was to grab a bunch of his thinning blond hair and snap his head sideways, hoping he would go sideways with it.

I chose the latter. The move didn't knock Captain Jay off of me as I had hoped, but he did stop pounding my head against the hard wood. He held his head and screamed. I held a handful of Captain Jay's hair.

Jay had had enough and limped back to his bar stool holding the side of his head and ordered another beer for both of us. By now, the remains of my Hawaiian shirt were on the floor, and what was left of his T-shirt was barely hanging around his neck. Everybody opposite us watched. A newcomer to the island came around the bar where we sat.

"You shouldn't be picking on that guy, he's smaller than you," he said, looking at Captain Jay.

Captain Jay looked at me and then back at the wannabe hero. We laughed.

"You guys are ruining everybody's night. You need to stop," he said.

Captain Jay and I looked at him then to each other.

"Let's do it."

We stood together to pounce on the guy, but he scurried out to the road before we made it to the door.

"He's fast," Captain Jay said, and we returned to our stools.

The bartender had not been happy all night. I didn't know why. As a direct result of our marathon brawl, he had sold more drinks than usual as the word got out about the brawl taking place at his bar. He only had to work one side of the bar, occasionally serving us our drinks. The ungracious prick evidently called the police. Alex and his brother Jimmy, both in police uniforms, poked their heads inside the bar the last time I was on my ass. They smiled and shook their heads as they retreated back out to the road. I was glad it wasn't Officer Pearson. He might have shot us.

Fran, the owner, came in, likely called by the bartender, looked around, rolled her eyes and stepped in front of us.

"You guys have to leave," she said.

"Why? We won't fight anymore," Captain Jay said and grinned.

"We have a dress code."

I looked over at what all of the other bar patrons were wearing. Tank tops, skimpy halter tops, bathing suits; one man wore a wet suit from an earlier night dive. A resident artist, who frequently sported a white rag mop on his head and told everybody he was a white Rasta, was there.

She saw me look to the other patrons and said, "You have to be wearing a shirt to be served."

"No problem," Captain Jay slurred. "Come on, Rookie."

I followed him out of the bar to his retail shop, which was part of the small, wood-sided building that separated the Backyard from the street and was only a few feet from the entrance to the bar. Jay took a key from his pocket, unlocked the door and we each grabbed a T-shirt.

"Hold on, Rookie. It might be a long night," he said, throwing a handful of shirts to me. We walked back to the bar, passing a friend who had seen enough.

"You guys are crazy," he said. "Maynard tried to sneak toward you guys with that fucking knife he carries down his pants. I don't see how it doesn't cut his dick off. Anyway, before Tommy Lowell left he told him that if he didn't back away h-he'd b-be w-wearing h-his knife up h-his ass."

I was glad Tommy was around to fend off any real danger. I hadn't seen him and was surprised he didn't kick both of our asses, though, just for causing trouble.

We stumbled back into the bar. Uncle John was gone. My new T-shirt read, "Mine your own fucking business." I thought that something was misspelled, but what the hell, I was looking at it upside down.

Jay put his shirt on. It had a picture of a guy sitting under a palm tree with two bosomy women, and I think it read, "It's here, wish you were beautiful." The side of the bar we'd occupied for most of the night was still empty. We sat down on our stools, Captain Jay proudly grinning at the owner and the crowd across the bar.

I don't know how many more times that night I was on the ground, either on top or on bottom. I don't remember leaving, but I woke up the next morning beat to hell and hung over. My arms and shoulders had purple dots where Captain Jay's fingers had grabbed me the night before. My hair had dried blood in it, I couldn't tell whose. The back of my head throbbed, and every muscle in my body hurt.

I heard a vehicle drive up to my house and the honk of a horn. I looked outside and saw a shirtless Captain Jay in his baby-blue Jeep, sitting tall with a smile just below his aviator sunglasses. I'd forgotten about the dive we'd planned. I grabbed my gear and limped outside, just in time to see Captain Jay lean out of his seat and vomit on my new concrete steps.

I wanted nothing more than to cancel and had the feeling, regardless of his body language, Captain Jay wanted to as well, but he was stuck with the dive. He needed another boat order and had invited a few potential boat buyers on a play dive on his boat, which was a similar, but smaller version of what Uncle John planned to build.

I begrudgingly climbed into the Jeep. "Where are we going today?" I asked Jay, looking at the patch of dried blood on the side of his head where there used to be hair.

"Mingo."

Good. Mingo Cay had a long, sloping reef with depths of forty to ninety feet with minimal current and was just a few minutes from Caneel Bay.

"I don't think I'll do any spear fishing today," I said and looked over at Captain Jay's purple bruises the size of finger tips on his upper arms and shoulders.

"Me either."

Jay drove to Caneel, and we met his guests at the dock. Gizmo had the boat and gear ready.

Everybody on board, Gizmo took the boat toward Mingo Cay, about a mile from Caneel Bay.

The seas were calm, but I felt very queasy and sat on the rail in case I needed to throw up. Captain Jay was a lightweight Elvis as he tried to joke and mingle with his guests.

Gizmo anchored the boat inside the reef close to shore and put the divers in the water. A few snorkeled to shore, opting not to put tanks on. Captain Jay and I swam slowly behind Gizmo and the guests who dove, letting the warm salty water nurse our wounds. A few yards in front of me Captain Jay went vertical, pulled his regulator out of his mouth, and threw up into the sea.

A cloud of mush and food chunks shot out of his mouth and sort of lingered. Some chunks floated up, some chunks sank, but the cloud drifted with the light current. Fish fed on the chunks. First small wrasses and sergeant majors, but then some larger rock hinds joined in.

At that moment I wished I'd brought my speargun.

Captain Jay put his regulator back into his mouth, took a short breath and then removed his regulator again, as if he was ready to feed the waiting fish again. Nothing happened. We slowly swam back to the boat. I couldn't wait to get home and sleep.

Chapter Twenty

"I must have a prodigious amount of mind; it takes me as much as a week, sometimes, to make it up!"
Mark Twain

We finished the inn, and the Condons decided not to build more units for the time being. They declared they were on a limited budget and wanted to rent out the three finished units above the cistern. I needed to find furniture, fast and cheap. I scoured the classified ads in the St. Thomas papers until I eventually found enough odds and ends to work. I found a warehouse full of rotting mattresses. The owner charged me thirty-five dollars for all of them. He just wanted them gone. I sent most of them to the dump but salvaged six, heavily-stained mattresses that weren't too moldy and aired them out for a week on the new deck that ran the length of the inn. The used sheets I bought would cover up the stains, I hoped. I was allowed to return to the Caneel warehouse to pick up some old rattan furniture pieces.

The ex-porn stars moved into one of the units. Black-belt Sherry rented the middle unit, and a group of young new rookies from the US moved into the last one, where they kept the porn stars busy, or vice versa.

We opened the laundry with coin-operated machines, but there was not enough room for the public to maneuver around each other and the machines. I hired a large lady from St. Kitts to put two "quats," her down-island name for quarters, into our machines to wash, dry, and fold laundry that was dropped off by islanders who either didn't have washers or had run out of cistern water. The ninety-thousand-gallon cistern made the laundry more profitable than the three rental units above it.

The group that purchased Gallows Point came down from New Jersey to ask me to build a resort for them, and again I told them that I would think about it. On their way to the ferry to return to New Jersey, they stopped by the inn and told me the offer would stand, and they would be happy to fly me up to the States to discuss it further.

I had offers to build homes for new land owners from the US and entertained a few of them. Driving out to see one of the lots, I heard the familiar screaming and cussing of Chainsaw Pete over the sound of his chainsaw somewhere deep in the bush off to the side of the road. He was busier, and bloodier, than ever.

I couldn't wrap my head around building one house at a time. My knowledge of construction and development had expanded rapidly. To me, building one house or ten houses at once was the same process, just a difference of scale. I couldn't see returning to where I started, building a single house. I declined all of the house-building offers, not sure what I wanted to do—familiar conundrum territory for me.

Walking through Cruz Bay thinking about my future one day, I ran into Charlie Kline, who had returned after being gone for several months to parts unknown. He sat on a bench in the park with a friend from New York—a short, pudgy man with a heavy New Yawk accent—and talked very fast.

"I see you've finished the inn in record time. What are you going to do now?" Charlie asked with his familiar gruff voice, a voice I'd missed in his absence.

"I don't know. I might take over Gallows and develop a project for the new owners."

Charlie smiled and said, "The place has been closed down for a while. Looks like they could use some help."

We were alone in the park. Nobody was near us to hear our conversation.

"My friend here, Joe, might have an offer for you."

Great, another house to build, I thought.

"Did you buy some land?" I asked Joe.

Joe and Charlie gave each other sideways glances.

"Joe is into a lot of businesses in New York and other places," Charlie said and looked at Joe before continuing. "He wants to disappear."

"What? What the hell does that mean?" I paused, not sure I wanted to hear any more. "Do you have a mean wife, or something?" I said with a laugh.

"Or something," Joe smirked.

Charlie took a deep breath, leaned forward on the bench and said, "It's not that easy to disappear. It has to be something plausible."

I wanted to leave but curiosity took over. I leaned forward, close to Charlie's ear and asked, "What the fuck are you talking about?"

"Look, everybody here knows you. You haven't screwed up. And everybody knows that you're a pretty aggressive diver, not afraid to dive in dangerous places."

"Yeah, so?" I said, waiting for the punch line.

Joe interrupted with, "I'll gives ya forty large to take me diving and let me disappear. Ya know what I'm sayin?"

"No. What's forty large?"

"Forty grand. *Dollars*," he answered, looking at me like I was from another planet. I wished I was.

"I still don't understand. You want to die? Sorry, but you don't look like much of a diver."

Charlie explained, "We were thinking that you could use Jay's Seabird, drop anchor maybe over at Cow and Calf. Swim around a while so other boats see you. There are always plenty of boats passing by, and people know you and the boat. They'll assume you or Captain Jay have divers in the water. Joe will hide below the rail until you come back. You'll sneak him through Fisherman's Pass at False Entrance in Benner Bay and drop him off on a houseboat a friend of his lives on in the bay."

Benner Bay was close to Cow and Calf on the southeast side of St. Thomas. In the bay was a funky marina and boatyard full of broken boats and aging hippies. Several live-aboard house boats were permanently anchored in the bay. The bay was surrounded by mangroves. There was also a half-sunken barge that had been converted to a bar and had become a favorite drinking hole, in spite of the curmudgeon bartender and his nasty parrot that had the run of the barge and bit freely.

The entrance to the bay was a narrow, dredged channel that didn't look anything like a natural entrance. The more natural-looking entrance was a wide opening in the mangroves with a shallow rocky shelf that didn't quite break the surface of the water. For a first-timer entering the bay, the wide, calm opening with houseboats flanking either side looked like an inviting entrance, and many of the unsuspecting boaters abruptly and destructively parked their boats on that hidden shelf—hence, the name, False Entrance.

But there was a way through False Entrance, known only to a few locals and Captain Jay. We called it Fisherman's Pass. It was a narrow opening in the barely-submerged shelf, hidden by the murky water of the bay and too shallow to cross over unless you had your boat up on plane, which required navigating it at high speed. You had to know exactly when to turn in order to miss the rocky shelf on either side of the Pass. The people who lived on the houseboats hated anyone with knowledge of Fisherman's Pass.

As with so many Island experiences, the first time I learned of Fisherman's Pass was with Captain Jay. We'd been on a play dive and were taking our St. Thomas divers back to their cars, parked at the boatyard at Benner Bay. We entered the beginning of the bay at the same speed we'd been cruising out in the open ocean, about twenty knots.

"Hey, Captain, don't you want to slow down a little?" one of the St. Thomas divers asked, laughing as though he knew Jay would slow the boat.

I looked at Captain Jay and saw the big Elvis grin.

Without slowing down, Captain Jay turned hard to starboard, almost knocking everybody off their feet and headed for the houseboats and the submerged rocky shelf. Everybody on the boat was familiar enough to know that this was False Entrance, not the correct entrance. All eyes and mouths were wide open, and all hung on to the nearest part of the boat, waiting for the crash.

We flew through False Entrance and between the houseboats, our wake causing the houseboats to bounce up and down unmercifully, producing more movement than they'd probably seen in a lifetime.

We pulled up to the dock from the opposite direction of the normal approach, getting astonished stares from onlookers in the boatyard.

"Welcome to Fisherman's Pass, boys and girls," Captain Jay said and laughed.

Charlie coughed, bringing me back to my present dilemma. Charlie and Joe's plan sounded pretty screwball to me.

I asked, "So I'm supposed to come back to Cruz Bay and report that my guest went missing?"

"Happens all of the time," Charlie said with a smug expression.

That was true. Charlie's partner got into trouble after losing a paying guest.

The guest had a heart attack underwater and floated out of view while Charlie's partner was crawling under a coral head trying to snare a lobster for his fledgling lobster roll business. The body was found the next day.

"I could get in trouble."

"You're not in the dive business, and he won't be a paying guest. You just explain that you took a guy out who claimed to be an experienced diver, and he got lost. Never surfaced."

"Yeah. But I'm gonna show up on Marathon Key in five years," Joe piped in.

I looked at the pudgy man and then to Charlie, winced and shook my head. Charlie sat back and smiled. He presented a proposal, for which I had no idea if he would be receiving money, and simply waited for me to decide if I would be part of it. I don't think he cared one way or the other.

We heard a commotion and looked up to see Cashew, the pseudo-Rasta molester of women who was wanted on several USVI Marshall bench warrants, running for his life through the park.

"He gonna be keeled. John gonna keel dat boy," a local lady screamed.

Several steps behind Cashew, and running just as fast, holding a machete above his head, was the barefooted, broad-shouldered John Gibson, the Tarzan palm tree climber. He was seriously pissed off.

They ran past us and up the hill. I rose and followed at a safe distance along with the rest of the crowd to see how this would end. In any case, it couldn't be good for Cashew, which would have pleased a lot of us.

Jeeps stopped. People walking through the streets stopped and stood wide-eyed as the two passed. I jogged up the hill so I would not lose sight of the chase, which was now outside the police station. That is where Cashew, the wanted criminal, made the best choice he had probably ever made in his life. He ducked into the police station. I couldn't see what happened after that, but I didn't hear any blood-curdling screams.

Charlie and his friend Joe were not far behind me. With the show over, Joe asked me to think about his offer and let me know that I had an open invitation to visit him in New York.

Chapter Twenty-One

"They did not know it was impossible so they did it."
Mark Twain

Uncle John finished the three boats and announced they were ready to make the trip from Florida to St. John. Victor, the local fisherman, had been convinced to place a deposit on one of the boats and would make the trip. Jay had convinced a couple of his wealthy regular Caneel dive guests to invest in his new dive boat, and he was looking for more. He pulled his Jeep next to my shack at the inn and shouted, "Come on, Rookie, we're going to go to Jost Van Dyke for lunch."

I stepped onto the wrap-around porch and took a deep breath, smelling the jasmine that grew on the north side of the porch. It was a Sunday and the weather was perfect. I smiled and asked myself, "When isn't the weather here perfect?" I looked to the road where Captain Jay waited. I needed no convincing. I grabbed whatever gear I thought I might need and hopped into the Jeep.

"Who's coming?" I asked Captain Jay, knowing that he would have invited more than me to a trip to Jost.

"My partner and his new wife are coming."

I smiled and said, "Captain Jay, I met your partner from Boston, and I met the guy from Minneapolis who was supposed to be your partner. Which partner is coming along today?"

"Neither. You haven't met this guy, yet. He is a Rockefeller heir. Nice guy."

"These guys are all partners with you on what, a fifty-thousand-dollar boat? Any one of these guys could buy a fleet of boats. Why do you need three of them?"

"They don't know each other. Don't say anything about the other partners."

I shrugged and decided it was best if I didn't know any more than that.

The two partners I'd met were wealthy men in their forties who loved to dive. They were frequent guests of the resort and usually brought their friends along on dives and acted like they owned the boat, which they did—or thought they did. They evidently didn't know each other but had invested in the same boat, not that it mattered. They were happy and could easily afford to be treated as "one of the boys" when diving with Captain Jay.

I smiled and said, "Fine with me."

We arrived at the resort. Gizmo and Scott were already on the boat.

"Hey, Scott. You have a day off. Good for you."

"Okay, Gizmo. Everting okay wit you?" I asked with a laugh.

"Everyting fine, Mr. Arlan," he said, returning the laugh.

Tied along the dock was Captain Jay's other boat, the Seabird. Captain Jay had hired a new guy several months earlier to help with weekend dives. Craig was a tall, lanky guy who could swim like a fish. His judgment was sometimes suspect, though. He waited on the dock for his guests to show up for a two-tank dive.

Captain Jay's new girlfriend arrived and stepped onto the *Jumbee Jay*. I helped her with her bag.

Captain Jay approached Craig and asked, "Where are you gonna take them?"

"I was thinking about Carval."

"Don't go to Carval. It's too rough today."

"But I was out there yesterday, and it was great," Craig said.

Jay leaned into Craig, who was a good four inches taller than Jay, and said, "Not Carval. Understand?"

Captain Jay's new partner, Gerald, showed up with his wife, and we motored out of the bay toward Jost Van Dyke.

We were enjoying a perfect day at the Sandcastle resort and restaurant on Jost Van Dyke, a place where you never needed shoes, everything under foot was sand. Sitting in a chair, you couldn't resist the urge to curl your toes up in the cool sand as you sat at a table enjoying food and drink.

During brunch the waitress whispered into Captain Jay's ear that he had a radio call from Caneel. Jay returned a few minutes later.

"We need to get back," was all he said.

Scott and I looked at each other and shrugged. Gerald and his wife looked a little perplexed but followed us to the beach to wade out to the boat which was anchored stern to shore, the bow anchor in deep water and a stern-line tied to a palm tree on shore. Gizmo was visiting family, and we had no way to contact him. We left him on the island.

Captain Jay was distracted and drove the boat with the large swells south toward the north shores of Congo Cay, Mingo Cay and Grass Cay. Carval Rock, closer to us, loomed large in the foreground, the swells from the Atlantic crashing into its rocky north shore.

I stood and carefully walked to the center console and said to Captain Jay, "Want to do some diving?" I'd hoped to get a smile.

"That's what you and Scott are gonna to do," he said, not smiling.

"We are?" I looked at Jay. "I was just kidding. It's pretty rough to be diving here."

"The Seabird is down there," Jay said and nodded toward Carval Rock. "Craig, that fuckin' idiot, brought his divers out here, where I told him not to go, and sank my fuckin' boat. The fuckin' idiot."

"Where are Craig and his divers?"

"They were picked up by the Tortola ferry. I couldn't get the whole story, but I guess they found a spot on the rock where the seas were calm enough to hang on until they could be rescued. They should be back at Caneel about now. The fuckin' idiot."

We bounced in the swells as close to Carval as we could. I looked down into the water. Visibility was excellent. I could see coral surrounding the rock ninety feet down.

"What side of the island is it on?" I asked Captain Jay.

"Don't know. We'll start lookin' here on the north side."

There were a couple of old tanks and some random gear on the boat, and Scott and I pieced together what we could while Captain Jay held the boat as still as he could.

"There it is," he shouted and pointed to the port side.

Sitting on a sandy patch ninety feet down was the clear outline of the blue Seabird.

Scott and I stepped from the dive platform into the water and swam toward the sunken boat. The heavy swells we confronted on the surface dissipated within ten feet. Fortunately, we were far enough from the rock and the underwater cut and weren't in danger of being swept through to the other side. We reached the boat in less than two minutes. As we closed in on the Seabird our vision blurred, and our skin burned. A barracuda hovered over the center console seat, looking like he was ready to take the boat for a spin.

Dive gear was strewn around the boat and we gathered masks and fins and weight belts and secured them in the stern and center console hold. It was obvious that Craig had prepared to dive when the boat went down. There was a trail of heavy weight belts that had been dropped on a path that led to the calmer south side of the rock.

There was no evidence they tried to anchor. Craig probably planned to dive there but brought the boat too close to the north face of the rock, where a reflecting wave bounced back over the bow, causing Craig to put the boat in reverse where a following wave breached the stern and filled the boat with water. The boat would have sunk, leaving the divers treading water on the surface.

After our initial assessment I surfaced and shouted to Jay that we were going to follow the trail of gear the divers had dropped and bring what we could to the surface. Captain Jay followed us as we grabbed all of the gear we could carry to the surface, including a couple of expensive underwater cameras.

"My skin is burning up," I said as I hung onto the dive tray as best I could in the rough sea. Scott was just as miserable and said as much.

Captain Jay said, "Leave the rest of the gear. We can return later for it. You guys better get up here and rinse the fuel off." Captain Jay didn't need for us to tell him about the fuel. Even in the rough water he could see the rainbow-colored hue that formed in the water above the boat before moving on with the current.

"I'm gonna to rig up some rope," Jay said as we climbed on-board.

Captain Jay's girlfriend handed us a bottle of dish soap. Scott and I stripped down to nothing and spread the soap over our blistering skin.

"What are you going to rig up?" I asked.

"We're gonna pull the Seabird up," he said matter-of-factly.

"How are we going to do that?"

Captain Jay tied three ropes to the frame of the boat and said, "Get your gear back on, Rookie. I want you to go back down and tie these ropes onto the bow cleat and the two side cleats. Use the bow line on the Seabird to hang on while I lift the boat."

"Are you fucking kidding? You want me to ride the boat up? Its weight will pull this boat apart."

"You have to. When you get to the surface you need to make sure the sea cocks are open. I'll keep the speed up and tow you around the sound until the water drains out through the sea cocks. Then you need to close them."

I stepped off the boat into the rough sea with ropes in hand and bobbed on the surface for a moment while clearing fog from my mask.

"Make sure you don't let the rail get in the way of the rope. And yank three times on the port side rope when you're ready," Captain Jay shouted as I sank below the surface.

I kicked down to the boat. The barracuda had returned to hover above the captain's seat. I tied off all three lines and secured one of the short tie off lines still on the boat to the bow cleat for me to hold onto if everything went to hell, which I was sure was going to happen.

I checked for anything loose, secured all hatches and made sure the sea cocks were open. I yanked hard three times on the port line that stretched up through the blue up to the distant outline of the *Jumbee Jay* and hung on for glory.

I heard the engine pick up RPMs above me. The Seabird bow rose, slowly. The fiberglass creaked loudly from the stress. I wondered which boat would be ripped in half first. The Seabird lifted off the sandy bottom, slowly at first, then more rapidly and at an unbelievably steep angle. I left the barracuda behind. An unsecured line that I hadn't seen earlier whipped through the water, snapping at me. We were moving through the water so fast I couldn't turn my head. If I did, my mask would fly off. I couldn't see Captain Jay's boat. The bow was at such a steep angle, all I could see was the bright surface drawing closer. I hung on to my line with one hand and the steering wheel with the other. Committing both hands to one or the other could have been a disaster. Holding on to the wheel kept me from flying out of the boat, and holding on to the bow line kept my weight off of the wheel which otherwise might have broken off. The noise of the water gushing past my head and the creaking of the fiberglass was deafening.

I was about to let go of both and abandon the Seabird. Then there was silence. The pressure on my mask was gone. We'd broken the surface like a nuclear submarine. For a second or two, the Seabird was flying—until gravity took over and it crashed back to the surface. My head hit the steering wheel, knocking my mask off. I almost fell on my ass, having forgotten that we were moving forward as fast as Captain Jay could pull us.

The boat was full of water and heavy and far from being on plane. I looked forward at Captain Jay's boat. Captain Jay was looking back at me with a frown. Scott and the other passengers were hunkered down staring at the boat's stern, which was taking most of the stress.

I hid as best I could behind the center console in case one of the lines snapped. The water level was now down to about my ankles, deeper near the stern. We picked up speed. Soon I felt the familiar sensation of the bow settling down on plane, the boat immediately moving faster and more smoothly.

After a few more minutes the creaking of the fiberglass stopped, and the water drained. I shut the sea cocks and steered the Seabird, matching Captain Jay's movements as we returned to the bay at Caneel. Captain Jay towed my powerless boat close to his mooring. I grabbed the buoy and tied off the Seabird before we slid past.

That was interesting, I thought as I secured the lines and waited for Jay to swing back and pick me up.

Captain Jay pulled the *Jumbee Jay* up to the Caneel dock. Scott, Jay's girlfriend, Gerald, his wife and I went to the bar for a desperately needed drink. Captain Jay went to kick Craig's ass.

I looked at Gerald and joked, "So, are you ready to invest?"

He eventually did. So did the other two, each convinced that they held a first lien on the new boat and never knowing otherwise.

Chapter Twenty-Two

"It is easier to stay out than to get out."
Mark Twain

The Gallows Point owners continued to call, and I continued to say *maybe* to their requests for me to visit them in New Jersey. Captain Jay prepared to go to Florida with enough crew to bring back the three boats Uncle John had built. Charlie Kline told me that he was going to his house in Queens for a few weeks and invited me up to visit with him and his friend, Joe, who still bugged me, through Charlie, about helping him disappear. A girl I had met on the island a year earlier had called. She lived in New York City and worked for the *Economist Magazine* and had invited me to visit. All things pointed to New York, and I knew how to get there—free. All I had to do was spend a day or two with the Gallows Point owners.

I flew to Newark on the Roach Coach, an Eastern Airline flight that left San Juan every night well after midnight and flew directly to Newark or JFK airports. My flight landed around five in the morning at Newark Airport where I had to wait until one of the Gallows Point partners picked me up. We'd agreed earlier that he would come at eight in the morning. He pulled up to the arrival curb in a new Mercedes with a big smile and a distractingly large gold watch on the wrist of the hand that held the top of the steering wheel. I threw my duffle bag in the back seat and received a limp handshake as I settled into the front passenger seat. The partner, George, was a fairly recent

Greek immigrant and ran a large seaside restaurant for his partners. With the perfunctory chatter out of the way before we exited the airport property, George proudly told me how much money his restaurant had made the last week, the price of his Mercedes and how much his forty-four-foot Swan sailboat was worth.

"We'll go for a sail while you're here. You'll love it. Ya like to sail, don'tcha?" he said, making me wonder how he'd picked up a perfect New York vernacular inflection so quickly.

"I live in the Caribbean, remember?"

"Yeah, but I'll betcha ya never been on a boat as nice as mine."

I shrugged and wondered how much more of George's bullshit I would have to endure before finding my way to New York City, where I really wanted to be.

"Hey Arlan, reach under your seat and pull out the case that's there."

I reached under the seat, felt a soft case and brought it up and into my lap.

George smiled and said, "Open it up."

I unzipped the bag and pulled out an Uzi submachine gun.

"It's an Uzi," George said smugly.

So, I thought and placed it back into the bag.

"You ever shot it?" I asked.

George's smile disappeared, and he said, "It's for personal protection, ya know. This is gangsta land, ya know."

He didn't say much the rest of the drive, and we ended up at his restaurant, a mostly empty spacious dining room with a view of the New York skyline. It obviously didn't open for breakfast, but I realized it could easily seat a few hundred people when open for lunch and dinner, likely concentrating on quantity, not quality. We drank beverages and made small talk while waiting for the other partners to arrive.

I had no intention of working with these men, not that they didn't need help. The plans they presented at the Gallows Point bar during their last trip proved that. The property, the island and the Caribbean deserved a lot better than what this partnership had proposed.

Gallows Point made up the south side of the main port of entry into St. John. Half of the five-acre peninsula had shoreline on Cruz Bay, and the other half, a palm-tree-lined rocky coastline, faced west to St. Thomas and the sunset. A few funky cottages, an open-air bar, and a couple of horseshoe pits had been built and operated by Richard "Duke" Ellington, a mystery writer who had bought the land from the USVI government in the fifties. He rented the cottages to tourists and ran the bar, which was the favorite hangout for the continentals living on the island during the fifties, sixties and seventies. Toilets broke, water ran out frequently, nocturnal rats slept behind wall hangings during the day and old refrigerators didn't keep food cold. When tourists complained, Duke would laugh, put a massive arm around their shoulders and herd them to the bar, where he plied them with free drinks until they forgot what they were there to complain about.

The property was one of the finest locations in the Caribbean, and the rumor was that Duke had made a fortune from the many options to buy the property, keeping the option money when the prospective buyers couldn't bring the required cash to the table on the closing date. It was emotion, not investment sense that led prospective buyers to Gallows. The property was that special.

Some argue that Gallows Point was the model for the fictional inn in Herman Wouk's, *Don't Stop the Carnival.* Others were sure that the story was based on either Villa Olga or an inn that used to be on Hassel Island, located in the Charlotte Amelia Harbor. Any of the three could have been the model to the fictional inn in Wouk's masterpiece about operating a small inn on a Caribbean island.

The group from New Jersey had money and had offered Duke full price for Gallows Point, and he reluctantly accepted. Duke and his wife moved to Florida, where both died of natural causes within a year.

A few months before I traveled to New Jersey the partners were on-island to informally present their plans for the property. There was no official announcement, but we'd heard that the partners were on-island and had been seen carrying rolls of architectural drawings. More people than usual showed up at the bar at Gallows Point every evening that week, hoping to see the plans. One evening a rolled set of architectural plans was placed on what was the focal point of the open-air bar at Gallows Point, a giant hand-painted round table depicting the island. Nobody made a presentation, the owners seemingly content just to mingle with the crowd. Dick Bramble finally meandered over to the round table, unrolled the drawings and started to flip through the layers of thirty-six inch by twenty-four-inch blueprints.

Most of us shuffled to look over Dick's shoulder at the plans. The first page was typical title and owner information. The name of the resort was to be called, Gallows Point Motel and Restaurant. Motel is usually the word reserved for places you drive to and from, hence the *mo* part of *motel*. I guess these guys were expecting that cars full of vacationing families, on their way to Philadelphia, would drive into the Gallows Point parking lot and check into a room. The second page was an artist's rendering that depicted a fireworks display from little Steven's Cay, a mile off of Gallows in Pillsbury Sound. It brought awkward smiles and a few coughs. The next few pages brought laughs and sighs from half-drunk, full-drunk and sober locals and continentals who'd gathered at the bar. They showed the developer's intention to level the center of the property and rebuild it with concrete cascading waterfalls that ran the entire property, from the road to the bay. The pages were rendered and colored in multiple Caribbean colors. It looked like Walt Disney puke.

The owners quietly retreated from the bar and quietly left the island the next day.

So I was in New Jersey, to be wined and dined and charmed, New Jersey style, into designing, permitting, and building a new resort on Gallows Point.

"We are prepared to double whatever your salary is and give you equity in the deal," one of the partners told me while we sailed into the East River on the Greek's fancy sailboat.

"I have been making thirty thousand dollars a year," I lied, and looked over to a waterfront restaurant with shiny silver siding. I was pretty sure that it was on the shore of Manhattan, where I really wanted to be. I wondered if they could simply drop me off at the restaurant.

They continued to negotiate, with themselves really. I was doing everything possible to get them to tell me to take a hike. By the end of the sail I had been offered ten times what I was presently making and an equity position, and more importantly, the project would be mine to create and develop, if I accepted the offer. They gave me everything I asked for, and a lot I didn't ask for. I'd have to think hard about this, but one thing was for certain—the project I would plan would look nothing like theirs. There would be no concrete cascading waterfalls or fireworks on Stevens Cay, and the name would not have "motel" in it.

I used the little car they gave me and drove into New York City to visit my friend at the *Economist Magazine*. While there, I called Charlie Kline to see if he was still in the area.

"Yeah, come over to Queens tomorrow," he said in his gruff voice. "Plan on staying the night. Joe wants to show you something."

I drove to Charlie's house using the directions he gave me. I had never been to any of the boroughs of New York. Coming from an island, and before that, a corn field, this place was intimidating. Paving and non-descript, multi-story structures covered one hundred percent of the land, creating a permanent grey, dirty look. Other than time spent in their cars, which also all looked grey to me, it seemed to be permanent indoor living for the residents of the indistinguishable neighborhoods that I drove through. There weren't a lot of people walking the streets, and I didn't see any trees, or anything else green. The deafening sound of traffic and horns replaced the deafening tree frogs I had become used to in the Caribbean.

Charlie was glad to see me and welcomed me with a beer and a refrigerator full of the type of food he thought I might like to eat while I was his guest. I smiled. He was polite in an old fashioned way, like a visit to one's grandmother's house—big smile and lots of food—but the last grandmotherly personality you would ever want to piss off.

"We're going to go to one of Joe's bars tonight. That okay with you?" he grumbled, politely.

"Does he still want to disappear?" I asked.

"It seems so."

"Charlie, I don't get this. Who is he running from? If it's the law then I would be an accomplice, if caught. If he's running from the mob or a drug dealer I'm just as likely to be killed. And what is with this bullshit that he is going to resurface on Marathon Key in five years?"

"He'll have to explain all of that. I'm just the middle man. He's glad you came to visit him on his turf. He wants to give you a dog and pony show. Prove that he's the real deal."

"Is he?" I asked.

Charlie smiled and said, "I guess we'll see."

We drove through the concrete neighborhoods to a concrete strip mall with a large concrete parking lot. Everything looked grey. A lot of cars were parked near one of the store fronts in the middle of the strip. All of the other businesses looked to be closed.

We entered and were immediately hailed by Joe from the back of the room, near the pool tables. He held a pool stick and laughed with a couple of big guys with crewcuts and tattoos.

"Hey guys, come on back. Harry, get them whatever they want to drink," Joe shouted to the bartender.

The room was filled with smoke and disco music blasting from a juke box near the bar and a cacophony of New York borough accents that I had a hard time following.

Charlie and I were led over to a booth. Beers were delivered, and Joe pulled up a chair, giving Charlie and me each our own side of the booth. Joe was obviously in charge of this place. He joked easily with the patrons who addressed him from their tables or bar stools. The two big tattooed men frequently whispered into Joe's ear and were sent off on some unknown errand within the bar.

"I'm glad yous guys came. How's everything on the island?" he asked, looking at me.

"All is fine. Thanks for the beer."

Charlie was quiet, as usual.

Joe went on to tell me about some of the businesses he owned and how well he was connected. To what, I never learned.

"Ya see, I'm connected. I can get anything done, and I'm a man of my word."

"Why do you want to disappear?" I asked.

"I tell ya that later. I want to prove to you that I can get things done first. Ya see, here's what is gonna happen tonight. Didja see that new Cadillac in the parking lot when you came in? The shiny blue one."

I hadn't noticed a Cadillac, just a bunch of big, ugly, grey cars. I had no reason to think there wasn't a blue Cadillac out there in the parking lot. I shrugged and said, "Yeah?"

"Ya see, we're gonna wait until closing and then leave to get in our cars. Only my new Cadillac, it ain't gonna be there anymore. Ha, ya get it?"

I did, but wished I hadn't.

"This is a new business for me. I'm gonna make ten large tonight. The car only cost me nine. Got it at a discount from my brother-in-law's car lot. Ha. And then, in a week or so, after nobody can find my stolen car, I get the insurance money," Joe said with a laugh and slapped the table. "I'll probably get eight or maybe the full nine back. This is gonna be good business."

Charlie and I looked at each other and laughed with him.

We spent the rest of the night listening to Joe tell us all about his deals. He always 'made out like a bandit.'

Close to closing time the crowd had thinned, and soon after we were the only people left in the bar, except the bartender and the two tattooed goons.

"Okay. Time to leave," Joe said and stood up laughing, giving us a wink.

He was the first out the door with Charlie and I right behind him. The goons stayed in the bar.

Joe stopped abruptly, causing me to bump into him.

"Oh, shit," Joe said, and stood with his mouth open and his hands spread, palms up, as if to say *what the fuck.*

I couldn't hold back the laugh. All of the cars were gone all right—except two. A few car widths from Charlie's car was a shiny Cadillac. I guess it was blue after all.

Charlie and I got into Charlie's car, leaving Joe shouting to his goons who were running out of the bar to see what their boss needed.

I laughed and said, "I don't think I'm going to take Joe up on his offer."

"Good idea."

Chapter Twenty-Three

*"Let us not be too particular. It is better to have old
second-hand diamonds than none at all."*
Mark Twain

I used Charlie's phone the next day to make plane reservations back
to St. Thomas. I needed to get my new Gallows Point partner's car
back to him and get up to Newark to catch a fight. I wasn't sure what
day I would leave, so I called two different airlines that flew from
Newark to St. Thomas and made about fifteen reservations on each in
different names for three different days ensuring I would have a seat. I
did this every time I flew, never knowing the exact day I would leave
until the last moment, and never making my scheduled return flights.

In the old days of flying, pre-9/11, and before computers and
added fees for just about everything except blowing your nose while
in flight, flying was a lot easier. Reservations were made without the
need for a credit card or a deposit. All you needed was a name, and
there was no added fee for changing the return portion of your flight.
It didn't matter that I had many reservations in different names. The
seats would all be reserved. I would usually decide at the last minute
which day I wanted to leave. I would check onto the flight using my
own name. There were always empty seats reserved under the other
aliases I used to make the multiple reservations around me. Sometimes I would reserve an entire row using my name and two made up
names, then fly in comfort with no other passengers in my row.

My reservation strategy only failed on a few occasions. If there were flight delays involving planes from the same airline going to the same place, the empty seats around me would fill up with passengers transferring from other delayed flights.

* * *

After agreeing to the terms of my soon-to-be contract with my new partners from New Jersey, I returned to the island eager to start a new project. I moved into Duke Ellington's old house, one of only three masonry structures on the Gallows property. Another was the Gate House, which would be the only original structure to survive the project I was soon to build. I think it's a gift shop today. The third was the Red House, adjacent to the house I moved into. The remaining structures were funky wooden shacks—the Yellow Cottage, the Green Cottage, the White Cottage and the Tree House, which was behind the bar and built on piers in and around a couple of mature trees.

For the next few months I had a crew clean the cottages up and get them ready for rental. My partners sent a new CJ Jeep down from the States, and I had a large enough bankroll from my new partners to have furniture built for the cottages and my office. It was always better to build furniture using termite-proof, pressure-treated lumber rather than buy stock furniture from the stores in St. Thomas, which would be consumed by termites in short time.

A couple of years earlier I had gone down-island for a month. When I returned I grabbed a beer and sat down in a wood-framed, canvas-seated director chair that had been painted white. The chair collapsed, sending me flat on my ass. The chair looked fine before I sat down. After the termites had their way, the only thing left of the chair's wooden frame was a spongy material held together by the undisturbed white paint.

Captain Jay had brought the three boats down from Florida without sinking any of them or getting anybody killed, but I understand that there were numerous close calls. Victor, the local fisherman proudly anchored his new boat in Cruz Bay. It could hold more fish traps than any of his competitors. He was happy. Captain Jay's new dive boat was bigger than his other diesel engine boat we had grown used to. He sold the hull of the Seabird after it sank. The old outboard engine didn't survive the sinking. The third Uncle John built boat was anchored in Cruz Bay, unsold.

I had a new boat, too.

One afternoon I sat in the park with Charlie Kline when a beat-up fiberglass boat with a small outboard engine motored into the bay and tied alongside the dock. Three grungy guys stepped off speaking Spanish.

Charlie walked out to where they had tied up and started a conversation. I was too far away to hear any of it. The conversation looked to be pleasant enough, if not a little too serious. I saw Charlie say something which brought a big smile to the three amigos who all shook Charlie's hand as he walked back to where I sat.

Charlie sat down and told me that the men he'd talked to were fishermen from Puerto Rico and had traveled from Ponce, a quaint fishing village on the south side of Puerto Rico, all of the way to the BVI, fishing along the way. They hadn't had much luck fishing and were out of money and fuel.

I said, "That sucks. What are they going to do?"

"They're going to take the next ferry to St. Thomas, taxi to the airport and then catch a Prinair flight back to Puerto Rico," he said with a smile.

"I thought you said they're out of money."

"Not anymore. You just bought their boat."

"What?"

"You're doing a lot of free diving, and you can't keep catching rides with Captain Jay. He's up to his ass in trouble with that new boat of his anyway."

That was all true.

"How much did I pay for that boat?" I asked as the Puerto Ricans took their few personal possessions off the boat.

"Two-thousand dollars. You better walk over to Chase Bank and get cash for these guys. They're not going to take a check."

I was flush with cash, thanks to my new salary at Gallows. I did need a boat, but wasn't shopping for one. And this thing was a real beater.

I walked to the Chase Manhattan Bank, kitty-corner to the park on the southeast side, withdrew two thousand dollars and walked down to the dock to pay for my new boat. Charlie, having checked out the hull and the engine as best he could, stood at the center console helm and declared that the boat was ugly, but solid.

"*El barco es muy bonito*," I told the Puerto Rican trio, trying to be friendly.

The man who seemed to be in charge smiled and took my money. He said, "*Es muy feo, pero solido*," repeating perfectly in Spanish what Charlie had said.

The Puerto Ricans joined the line to board the ferry to St. Thomas, and I jumped onto my new boat. It was an old Sea Craft, and it needed a lot of work. I ended up painting it dark blue and bought a new Evinrude outboard engine. The boat served me well for the next few years, and the boat and I were almost inseparable during that time.

***

I was bothered by what Charlie had said about Captain Jay being up to his ass in trouble with his new boat. He still owed Charlie money, and his retail business seemed to be failing. It was only open a couple of days a week, and his attempts at long-lining for swordfish failed as well.

I went long-lining with him once. He bought a half-mile of floating line coiled on a large wheel, attached it to the stern of the *Jumbee Jay* and headed out to the Puerto Rican Trench late in the afternoon, arriving well before sunset. We drifted with the westerly current and slowly let out the buoyant line from the wheel, attaching shorter lines every fifty feet with large hooks on the end baited with squid. The shorter lines were weighted and sunk to a depth of sixty to eighty feet. At either end of the half-mile of surface line were buoys with strobe lights attached. We followed the two strobe lights at either end of the floating line, which was drifting at the same pace as our boat. By midnight we were ready to catch swordfish, the cash crop of long lines. It was easy work after placing the long line. We simply waited until morning to haul in our catch.

I tried to sleep, but Captain Jay had a giant spotlight pointed down into the sea. The bright light attracted a shark that he shot at with his Mini M14, jolting me out of my short naps.

"What the hell are you doing?" I shouted from the small, humid cabin, which I shared with fenders, extra anchor line and dive gear.

"I'm killin' the damn sharks that might bite our asses when we're snarin' lobster. Don't you know nothin', Rookie?"

"Jesus," I said under my breath and lay back on the hard foam cushion.

At daylight, Jay, Gizmo and I reeled in the line, hoping it was full of hooked swordfish. We pulled in several baitless hooks and two very alive and very pissed off dusky sharks, which Jay dispatched with his Ruger Mini M-14 and dumped back into the sea.

What a waste, I thought, and almost said. But Jay had the weapon in his hand.

I was young and didn't know much, but I felt that Captain Jay was imploding, though I didn't have sufficient confidence in my opinion to express it to him. It was as if Captain Jay had to have bigger and faster everything to keep his image as king of the island, an image that was slipping away thanks to all of the newcomers who didn't give a damn about the locals or the continentals who had pioneered the lifestyle they now enjoyed. Captain Jay's side ventures failed to pan out financially, mostly because of his lack of focus and inability to run them professionally. I wasn't sure how or if he made money with his dive business. The big boats, though impressive looking, were fuel hounds. Charlie constantly reminded Jay that he would make a lot more money if he got rid of his big show boats and simply used a few rubber dinghies to dive the immediate area. Charlie was right.

I was also getting an uneasy feeling that Captain Jay was bothered that I was having more success on the island, while he was struggling. I hadn't yet heard him complain about financial problems, but that was relative since he didn't understand basic accounting or the difference between gross and net. He never appeared to be depressed or moody. On the surface, which is what any of us ever saw, he was still Captain Jay, king of his domain. But the chinks in his swashbuckling armor were growing.

Chapter Twenty-Four

"The lack of money is the root of all evil."
Mark Twain

I'd hired and fired two different architects for the Gallows Point project who didn't seem to understand what I wanted for Gallows, or maybe I couldn't explain it. I was a rookie, after all. The third architect I hired, Denny Stockman, was the ex-partner of the last one I fired. Denny not only designed Gallows Point but most of the future projects I was to build on the island. He came up with some great vernacular designs that were almost genius in their simplicity, and our projects never lost roofs in hurricanes, which became the litmus test for quality of construction and design in the Caribbean. It paid to recognize local history and expertise by following the design wisdom of predecessors.

The quintessential Caribbean-styled buildings found in tourist brochures and throughout the islands didn't happen by accident. The designs came out of two things—available materials and hurricane protection.

Hundreds of years ago, the primitive, mud-coated waddle and daub gave way to the Caribbean-style when Europeans arrived to the islands. Stone was readily available and was mortared together using sand and molasses. Sometimes the sugary mortar was mixed with dyes from plants to give it a pink hue.

Hip roof styles, framed from indigenous mahogany and other hardwood trees, didn't overhang the stone walls they were built upon.

Instead, where shade was needed, a simple shed roof was attached to the stone walls.

During hurricanes, occupants huddled within the stone walls under the hip roof. An overhanging roof would have allowed wind uplift, tearing the roof from the stone walls, taking with it the only structural integrity that kept the walls from collapsing onto the people below.

If an exterior shed roof was destroyed in a storm, nobody was hurt, and cheap, or free, labor made it easy to rebuild them. Later, Portland cement was used to pour tie beams and ring beams at the tops of the walls, lessening the structural need for a hip roof. But, by then, the hip roof design had become typical and one of the main elements of Caribbean-style architecture. I was always amused by the new builders who would arrive to the islands and attempt to incorporate large, uneven roofs with giant overhangs into home designs that should have stayed in California, or other areas that don't see two-hundred-mile-per-hour winds. I once saw one of these roofs fly over my house and into Great Cruz Bay during a hurricane. It looked like a giant flying nun's cap just before crashing into the sea.

While Denny Stockman poured his energy into the design, I was busy writing the required environmental assessment report for the project. In the interim, I had leased the bar to an old-time continental who had been drinking at the bar since the early fifties and put a fresh coat of paint on all of the cottages. I rented the cottages to tourists for a while then closed down the rental operation and let my friends and workers stay in them. All of the wood cottages would be razed once construction on the project started. The concrete cottages would be used as needed, then demolished as the project grew.

Captain Jay took the Tree House behind the bar. Tommy Lowe had agreed to be my construction foreman and moved into the house on the point. I filled the others with friends or friends of friends who needed temporary housing while they were getting back on their feet after any kind of disaster. As long as they didn't complain about the bad mechanical systems and nonexistent room-service, I didn't charge anybody anything. It was good to have us all at the same address. Tommy and Jay had been on the island longer than I, but at the ripe old age of twenty-six, I was part of the old guard, no longer a rookie—except to Captain Jay.

Though I was free-diving more and more, Tommy and I frequently went on play dives with Captain Jay on his new boat. I even occasionally helped Captain Jay take his resort guests diving. On one of these dives, Captain Jay had taken his resort guests way around the island to Eagle Shoals, a reef that was just below the surface and only exposed when the seas were heavy. It could be a challenging dive and most operators stayed away if the current was strong or the seas high. On this day the sea was calm with no current to speak of, and the visibility was more than eighty feet.

Jay led the group of six divers around the reef. I followed, urging stragglers forward when they stopped to explore the more subtle beauty of the coral reefs that Captain Jay and I found boring—sponges, anemones, crustaceans, echinoderms and the multiple species of colorful aquarium fish, all far too small for our spearguns.

Captain Jay kicked up a small, five-foot nurse shark by grabbing its tail as it quietly rested under a large coral head. Startled, it swam in a large arc among the divers before settling in a large hole in the coral where it met the sandy bottom. The docile nurse shark, a giant catfish with small teeth, posed no threat to the divers.

Resort dive guests have varying reactions to large animals under water. To some, every big fish is a shark, and they become frightened, sometimes causing us to chase them down and keep them from kicking too fast to the surface. Others wouldn't know a shark from Flipper and seem either oblivious or too frightened to flee when confronted.

Captain Jay and I once had a group of divers in the water on the west side of Congo Cay, where a fairly aggressive twelve-foot bull shark had often been spotted. We'd finished our tour of the area and returned to the boat. Everybody had plenty of air left so we hung out below the boat, enjoying the exceptional visibility. The big bull shark appeared out of the blue and swam non-aggressively through the group. Jay and I nodded to each other, knowing we needed to get the most timid of the group up to the boat. Jay escorted three of the divers up to the dive platform where Gizmo helped them onto the boat, then returned while I was herding the remaining divers into a close group. The shark swam around us and showed no aggression.

After several entertaining minutes I checked the divers' air gauges. We needed to surface soon. For the hell of it, Captain Jay swam over to me and locked his arm in mine. He motioned for us to swim together toward the bull shark. It was too much for the shark, and with two swipes of his tail he was gone, lost in the blue-grey backdrop. We escorted the remaining divers to the boat, where they couldn't stop talking about the big shark they had swum with.

One of the ladies Jay had brought up earlier looked at us questioningly and asked, "You mean that big fish swimming around us was a shark?"

The group of divers at Eagle Shoal reacted calmly to the nurse shark. I'd seen Captain Jay leave the group and swim to the edge of the reef. I swam ahead of the group and saw Captain Jay with his head under a coral head looking for the nurse shark he had molested. I signaled for the divers to stay put on the patch of sand next to the coral.

The coral head that the nurse shark swam under was just large enough for the shark and seemed to be a tunnel with an opening on the other side. I looked at the group and gave them the thumbs up signal. They all looked at their air gauges and returned the thumbs up signal.

Everybody was good.

Captain Jay pushed his head out from under the coral head, unbuckled his tank and slipped it over his shoulders, letting it rest on the sandy bottom next to the coral head. He saw me and smiled through his mask. Keeping the regulator in his mouth he crawled under the coral head, clearly showing off, to what end I had no idea.

Jay was so far into the hole his regulator hose had stretched to its max and the tank dragged a few inches before hooking onto the coral. He abandoned the regulator for a short while then came scooting out backward grasping for his abandoned regulator, which had been caught up in part of the coral. I swam the three feet between us and shoved my regulator into his mouth.

The diving group looked disinterested, at best. They had no idea what we were doing. I didn't either. Captain Jay gathered his regulator and motioned for me to swim to the other side to block the shark's escape.

I shook my head and motioned back to the divers. He glared at me from behind his mask. Knowing he wasn't going to give up, I swam over the three-foot-tall coral head and hovered near the entrance of the other side, giving the nurse shark plenty of room to swim past me if Jay prodded him out of his hiding place.

I could see the group on the other side of the coral trying their best to stay stationary on the sandy bottom. They looked bored. I couldn't see Captain Jay but heard a loud, bubbly scream from under the coral head. I looked over the top of the coral head to see Captain Jay backing out as fast as he could and the nurse shark wriggling past him on his way to a new hiding place. Jay's right hand held onto a bloody left elbow and bicep while frantically searching for his regulator.

I sprang over the coral head and, once again, shoved my regulator into his mouth. The group of divers back-pedaled a few feet. A couple of them looked upward toward the boat. I then helped Captain Jay put his tank back on and lead the group back to the boat.

It was a long ride back to the resort. The divers were quiet as Captain Jay joked of the experience, slapping me on the back trying to get me to laugh along with him. I didn't. As we disembarked I looked at Captain Jay's wound. The cuts on his arm weren't deep. The bruising would be worse.

* * *

A few weeks later I ran into Uncle John at the Gallows Point bar.

"Uncle John. I didn't know you were coming to visit. Are you staying with Captain Jay?"

"Yeah, I need to sell that damn boat. It's just sitting in the harbor. There doesn't seem to be much interest in it."

"Where is Captain Jay?" I asked, hoping to change the subject. I knew that Jay was trying pretty hard to sell the boat and was pretty frustrated that there were no buyers.

"He's up in the Tree House."

I walked behind the bar to the Tree House, stood at the bottom of the steps, and shouted, "Inside?"

"Fuck you," an unseen Jay shouted from above with a laugh.

Captain Jay's girlfriend came out and walked down the stairway to where I was standing, gave me a hug and said that she was going to have a beer with Uncle John. I walked up the steps through the open sliding glass door into the kitchen.

"Hey, Rookie. What's up?"

"I'm just checking in with you. How long has Uncle John been here?"

"I don't know. He's pissed off because his boat isn't sellin'. He's thinkin' about takin' it back to Florida. But the engine is screwed up. We need parts from the US. It's gonna take a while to fix it."

"How's your business? I see that your shop is closed most of the time."

Captain Jay's facial features hardened, and he said, "What the fuck is it to you? You're the big-shot developer now. What do you care?"

"Jay, if you're having problems maybe I can help."

"Okay," he snarled, "Give me fifty-thousand dollars."

"I… I wasn't thinking about that kind of help. I don't have fifty-thousand dollars."

For reasons I'll never know, Captain Jay grew angrier. He walked up to face me, his nose a foot from mine. I didn't back off.

"I knew you wouldn't help me. You're a pussy."

I'm not sure why, but his comment pissed me off. My smile gone, I said, "Maybe you should stop trying to impress the rich dudes at the resort and stop giving them free dives and boat rides to Jost and Virgin Gorda or any other place whenever they ask. Maybe you ought to close that stupid retail shop and concentrate on what you do best, like taking paying customers out diving, and not so far away from the resort. And what the fuck was that stupid stunt with the nurse shark a few weeks ago?"

Captain Jay's face turned as red as it had when the gun-happy policeman slapped him around in the back of the police car. "I ought to beat the shit out of you, Rookie."

I can't say that I was shocked, but I wasn't comfortable. I didn't know what to do. I probably should have backed away, but like a rookie, I just stood there, looking stupid. Captain Jay must have taken that as a sign to start the fight.

He pushed me hard against the wall a few feet behind me and came at me fast. I did the only thing I could think of without starting a fisticuff battle, which I think would have been a disaster for me.

As he approached I ducked under him, grabbed the backs of his thighs, placed my shoulder into his gut and lifted him—classic football tackling form. I wasn't going to let go and give him room to kick my ass, so we hung there. He hit me in the kidneys and tried to wriggle out of my grip. I held tight but was top-heavy and staggered around the room with Jay across my left shoulder, bouncing off a wall, then the kitchen counter, then another wall.

The Tree House was built up above the ground on a wood frame that was way under-engineered. Each time we bounced off a wall the house shook.

I heard voices from below us near the steps, probably attracted by the sound of four hundred pounds of human flesh pounding against flimsy plywood construction.

"What's going on up there? You guys all right?"

It was Uncle John's voice.

All Captain Jay or I could do was grunt.

Nobody climbed the stairs to check.

Captain Jay finally got enough leverage by pushing his legs hard against the kitchen counter, sending me backward, which was a stupid thing for him to do. My backward momentum sent his head into the wall behind us. We bounced off, and I spun around and fell backward, Captain Jay's nose hitting the edge of the kitchen counter on our way down.

He rolled off of me and I got to my feet. Captain Jay was on one knee with his left hand holding his nose. Blood spilled from under his hand. He stood up, turned the spigot on in the kitchen sink and leaned over it, cupping handfuls of water onto his bloody nose. I waited for him to attack.

"Hey, what are you guys doing up there?"

A different voice now. Still, nobody ventured up the steps.

Captain Jay looked over at me, blood still coming from his nose, smiled and said, "Shit Rookie, I think you broke my nose."

"I didn't do it. You're the one who knocked us into the counter." I sensed the anger had left him, but was ready for the next round if it came. I hesitantly said, "Come on, I'll buy you a beer. Or maybe take you to the clinic. How bad is it?"

"You got lucky, Rookie. I'll live."

I walked out onto the deck and saw that we had an audience. Half the bar had cleared out and stood in the driveway below the Tree House.

"Thanks for the help," I said and smiled down at the group.

Captain Jay walked out behind me with his bloody nose and Elvis grin.

"Looks like you didn't need any," Uncle John said and laughed.

Captain Jay's girlfriend nursed his nose while we enjoyed a few beers at the bar.

The fight was over, for now, and I didn't even know why it had started.

Chapter Twenty-Five

*"Plan for the future because that's where you are going
to spend the rest of your life."*
Mark Twain

Before Uncle John returned to Florida we had gone on a play dive.
As we headed out of Cruz Bay, Uncle John looked at his unsold boat
and said to nobody in particular, "I wish that damn thing would sink."

Tommy and I laughed but not hard. Captain Jay's face hardened.

The boat had become a burden that Uncle John probably wished
he had never built. The care and feeding of a boat, even one that mostly stayed at anchor, was a chore. He needed to sell it.

We motored over to the east side of Flanagan Island, off the east
end of St. John. There was a pretty nice reef that ran parallel to the
island about two hundred yards from land. The depth was a consistent
sixty to eighty feet. The seas were fairly large, and there was a south
to north current. We decided to drift dive. Gizmo was off to Jost Van
Dyke for a while so Uncle John, who was not a diver, agreed to follow
our bubbles as we dove with the current, picking us up when we ran
out of air.

Tommy, Captain Jay and I put on our tanks, grabbed mesh bags
and spearguns and stepped off the platform.

We swam to the top of the reef and loaded our spearguns. A
large ole wife, or queen trigger fish to the rest of the world, hung in
the water just over the grassy area on the shallow side of the reef. I

swam over slowly, skirting him as if I was going to swim far to one side. Fish have brains the size of peas, but sometimes you have to use subterfuge to get close enough for a shot, especially fish that live out in the open versus those that spend most of their time sticking their noses out of coral heads, giving them no place to run and making them easier targets.

If I'd been free diving I could have approached the fish more directly. The bubbles from scuba tanks make fish wary. If I wasn't carrying a speargun, the fish would probably have come up to be petted. Fish sense spearguns, particularly Nassau groupers. You hardly ever see them when you are spear fishing. Yet, when you dive without a weapon, no matter how many divers are present, Nassau groupers come up to you like trained dogs.

I kicked slowly past the ole wife, my speargun pointing away from him. The fish was typically curious and kept its position in the water, but its eyes followed my movements. I continued pointing my body away from the fish but brought the gun up and out to my side and pulled the trigger. Spearguns are notoriously inaccurate, particularly when shooting at a moving target. You want the fish to be as still as possible when you take the shot. To do this you have to anticipate which way the fish will bolt once they realize the gun is pointed at them, which they inevitably do. At the last moment, just before bolting, they get a distant look in their eyes. If you wait beyond that, you've already missed.

I hit the ole wife mid-body then held the gun between my knees and pulled the spear with the thrashing fish toward me. Play dives were competitive with respect to spearfishing, and we bagged our own fish, but Tommy could see that my fish had a lot of life in him, and he came over to help me bag it.

I knew this species of fish had a long, hard spine in their dorsal fin that could lock into place. It had multiple uses, one being a weapon that you had to pay attention to while placing it in the bag. I was about to learn another thing about this fish. Tommy held my mesh bag open. I grabbed the spear and slid the stainless flange up the shaft to lock the spring loaded barbs flat against the spear so I could pull it out of the fish. I carefully grabbed the ole wife behind his gills and moved him up and off the spear and used both hands to push the fish to the bottom of the bag. I nodded to Tommy, which meant that I was going to release my grip and pull my arms out of the bag so he could close it as quickly as possible. I let go and pulled my arms up.

Ouch! Damn.

The ole wife came out of the bag with my arms, its mouth attached to my right palm, which I had apparently held too close to its mouth. The fish was not letting go. Tommy laughed, bubbles shooting out around his regulator. Captain Jay swam over to see what was going on. He looked at the ole wife attached to my hand at the entrance of the mesh bag that Tommy still held open, and bubbles shot out around his regulator as well.

I looked at both pleadingly while trying to pull the fish's strong teeth off my hand and noticed that the fish didn't have teeth. Not normal teeth anyway. But, rather, two sharp incisors, one on top of its mouth and one on bottom. They followed the contour of his mouth, forming a pair of curved nippers. I learned later when I went to the library to research this menace of a fish species that they use these nippers to eat nasty things like sea urchins. They turn the spiny sea urchins upside down and then nip the roe from the urchins exposed underside. They also use the nippers to nibble away at thick conch shells, turning and breaking the shell into small pieces until they reach the meat deep inside.

At the moment, one of these conch-shell-nibbling bastards was taking a chunk out of my hand. I couldn't pry his mouth open. Tommy reached in and grabbed the fish and pulled.

Ouch, ouch, ouch!

The fish came away with a large chunk of my glove and a somewhat smaller chunk of my hand.

It was my turn to hold the bag open for Tommy, who cleanly placed the misbehaving ole wife into the bag. I closed it, and we continued our hunt, a small bit of cloudy, green blood trailing behind my right hand.

Our plan had been to stay together so that Uncle John could more easily see our bubbles in the heavy seas. I hadn't heard the boat engine for the last ten minutes. Who knew what Uncle John was following, but it wasn't us. Captain Jay swam after a large Nassau grouper that bolted out of one coral head and down the reef into another. Tommy and I followed with our spearguns ready. Jay lost the grouper and turned to us with a shrug. A Nassau is considered a delicacy that all of us would have liked to see as dinner later that evening. We hunted the coral heads for the fish, spreading out to look in different, but interconnected holes in the coral. One hole harbored at least six spiny lobsters, their long antennae sticking out from the opening, waving back and forth with the movement of the sea. A good catch most days, but we were hunting fish.

The Nassau had hidden deep in the same hole and bolted past the lobster. It was fast. Tommy tried to line up a shot but the grouper made it safely to another deep hole. I stuck my head into the hole as far as I could. There were no grouper, just a couple of small lobsters and the gaping mouth of a very large green moray eel inches from my mask. Lobster and eels have a symbiotic relationship within the reef system, frequently sharing holes in the coral, choosing mutual protection over the urge to eat one another.

I backed out of the hole and saw the grouper escape from another opening in the coral a few feet away. Tommy took a shot and missed. The grouper turned toward me. I shot and missed. Captain Jay looked over and swung his gun, which rested at his hip, toward the fish. Without aiming he pulled the trigger. Head shot.

Tommy and I shrugged at each other in disbelief and left Captain Jay, the lucky son of a bitch, to bag his own fish.

Minutes later I spotted a yellow fin grouper, and I took off after it, leaving Captain Jay and Tommy on the deep side of the reef, knowing I'd be on my own the rest of the dive. The current was too strong to swim sideways very far and made it almost impossible to swim against it. I'd take my chances and hope Uncle John had a reasonable idea where to find us when we surfaced. I never found the grouper but later managed to bag a tiger grouper and a dog snapper.

My hand still hurt like hell from the ole wife bite. My air was okay; I had about a thousand pounds left, but I was done fishing, and I hadn't heard the boat since we dropped into the water.

I surfaced with the bag of fish and needed to see where in the hell Uncle John had gone. The swells were huge. I had to wait until I was at the crest of a swell to see any distance, and then I had to hope that the boat was not hidden in a trough. For several minutes I was lifted up and down in the heavy rolling swells and didn't see anything except Flanagan Island, which was a couple of hundred yards to the west. I decided to stay on the surface and swim to the island. Who knew how long it would take Uncle John to find me, if at all.

A large crest picked me up, and I saw the boat for a few seconds. It was all the way back where we went in. I could see Uncle John on the bow searching for us, which was strange. He knew the current would take us north.

I stayed on the surface and snorkeled toward the island, conserving what air I had left, in case I needed to go underwater again, for any number of reasons. I was on constant lookout for shark beneath me, my fish and bloody hand being a pretty good invitation. Rising up and down with the waves I was about halfway to the island when a large swell dropped me close to Captain Jay and Tommy. They were both out of air and huddled together. I was glad to see them. They were turned away from me and hadn't seen me yet.

"You better not have dropped your fish," I shouted over to them from the next crest.

Jerking their heads toward me, Jay raised his mesh bag partially out of the water and shouted back, "I'm not losin' *my* fish. You still got yours?"

I raised my heavy bag as best I could.

Jay nodded and shouted, "Have you seen or heard the boat?"

"Yeah, your uncle is way back where we went in. He's lost us. I was swimming for Flanagan when I ran into you guys. We might as well keep going in that direction."

They both agreed, and we kicked toward the island. A few minutes later we heard the boat. It was close. The bow came over the crest of the wave next to us.

"I think he's going to run over us."

We scrambled out of the way. Both Captain Jay and I dropped our bags. We had no choice. I was glad I had saved some air. Uncle John cut the engine, walked to the stern and shouted for us. We were a few yards off his port side, close enough that I didn't need to shout when I raised my speargun, which was still loaded, and said, "I'm about to shoot you in the ass."

Uncle John turned around and saw us. I think he thought I was really going to shoot him. He was genuinely apologetic as we swam to the bouncing dive tray and handed him our gear. I put my regulator in my mouth and dove for the two bags of fish we dropped.

Everybody safe on board, I held up the mesh bags and told Uncle John, "You don't get any of these."

"Shit guys. As soon as you went in the water I lost your bubbles. It was too rough."

"What the hell were you doing way back where we started?" I asked.

"Hell, I went up and down the length of the island twice looking for you guys. I couldn't see anything in those swells. I'd go a hundred yards or so, cut the engine and yell for you."

We headed back toward Cruz Bay, drinking beer and giving Uncle John a hard time for losing us. We also gave Tommy a hard time for not spearing any fish.

I had no idea that was the last play dive Captain Jay and I would ever share.

Chapter Twenty-Six

"Eat a live frog first thing in the morning and nothing
worse will happen to you the rest of the day."
Mark Twain

There was a reason why nobody had been able to develop Gallows
Point. It was damned difficult. I've often wondered if an older and
more experienced version of me would have taken on the project.
Probably not. Being a rookie had its benefits. I had no idea I couldn't
do it so I trudged forward.

Tommy, Denny and I sat through a multitude of meetings with
wannabe builders, landscapers, extended aeration sewage system
experts, reverse osmosis experts, government officials, marketing
experts, financial institutions and, occasionally, my partners. I completed the environmental impact report, all two hundred eighty-seven
pages, and presented a draft to the staff of the government agency that
would review it.

"Uh, this is pretty long. Can you shorten it by maybe half? Or
more?" the director asked.

I smiled, tucked the report under my arm and walked dejectedly
to the parking lot and my car. I'd spent months researching and writing the report. I guess the agency's staff didn't appreciate the detail
I'd put into the report like references to Dr. Chang's studies in Hawaii
that reported the efficiency of twenty different roof materials to collect water, depending on the amount of individual rainfall events, al-

lowing for evaporation, friction, wind and the level of imperviousness of the roofing material.

The island had just entered another off season—the quiet season, the down time—when a collective sigh of relief resonated throughout the island's residents. It was the time we locals begged for after having experienced months of a love-hate relationship with the people who spend their money to temporarily experience our little piece of paradise and who, simultaneously, keep us in business and drive us crazy.

Most of the restaurants and shops were closed. Lots of people, who'd worked their butts off during tourist season, were off-island enjoying some time away. Tommy was on a cruise with his girlfriend. I told him that he'd eat and drink too much and get seasick. He did. Charlie was someplace secret, probably in the middle of the next geopolitical hotbed that we'd read about in the newspapers in a few months.

I enjoyed the quiet time because I was immersed in the planning process and needed all the time I could get to understand my new profession—and rewrite the environmental impact report.

On a quiet Sunday afternoon Captain Jay charged through one of my always open doors and said, "Hey, Rookie, I need your help."

He didn't wait for a response. He paced through my office with some old towels and a two-gallon can of kerosene and set them on my deck. I put my papers inside the books that were open, closed the books and shoved my work to the side of my desk. I wouldn't protest. It would have been a useless effort, and I was curious to see what trouble he would bring to the island, and us, next.

"We need to make a fuse," he announced.

I laughed and shook my head. *Fine. Bring it on,* I thought.

"I'm gonna burn up Uncle John's boat. It's not selling. We can collect the insurance money."

"What? Are you crazy?" I already knew the answer to that, but this was insane.

Captain Jay paid no attention to me and rolled up one of the small towels, dipped it into the kerosene and tried to light it. I shrugged, pretty sure he was blowing smoke, convinced I could talk him out of this hare-brained scheme if he persisted. I decided to play along and grabbed a towel and the can of kerosene.

"This stuff is hard to light," I told Jay while we struck matches and tossed them toward the kerosene soaked towels. "What is this fuse for anyway?"

"I already told you, Rookie."

"I mean what's it going to lead to? You got a bomb?" I asked with a sarcastic snort.

Captain Jay paused, looked at me and very seriously said, "I'm gonna pour some kerosene in the bilge. Then I'm gonna fill my jerry full of it, haul it onto the deck and light it up with this fuse." He held up the towel he had rolled up and dipped into the can of kerosene.

"Jay, you're going to need a longer fuse than this. You won't have time to get off of the boat, if the kerosene ever lights." I struck another match and held it against the kerosene-soaked towel I had rolled up and placed by my feet. It didn't light. "Look," I said and pointed to the wet towel at my feet.

Captain Jay shrugged and lit another match.

We finally got one of the towels to burn, uncontrolled.

"This looks pretty inexact to be relying on as a fuse."

We experimented with different ways to twist and tie the towels. Sometimes the flame went out before it reached the halfway point. Other times, the towel would burn so rapidly we had to pull our hands away as soon as we lit them. They burned more consistently when rolled tight with no twist. We were like kids playing with firecrackers, laughing each time the towel would burn.

I finally said, "Jay, isn't there a better way to do this?" I wasn't trying to encourage this ridiculous scheme, but I was engrossed in the moment, the puzzle of how to create the perfect fuse.

He rolled up another towel.

I looked at it. "Wait, let's use some string to tie the towel and make it a little more uniform."

While wrapping the string around the rolled towel I came to my senses and realized how absurd this was. I asked Jay, "What is your plan? What are you going to tell people? What's going to cause the fire?"

"The engine parts came in last week, and I hired a diesel mechanic from St. Thomas to put the engine back together. He's been workin' on it almost every day. There are solvents and crap all around the boat."

"You are going to burn it up while he is working on the boat? No licensed diesel mechanic is going to leave solvents and crap lying around the boat overnight."

"Nobody is going to think of that," he said and grabbed another towel.

We tied the next one up even tighter. It burned with a slower consistency. But it was not a reliable fuse.

"So, what are you going to do, dinghy out to the boat and light a fuse and hope that nobody sees you? Hell, just about every boat in the harbor is a live-aboard. They all know you. And how are you going to keep Lisa from knowing what you're up to?"

"Jesus, Rookie, I've thought about that. I'm gonna get in an argument with Lisa and tell her I'm gonna sleep on the boat. I'll paddle my dinghy out to the boat. It'll be dark, and if anybody sees me it won't be a big deal. It's my boat."

"Then what?"

"The kerosene will burn slow. I'll slip into the water after the boat is burning pretty good and swim to shore. I'll tell everybody that I was smokin' and somehow the boat caught on fire and that the fire grew too big to control so I abandoned ship. Everybody will think it was caused by the work being done on the boat, with all those solvents bein' left out and shit," he said, proud of his strategy.

We tied another towel up, and it didn't burn at all. It was too tight.

"This is stupid Jay. What if the kerosene explodes?" I asked, figuring that he might see this as just another obstacle.

"Kerosene doesn't explode, Rookie," he said with a laugh, tying up another towel and lighting it.

It was the best yet, but still far from anything I would trust.

I changed the subject and talked about some new mahogany spearguns made in Australia that I had seen advertised in a dive magazine.

"They would be great. Neutral buoyancy. Quicker to get on target. Not all of us are as quick on the draw as you," I said, still amazed at the shot he had made on the Nassau grouper during the last play dive.

"You can use my shop to order a couple. We'll get a discount."

"Great. Thanks."

Captain Jay seemed satisfied with the last attempt at building a fuse. He grabbed the remaining towels, string and fuel tank and stepped into his Jeep.

"Jay, this is all bullshit, isn't it." It was a statement, not a question.

"You got a problem with it, Rookie?"

"I sure do. It's a fucked up plan."

Jay's eyes narrowed, and I saw a flash of anger.

"What are you gonna do? Stop me? Tell somebody?"

"If I have to, yeah."

Captain Jay's anger was gone in an instant, replaced with the Elvis grin. He said, "Awe shit, Rookie. I wouldn't do somethin' stupid. These fuses aren't ready. We'll work on them this week sometime. It was fun, wasn't it?"

"Yeah, it was fun," I said, not sure what Captain Jay was going to do.

Jay must have sensed my concern. He leaned out of the Jeep, patted my shoulder and said, "Don't worry, Rookie. You don't need to tell anybody. I'm not gonna burn that fuckin' boat up. I think it would be better to take it out to Carval and let it accidentally break free of the anchor and smash up against the rock." He grinned and squeezed my shoulder. "That would be a sight, wouldn't it, Rookie?"

"No."

Captain Jay put on a fake look of disappointment and said, "Well, fuck it then. Nobody wants to have fun anymore. This island is getting filled with pussies."

I let out a sigh of relief as Jay drove out of the driveway and onto the road. He turned in his seat toward me and shouted, "Look into underwater drills. Maybe that's what I need." I heard his laugh halfway down the hill to Cruz Bay.

I went back to reviewing my architectural drawings and environmental impact report. I didn't think much about the fuse, or any of Captain Jay's ridiculous schemes the rest of the day.

I should have.

* * *

KABOOM!

I was shaken out of my sleep by the loudest explosion I have ever heard. I opened my eyes. The open windows and shutters let in a bright orange aura from all sides of my house.

I sat up, disoriented.

Then there were two smaller successive blasts. Glasses in my kitchen rattled with each one.

I ran outside. All of Cruz Bay was enveloped in a surreal orange light. Dinghies came alive and zipped around the bay. Captain Jay? I wasn't sure. Even if he was stupid enough to do it he was going to use kerosene, and kerosene doesn't explode.

This has got to be something different, I thought. *Where the hell is Captain Jay?*

I ran to the Tree House. Lisa stood on the porch, trying to see the source of the explosions. We could both see flames shooting above the trees that were blocking our view of the part of the harbor that was on fire, where Uncle John's boat was anchored.

"Where is Jay?" I looked up at Lisa.

"I don't know. We had a fight, and he said he was going to sleep on the boat," she said, wide-eyed.

Shit.

"What were those explosions?" she asked.

"I can't see what blew up. Looks like something in the Creek. What boat was he going to sleep on?" I asked, knowing the answer.

"I don't know. He didn't say."

"I'm going to go down to Cruz Bay to find out what's burning," I told her, not really sure if that was what I was going to do.

Three explosions? That didn't make sense. If it was his boat burning maybe something else caused the explosion. Maybe Jay went out to his dive boat at the resort to sleep. Maybe it was something on shore on the far side of the harbor. I needed to know what had blown up.

I was in my Jeep when I saw Lisa run up the hill toward me. "It's Jay. You have to come. He's down in the bay."

We ran to the waterfront. The sky was still orange, illuminating everything in the bay and half the village. Captain Jay spoke but I couldn't see him. I stepped into the water and he spoke again. He was right in front of me, submerged in water up to his chin.

"Lisa, go get a blanket." She ran up the hill toward the Tree House.

"Good. She's gone and I can tell you my plan." His voice was quavering as he spoke.

"What plan? What the fuck are you talking about? Where's your dinghy? Are you hurt?" I asked.

"Rookie, I'm all burned up. I took my forty-gallon plastic jerry jug and filled it with gasoline, instead of kerosene," he said, shivering. "Like you said, I was worried that the kerosene wouldn't light. But the last few fuses I made were slow burnin' enough, so I made a longer one from a large towel. I thought I would have plenty of time to sneak back over here. I took the cap off and put the fuse in. But it was heavy. I must have spilled gasoline all over when I was carrying it onto the boat."

I stepped further into the water toward Jay.

"When I lit the fuse the whole thing blew up. I was blown into the bay. The dinghy was on fire. I swam over here. I didn't know what else to do."

I couldn't tell how badly he was burned because most of his body was underwater.

"Jay this is a total fuck-up. Come on. We need to get you down to the clinic." I stepped into deeper water so I could help him to shore.

"No, I need to swim back and go to shore near the boat. Other-wise, everybody is gonna to be suspicious, includin' Lisa."

The whole scene was surreal. A better person would have waded out and retrieved Captain Jay. I hesitated and looked back up the hill to see where Lisa was. I was still the rookie, waiting for someone else to take charge. When I turned around Jay had disappeared into the black water of the bay. He said he was burned but didn't act terribly injured. Other than the shivering, which could have been normal, it was after two in the morning, he seemed to me to be relatively fine. I walked up the hill toward my office. Lisa came out of the Tree House with an armful of clothes.

"Where's Jay?" Lisa asked.

"I think he's drunk. He swam back to the boat. Wait here to see if he swims back. I'll head down to Cruz Bay and pick him up."

By the time I settled Lisa down and reached my Jeep, a police car had sped up the hill and stopped next to my Jeep. It was Alex.

"Mr. Arlan, Captain Jay is in de water by de clinic. He not comin out a de unless you der wit him."

"Okay."

I drove to the waterfront and parked across from the clinic. Alex parked next to me. The sky was no longer orange. The hull of Uncle John's unsold boat was anchored seventy yards from shore. What was left of the boat was barely afloat and smoky flames rose a few feet from the center of the fiberglass soup.

Captain Jay crouched in about three feet of water. Only his head above his nostrils showed. He shivered.

Alex said, "You must go and get him."

I was already on my way.

I waded into the water and took Jay's arm.

"Rookie, I'm all burned up."

I helped him to his feet, and we waded out of the water onto the beach and under a street light. His shirt was almost burned off his body. His shorts were still in one piece. Skin hung from his arms. His feet looked pretty bad, too. His face didn't seem to be burned, but his neck was a mess. It seemed that any part of his body not covered by clothing, except his face, was badly burned.

I helped Jay walk across the road to the clinic, which was nothing more than a first-aid station. The on–duty nurse met us in the road and helped me get Captain Jay over to the emergency room in the clinic. She made a phone call to the new doctor on the island, Dr. Allah.

We helped Jay onto the table where the nurse cut his remaining clothes off and started to administer an IV of saline. I stood there while Jay shivered.

"I have to pee," Captain Jay said with a shaky voice, looking at me.

What was I supposed to do? He couldn't get up. Where are the other nurses? The nurse handed me a plastic pitcher and nodded toward Jay's penis.

Jay shivered and tried to roll over on his side to pee in the pitcher that I held in front of his penis.

The nurse, busy with the IV, looked over and said, "Help him, me son."

"You want me to hold his dick?"

The nurse snickered and turned back to work on the IV bag.

Jay pissed all over the floor.

Dr. Allah arrived a few minutes later. I stood back while he solemnly examined Captain Jay. He then led me to the other side of the room and said in a low voice. "He is in shock and he may not make it."

What?

"We need to get him to the hospital on St. Thomas."

The irony of that statement amused me. The island had an ambulance boat, but it was frequently broken down, as it was now, and rarely repaired because of lack of funds. Whenever it was down, Captain Jay was always there to offer his boat to ferry critical patients to St. Thomas and never asked to be compensated.

I was stunned.

What would Captain Jay do? I asked myself.

I cocked my head when the answer came. I became Captain Jay and took charge.

"Okay Doctor. I can take care of this. Keep him alive."

I drove back to Gallows to collect Lisa. "Pack a bag. You're going to St. Thomas for a while," I told her, not giving her an explanation.

Next, I rounded up a sleepy Gizmo who had been shacked up with a heavyset blond lady from the US.

"Gizmo, I'm taking you to Caneel to get Jay's boat. Meet us in the Creek across from the Clinic."

I returned to the Clinic with Lisa. It was about four in the morning. Uncle John's boat smoldered, and a few dinghies buzzed around the bay. Captain Jay was heavily sedated and ready to go.

"Is there an ambulance waiting in Red Hook?" I asked Dr. Allah.

"It will be there in thirty minutes."

Gizmo docked in the Creek across from the clinic. We put Captain Jay on a stretcher, and Gizmo and I carried it to Jay's boat. A volunteer nurse was called to make the trip with Lisa and Gizmo.

I needed to stay to run interference with the police and anybody who asked too many questions. I would go to St. Thomas in a few hours.

Chapter Twenty-Seven

"A clear conscience is the sure sign of a bad memory."
Mark Twain

A few sleepless hours later I was on my Sea Craft heading to Red Hook. I had called the hospital before I left and was able to find out from Lisa that Captain Jay was no longer in shock and had been placed in isolation, whatever that was. What I really needed to do was get more details from Captain Jay before facing the gauntlet of questions which were sure to come in the next few days and weeks. Other than what he had told me while squatting chin-deep in the bay, I was as in the dark as much as anybody else, except for one thing—I knew this was no accident.

Like many other St. Johnians, I kept a beater car in Red Hook that allowed me to get around St. Thomas without having to rely on taxis and surrey buses. My St. Thomas beater was a well-used, rusted, lime-green BMW 2002. Those little cars came in all sorts of bright colors and were popular in the early seventies. They were small and maneuverable, great on gas and, as evidenced by my car, could accumulate hundreds of thousands of miles on the odometer before they died.

I tied my boat up at the Red Hook Marina and walked to the parking lot where I kept the car. A couple of minutes after starting it up I noticed the temperature gauge move from cold to hot, where it stayed for a few seconds, and then returned to cold, never moving again during the drive to the hospital. I didn't have time to stop and look under the hood at an engine that I knew nothing about. It was still running, which was all I cared about.

The hospital was in the center of the island, about thirty minutes from Red Hook, in a funky area of St. Thomas flanked by Lionel Roberts Stadium and scores of rundown houses. I had driven to within a block of the hospital grounds when the BMW stalled. As it lost power I coasted to the side of the road into an available diagonal parking space near the stadium. I was anxious to see Captain Jay but needed to at least take a cursory look under the hood, not fully sure what I was looking for. I opened the hood and looked at the engine.

I don't have time for this, I thought. I closed the hood and walked toward the hospital, but curiosity got the best of me. I backtracked and opened the hood again. The radiator was gone. I closed the hood and walked on, wondering why someone would take the time to steal the radiator from my beat-up BMW 2002. It's not like there was a big market for these cars. There weren't a bunch of them driving around St. Thomas. I found out why later when I ordered a new radiator from a local parts dealer. It was a fifteen hundred dollar part, more than what I'd paid for the car. I wished the thieves had stolen the car instead. I had insurance to cover that.

I walked into the hospital and found Captain Jay's room. Lisa was asleep in the only chair. Jay was in a bed with his arms and legs strapped and spread-eagled, held up by lines hooked to the ceiling, the theory being that the wounds healed better if they were not touching any bedding and were kept unwrapped and open to the air. This all seemed logical until, after closing the door, I saw clouds of dust billow up from under the door.

I opened the door to see a janitor sweeping the hallway floor with a push broom, forcing the tropical dust to billow up through the one inch opening at the bottom of the closed door, which was at the end of a short hall.

Lisa woke up. Jay was still drugged out.

"How is he?" I asked Lisa.

"He was awake a while ago and was asking for you. The doctor I talked to is kind of a jerk."

"That's typical. They don't usually like talking to laypeople, unless they're trying to get laid."

"He was young and arrogant," Lisa said, looking around for her bag. "Are you going to stay a while? I need to get something to eat."

"No problem. Take your time. I would offer you my car, but it seems to be missing its radiator. I'll be here when you get back."

She left and I sat in the chair, waiting for Jay to wake up.

"Hey, Rookie, can you cut me down?" Captain Jay joked while I nodded off in the chair.

"Not until you promise Lisa to me as long as you are tied to that ceiling."

Jay looked a bit puzzled.

I said, "I'll give you our first-born son."

Partially awake from his meds, Jay laughed.

I moved the chair closer to his bed and said, "Listen, I need to know what the hell happened. Shit is going to hit the fan, and I'm going to be in the middle of it." I paused and said, "I heard the first explosion. That must have been your jerry jug of gasoline. Jesus. I couldn't imagine that you would have done that. I thought you were going to use kerosene."

He looked at me blankly.

"I heard two smaller explosions a little while after that." I raised my eyebrows, waiting for a response.

Captain Jay shrugged, as best he could with arms stretched upward toward the ceiling. "Must have been the two propane tanks. They were for the stove in the galley."

"Makes sense. You didn't hear them explode?"

"No."

"Okay, here's what I'm going to tell people. You were on the boat because of a fight with Lisa. The boat was having some work done on the engine. You were smoking a joint, or cigarette, the joint being more plausible to those who know you. Somehow the boat blew up, and you were blown into the water. Sounds like a bullshit story, but that's all I can think of."

I waited for Captain Jay to absorb this.

"Sounds good, Rookie," he said and went back to sleep.

* * *

When Lisa came back I took a taxi to Red Hook and to my boat. I anchored my boat in the bay a few yards from Gallows and walked up to my office. Tim McQuin was waiting for me.

"How's Jay?"

"He's fucked up. We have to get him out of that hospital. He'll die from an infection in there."

Tim had first-hand experience with the non-accredited hospital on the big island. A few years earlier he and his wife had dropped me off at my house after a party and headed for their home on East End. The British-made SUV Tim drove lost its brakes on one of the many steep downhill stretches of road. At the bottom of the steep decline was a ninety-degree left turn. If you didn't make the turn you would go over a fifty-foot cliff and into the sea.

Tim tried to slow his speed by steering into the tamarind brush on the sides of the road. Hidden in one of the tamarind patches was a large blue bitch boulder. He hit it on the passenger side of the vehicle, throwing Mary out and against the rock. Tim got the vehicle stopped before it plunged into the Caribbean and searched for his wife. He found her in the bush with several major bones crushed.

He ran to the closest home for help. The ambulance boat was working, and Tim got her to the St. Thomas Hospital, where he quickly realized that the doctors there had no idea how to treat the severity of Mary's injuries. He was desperate and found an air ambulance service out of Miami to transport Mary to a US hospital. She returned to the island a year later, one inch shorter from her injuries, but alive.

"What happened? What caused the explosion?" Tim asked me.

I had two or three close friends on the island I probably could have trusted with what I knew. Tim would have been one of them.

But I couldn't bring myself to tell him, or anyone. I told him the story Jay and I had agreed to. I'd tell Tim the truth after I found out a few things.

"I need to call Uncle John. We need to get him to the States. Uncle John would have had insurance. Maybe we could get the air-ambulance service you used for Mary and get him to a burn center somewhere."

"Okay, I'm heading over to the hospital to visit Jay. I'll see you when I get back," Tim said and drove away, Blue next to him in the small truck.

* * *

"Uncle John? Listen. There has been an accident."

There was a long pause.

"Jay was sleeping on your boat, and it blew up."

"What do you mean, it blew up?" he asked incredulously. "Where's Jay?"

I filled him in on the extent of Jay's burns and the details of the explosion.

"Diesel solvents don't explode," Uncle John said matter-of-factly.

"Well, I don't know exactly what caused the explosion," I lied. "But your boat is nothing more than a soup bowl filled with melted fiberglass, right down to the waterline."

"Shit. That damn boat wasn't insured. I should never have built it."

It was my turn to pause.

"You had no insurance? But the last time you were here you said you wished that it would sink. We all heard you say that as we passed it on the way to go diving."

Uncle John said, "Well, uh, I did say that. But that was just a figure of speech. I just meant that I wished it didn't exist. Why? It's my loss." After another awkward pause, he said, "What's going on? Did Jay do something stupid?"

This answered one question that had been gnawing at me—did Uncle John ask Captain Jay to sink the boat? With no insurance there was little chance of that.

"Do you know if Jay has health insurance?" I asked.

"No. I don't know. But knowing Jay, he probably doesn't."

"Look, Uncle John, we need to get Jay to a US hospital." I explained the situation at the St. Thomas facility.

John blew out a deep breath and said, "I live near Titusville. The space center is near here and they have a special burn center set up for the astronauts. I know one of the guys on the board of directors. I'll talk to him and call you later. Can I reach Jay at the hospital?"

"Yeah, Lisa's with him. You can at least call the switchboard and talk to her," I told him and hung up.

I told Tim what had happened after my discussion with Uncle John. He and I visited Jay the next day. On the way up to his room we stopped to talk to the doctor in charge to tell him we were going to try to transport Jay to a hospital in the US. The little prick told us that his hospital offered excellent care, and he would not release his patient. Tim and I thought we had made solid arguments why it would be better for Jay if we got him to the States. The doctor was so arrogant in his refusal that Tim and I simply looked at each other, shrugged and walked away. *Wrong and strong,* I thought.

"What a little arrogant prick," Tim said under his breath.

We took the stairs up to Captain Jay's floor. I looked at Tim and said with a laugh, "I don't think the asshole understood that we weren't asking his permission. Uncle John called last night. There's room at the burn center up in Titusville, but we need to supply insurance information."

We walked into the room. Lisa sat on the edge of the bed with an awake and smiling Captain Jay, who still had all four limbs spread-eagled and tied to the ceiling.

"We can come back after you finish your S&M session," I said.

Jay smirked and said, "Funny, Rookie. Why don't you come over here so I can kick your ass."

"How are you going to do that? Looks like right now you can't scratch an ass, let alone kick one."

Captain Jay put his best face forward, but it was obvious that he was in significant pain. The burns looked bad.

"Listen guys," I started. "We're working on getting you to a hospital in the US. Can you handle a move?" I asked Jay. He smiled and nodded. Before he started asking too many questions I turned to Lisa and said, "It would be good if you went with him."

She seemed too tired to agree or disagree. "Okay."

"Why don't you head back home with Tim? I'll stay here a while with Jay."

She nodded and they left together. I needed to talk to Jay.

"What's going on, Rookie?" he asked in a semi-lucid state.

"We are working on getting you into the space center burn unit up near Uncle John's place. Do you have health insurance?" I asked, pretty sure I knew the answer.

"Hell no. Who does? Won't the boat insurance take care of this?" he asked.

I stalled and finally said, "There was no insurance."

Whatever best face he wore earlier completely collapsed. I had to tell him what we were planning so he could be prepared when we came to get him. It was going to be a rough ride.

"I don't know how, but we are going to get you admitted into the burn center up there. Tim knows a hospital Lear jet we can hire to get you there from here. They're in Miami and told us they could be here within three and a half hours of our call. The plane is fully equipped and comes with a nurse. There will be room for one more, and I think Lisa should go, too."

"What about the cost and no insurance?" he asked.

"Tim and I will fund the jet. I'm going to have to bullshit our way through the hospital admittance people."

"You're good at that, Rookie," he said and smiled.

"Never be as good as you."

* * *

Lisa was packed for the trip to Florida, and she and Gizmo went to see Captain Jay. Tim and I were at his restaurant. I had called the burn center earlier. Thanks to Uncle John, they were expecting my call.

Tim had asked me before the call, "What are you going to do about the insurance issue?"

"I've thought about that. I'm going to use the name of the big insurance company on St. Thomas and make up a policy number. It's Friday. We'll get Jay up there tomorrow. Chances are slim that the admissions people will call or even reach the St. Thomas insurance office on a Friday afternoon."

Tim laughed. "They'll call soon enough."

"Once Jay's admitted he's Uncle John's problem. I can't see them tossing Jay out on the street in his condition."

"What about the prick doctor?" Tim asked.

"I've got that covered."

We planned for Tim to call the air ambulance about ten in the morning the next day. The Lear would be at the St. Thomas Airport by two in the afternoon. I thanked our lucky stars we lived in such a small place—a place where a lot of people owed Captain Jay favors for the countless lobster and fish or boat rides he had handed out like candy.

Tommy Lowell was to take two of our biggest, meanest-looking construction workers to Red Hook at ten on Saturday morning. I called a taxi driver on St. Thomas who owned a big van and owed a few favors to Captain Jay and asked him to be at Red Hook to pick us up. I borrowed a wheelchair from the clinic on St. John. They were more than happy to oblige, since they had used Captain Jay's boat many times. I was also able to get them to give me a few Percocet tablets for the flight after telling the doctor of our plan. When I told him who the attending physician was he smiled, told me he knew him and gladly handed over the pain meds and also gave me some sterilized wrap for Jay's wounds. I guess I wasn't the only one who thought the little St. Thomas doctor was a prick.

Tim and I and the wheelchair met Tommy and his thugs at the ten o'clock ferry. They weren't thugs, really. They were nice guys who worked for me under Tommy's supervision. But they were big and, today anyway, would be thugs.

Lisa was at the hospital. I had called her earlier to tell her when to expect us. I had also asked Gizmo to be there. I had no idea how many of us were going to be needed, but the more the better. We piled into the van in Red Hook and headed to the hospital, arriving a little after eleven. I asked the driver to stay in the parking lot and told him I would send someone down when we were ready to go to the airport. At that point he was to pull into the emergency entrance, engine running.

Our entourage, Tommy, Tim, the two big thugs, the wheelchair and I, all headed for Jay's floor, getting strange looks from everybody we passed, especially a couple of security guards, who wisely chose not to ask questions.

Lisa and Gizmo were in the room. Jay was in a drug stupor, which was good. We wrapped his wounds with the sterile gauze, released him from his S&M straps and got him into the wheelchair without incident. A curious nurse poked her head in the room, stared for a moment, wide-eyed, and ran down the hall screaming for the doctor.

I sent Lisa and Gizmo down to alert the taxi driver that we were on our way and grabbed the medical chart clipped to the end of the bed. Tommy and his thugs ran interference in front of us. Tim and I took turns pushing the wheelchair, making sure Jay didn't slip out. We were at the elevator when the little shit doctor saw us.

"You cannot take my patient from this hospital," he sputtered, as authoritatively as he could muster.

We laughed.

"Security is on its way up," he said, trying to intimidate us.

"Th-they b-better have a f-fucking army," Tommy stuttered.

We all laughed, except Jay. In his stupor he could only mutter words we couldn't understand. But, even through the pain and the drugs, he was smiling. He was probably telling the doctor to fuck himself and enjoying the adventure.

The doctor was now thoroughly confused and beside himself with anger. I couldn't imagine what was going through his brain at that moment, and I didn't care.

The elevator door opened and we all got in, the doctor standing outside the door screaming for security. The door opened on the ground floor, and we made a quick exit toward the emergency entrance where the taxi would be waiting. Two unarmed security guards, who had obviously been alerted by the doctors and nurses we just left behind, ran around the corner to intercept us. They looked like the same guards we saw on the way in. Tommy and his thugs smiled at them. They just stopped and stared. We pushed Jay past them and out to the van.

There wasn't enough room in the van for everybody. Tommy and his guys found their way back home. The rest of us got Jay into the van and drove to the airport. A US Customs agent, originally from St. John and a friend of Captain Jay, was there to meet us, as planned. He took care of the paperwork. The Lear was waiting, engines running. A nurse came down the steps and helped us load Jay and Lisa into the jet.

Gizmo, Tim and I waved goodbye. I watched the jet until it disappeared into the high clouds and couldn't help feeling that a very special time in my life was nearing an end.

Chapter Twenty-Eight

"The only difference between reality and fiction is that
fiction needs to be credible."
Mark Twain

The first week after the explosion was fairly normal on the island, relatively speaking. Uncle John was able to keep Jay in the burn center, the insurance issue not being an immediate problem. I had to field many questions about the explosion from people I passed on the street or on the ferry.

"I don't know. I hadn't heard that. I'll try to find out," were my perfunctory retorts.

One lingering problem for me was the rumor that Jay's business enemy, Stu Black, the man who was on the bad end of the high-speed dinghy chase a few years earlier, was responsible.

I ran into two rugged St. Thomas divers Jay and I would sometimes go on play dives with.

"I heard that fucking Black did this," one of them snarled. "You guys caught him on Captain Jay's boat once before."

"We're going to take him for a swim out at the drop-off, only he won't be coming back," the other one growled.

I knew they were serious and had pieced together enough during our dives to know they could do a lot of damage if they wanted to.

I said, "I don't know. I was on the boat that day with Jay. There was a lot of work being done on the engine, and all kinds of flammable liquid and rags were lying around."

If I couldn't get these guys to back off, I was going to have to tell them what really happened. Once the truth came out, who knew how much legal and criminal trouble Captain Jay would find himself in? I asked them not to do anything until we could all talk to Captain Jay. They reluctantly agreed but told me that if they found any proof that Black was involved they would do what they thought necessary to make things right. I was pretty sure they weren't going to be able to find any proof. The boat, a bowl of melted fiberglass, had already been hauled away. I have no idea where it ended up, probably on the bottom of the ocean.

* * *

The public hearings for Gallows were scheduled, and if successful, we would be ready to start construction. I was optimistic and started making rounds with the island realtors to tell them about the project. I had talked to three of the four real estate brokers in town about my plan and called for a meeting with the fourth broker, Forrest Fishman. Forrest had come to the island many years earlier from California. He was of slight build with a big, toothy smile and sandy hair—a Jimmy Carter look-alike. He told the best jokes on the island and occasionally played tuba solo. His office was across from the Creek and a concrete bulkhead where barges came to the island to offload containers and bulk construction materials. One particular rusty-brown piece of junk, a five-hundred-ton barge owned by a local St. Thomian, made its way into the Creek once a month with a couple of hundred tons of river sand or gravel for the new concrete batch plant on the island. The barge was impossible to ignore, not only because of its bulk but also because of the noise emanating from the barge's engines and off-loading operations, which was clearly evident as I drove parallel to the bulkhead on my way to Forrest's office. I watched and wondered who would trust the vessel's seaworthiness enough to step on board to work on it.

The barge was so large it could barely fit into the Creek. Prior to its arrival on St. John, anchored sailboats would be asked to move so the barge would have a wide enough path to get through Cruz Bay and into the Creek. Once a path was cleared, the behemoth would slowly approach the bulkhead, lowering its ramp onto the pavement as it bumped the concrete retaining wall.

On this day the wind caught the bulky mass and, even when the barge was tied off to the giant cleats bolted to the concrete bulkhead, the captain had to keep the engines running with a little forward thrust so that it stayed in place and didn't drift off the wall.

Forrest was outside his office watching as two front-end loaders started to dig into the gravel on the steel deck of the barge and then take their loads to one of four fifteen-cubic yard dump trucks waiting next to where the barge was parked. The trucks would deliver their loads up to Iva Moses' land, where the batch plant was located, and return to the Creek for the next load.

Forrest had draped his tuba over his shoulder and played marching songs intermittingly while we talked. The engines were loud, but as more gravel was taken off of the barge the steel buckets on the front of the loaders scraped against the steel deck of the barge, creating a loud metal-on-metal grating sound made worse by the amplification caused by the hollow design of the barge's metal hull. As the load lightened, the barge rose, exposing more of its mass to the strong winds.

After thirty minutes of jokes and real estate conversation Forrest smiled, pointed to the barge and said, "I saw this coming before you came. This is going to be interesting." He put his lips back on the mouthpiece of his tuba and forced out the beginning of another marching song—one that sounded remarkably like the last two he'd played.

During the next thirty minutes our conversation about real estate ceased altogether. A crowd started to gather—not to listen to marching songs. The tuba was just Forrest's way of providing music for the drama we all saw developing with the barge—and the wind.

The barge was almost completely off-loaded with just a few more screeching loads remaining on the boat, and the captain was already having a difficult time keeping his barge against the concrete wall. The crowd grew. The tuba was still bad, but appropriate.

The captain had his crew untie the barge, and he gave the engines all of the thrust he dared as he inched his way from the bulkhead against a heavy crosswind.

The Creek was also the home of the National Park Service, its headquarters housed in a funky wooden building painted national park green that rested on a long dock that jutted into the water parallel to the bulkhead and about two hundred feet to the west, downwind of the struggling barge. Alongside the national park building, tied up to the dock, were three national park fiberglass power boats painted the same ugly-green as the building.

The inevitable played out very slowly. At least thirty people had stopped to watch the show. Some of them grabbed chairs from Forrest's office and brought them out to the road to sit and watch.

A five-hundred-ton barge in motion represents a lot of inertia. It's hard to get one underway, and even harder to get one stopped. It's particularly hard to control if it lacks sufficient power to fight wind or current. The captain's difficulty in maneuvering the barge was exacerbated by the lack of space in the Creek. At the same speed the barge was backed away from the bulkhead a crosswind pushed it sideways toward the national park dock and building.

We were mesmerized as if watching the climax of a good movie except, instead of dramatic background music, we had marching songs. What's going to happen? Which will win the battle—the wind or engine thrust?

Nobody thought to warn the people in the national park building of the big barge coming their way as more drivers in passing cars stopped and parked to join the growing crowd. Pedestrians from the nearby post office stopped what they were doing and watched.

The barge slowly drifted toward the national park dock, the captain desperately trying to turn the already sideways barge into the wind and, maybe, out into the bay. There simply wasn't enough room. The tuba stopped playing. Nobody talked. Twenty feet—fifteen feet—ten feet—five feet—then an ugly hard plastic crunch followed by a deep, resonating thud. The building visibly shook. Glass windows shattered. The crowd, at first shocked into silence, laughed and applauded. Forrest played the tuba again. Park rangers ran out of the building, looking around trying to figure out what had hit them.

Though we heard the outcome, the barge was so large it blocked our view. A few of us walked over to the park dock to see that two of the three boats had survived. The captain had been able to turn the barge slightly so it didn't hit quite broadside. The port corner of the barge hit the third boat. Pieces of green fiberglass were wedged between the barge and the dock. Park rangers and secretaries talked among themselves, though it was hard to hear their conversations because the engines of the barge were at full throttle as the captain pivoted off of the park dock and brought the bow into the wind. He could now maneuver the barge, under full power, out of the Creek and through the path made by boats that had moved earlier. We watched the barge leave Cruz Bay at an angle similar to that of a car with a broken leaf spring, the wind still having its way with the empty barge as it slid out into the open ocean.

Forrest and I walked back to his office. Several park rangers stood on the edge of the dock where the smashed boat had been tied.

***

I received my first phone call from Captain Jay later that week. It was two in the morning.

"Rookie?" a strained voice asked. It was a shadow of the larger-than-life blond Elvis voice.

"You've got to come up here. You've got to come up and put a bullet in my head. I'm serious. Real serious. I can't take the pain."

I had no idea if this was theatrics or real.

"Captain Jay, hang in there. I'll talk to Uncle John tomorrow. Is Lisa there?"

"She went back to Oklahoma to stay with her mother. You have to come and shoot me. You have to. You're my friend, aren't you?"

"Yeah, but—"

"You don't understand. Every night the nurses put me in a big tub full of water and scrub the burns with sand paper, I think. The pain is unbelievable. Just come and kill me. Tonight."

"Don't they give you pain medication?" I asked.

"No, the fuckin' doctor thinks pain meds are overused and addictive. The prick won't give me any."

That didn't sound right. He was out of his mind and in tremendous pain.

"Look, Jay, I can't do anything about this tonight. I'll call some people tomorrow. I need to hang up now."

I could hear "Tonight, you have to kill me tonight," as I hung up the phone.

* * *

The next day I went to Tim McQuin's office and told him about the call from Captain Jay. Blue skulked in the corner. I stayed on my side of the office. We called the burn center. After being passed from administration to the floor where Jay was being treated, and through two more nurses, I finally got to speak with the doctor. I told him about Jay's call. He grunted and mumbled and told me he didn't have time to listen to me.

"But he needs pain meds. Anybody can see that."

"He can get through this without pain meds," the doctor said to me condescendingly. "Maybe you should let me do my job, unless you are going to tell me that you know more about treating burn patients than I."

I looked over at Tim. Without taking the phone too far from my face I said loudly, "What a jerk."

Blue growled.

"Jay is one of the toughest guys you'll ever meet. Maybe we should strap you down in a chair and give you a massage with an electric sander. Think you could take that?"

"Are you immediate family?" he asked, in a tone that made me want to send Blue through the phone to bite the prick's head off.

I hung up.

"Tim, I can't do much about this. I'm up to my ass with my Gallows Point project. You can't do much about it. You are up to your ass trying to run a restaurant."

He smiled. "How many investors does Jay have on his boat, again?" he asked, still trying to register what I had told him earlier about the three first liens in the names of three different investors for Jay's new boat.

I had taken over Captain Jay's retail operation. It was in shambles. I discovered the boat documents in a file behind a stack of T-shirts. I knew all of the investors. I had been diving with all three of them. I knew that they didn't know each other or that they each held a first position lien on Jay's boat. I wasn't going to tell them, either.

"We need to bring one of them into this hospital mess. They're all wealthy and can probably help to throw some clout in the right direction," Tim said.

"You're right. I'll call Gerald. You take the guy in Minneapolis. If they don't come through I'll call the guy in Boston."

Later that night I was awakened by another disturbing call from Captain Jay. It was a repeat of his first call. I received these calls every night until Sam Halverson, the investor from Minneapolis, flew his private jet and his private physician to Florida.

Tim had contacted Sam and explained the situation. I guess Sam called the doctor at the burn center and didn't care much for the guy or the way he was treating Captain Jay. After reviewing Jay's charts and having a face-to-face meeting with the doctor in charge, Sam and his private physician decided to visit the hospital administrator. I have no idea what was said, but a new doctor was put in charge of Jay's treatment.

Sam called me and gave me the short story. He also said that he would take Jay up to Minneapolis to recover once he was well enough. He asked about Jay's businesses here.

"I closed the retail shop," I told him.

"Good, I never knew why he opened that damned thing. What about the dive business?"

"I'm helping out with the business and some of the diving when I can. Gizmo and Scott are doing a good job, saving Jay a lot of money. We decided that the dive trips would stay close to home. No showboating, so to speak."

We laughed.

The late-night phone calls stopped. They were replaced with happy daytime calls. Some sounded too happy. I guess the pain meds were working.

Chapter Twenty-Nine

"Clothes make the man. Naked people have little or no influence on society."
Mark Twain

Captain Jay had been gone almost a year. Most concerns about the explosion had calmed down. There were so many changes on the island it was easy for us to forget about Jay's troubles. It was like watching a puppy grow. Every day brought something new, and just like a puppy, the island became a little less cute and more adult-like. I wondered if I would have to grow up.

More people moved to the island from the US, and many of my older West Indian friends seemed to be retrenching into the bush. Rare were the days when continentals walked through Cruz Bay laughing, blending in and getting deep, heart-felt laughs and hugs from the local West Indians. I heard the once omnipresent *okay* less and less as I walked through the village. Only the locals and Charlie Kline would politely shout *inside* when coming to visit me. I hadn't heard the term *continental* in over a year.

Many of the older continentals moved back to the US or simply disappeared without telling anybody they were leaving. Health and aging issues were partly to blame, but some were sad to see the way of life that held them on the island like a magnet fade away. My construction mentor, Dick Bramble, moved back to New York State and died within a few months.

New shops and restaurants opened up not just in Cruz Bay but all over the island. Nothing fancy, just shacks on the sides of the roads for the most part. Two new dive operations opened up in Cruz Bay. Police officers from St. Thomas waved drivers through at the ferry dock, not allowing any driver to hold up traffic by waving their arms and stopping to talk to friends, unless they were related to the officer.

The government's effort to rid the island's police force of nepotism by rotating officers to different islands and enlarging the force brought new policemen and women from all over. One was a very nice black lady from New York who had moved to the islands a few years earlier and took whatever tests were needed to become an island policewoman. Her name was Yvonne. She had orange hair and breasts that were freakishly large. Holding a conversation with Yvonne was impossible. There was nothing sexual about it. It was like trying to hold a face-to-face conversation with a person who has crossed eyes—you didn't know which eye to look at. In Yvonne's case, you had to give her a lot more distance than you would give in a normal face-to-face interaction, and at that distance it didn't take much wandering for your eyes to be talking to her breasts.

She and another female officer caught me skinny-dipping in Frank Bay with Sid, a long-time island friend. They didn't so much catch us as they were called. My old angelfish-eating friend, Miss Gwennie, spotted us frolicking around naked in the shallow water from her house up on Goat Hill. We were a fair distance from her house, and it would have been hard to recognize exactly who was swimming naked in the bay. I think she called the police before she recognized us. At least I would have liked to think of it that way.

When she was sure who it was, she shouted down from her porch.

"Mr. Arlan, me son. Shame on you. Wa you and yo girl fren be doin showin yo private parts to all of da world?"

Then she turned her two hundred-and-fifty-pound body around, hiked up her dress, shook her ass at us and shouted, "You gonna to be so rude? I show you rude back."

We laughed and thought we should probably leave. Before we could get out of the water, along came Yvonne with her built-in partners and another female officer in a shiny new police car. They stood on the beach a few feet from the water.

"Arlan? What are you doing? We got a call from your neighbor. She said some people were swimming naked in front of her house. It's against the law, you know," Yvonne said, trying to be serious, but her lips were curled up in a slight smirk.

The other officer didn't say anything, but she too wore a smirk. Sid and I wore a smile and nothing else—and they knew it. Our clothes were piled at their feet.

I don't think they would really have arrested me, but they had to look professional in front of Miss Gwennie, who was still watching from her porch. But I did think they were going to embarrass me by making me and my shriveled pri*vate* part come out of the water.

Directly across the street from the beach was the retired Italian doctor's house. His teenage grandson was visiting from the US. He evidently saw the police car parked in front of his grandfather's house and came out to see what was going on. I knew him from previous visits. Sid knew him, too.

Yvonne and her partner didn't seem to be as interested with Sid. She swam down the beach away from us and motioned for the teenage kid to follow. While I was stammering my way through any excuse I could think of to stay in the water I looked over and saw the kid wade out into the water and hand Sid the T-shirt he had been wearing. Sid put it on and swam back toward me, standing up in the shallow water to show the police that was she breaking no law. It was a large T-shirt.

"I asked the kid to go get some shorts for you," Sid whispered to me.

"Arlan, you need to come out right now," Yvonne demanded; no smirk this time. She wasn't going to give the kid time to return to his grandparent's house and dig around for a pair of shorts.

The kid was smart, though. He saw what was going on and disappeared behind a large boulder. He came back out with his shorts on but his underwear in his hand. Sid climbed out of the water and retrieved the underwear. We weren't hiding any of this from Yvonne. We couldn't. We were all just a few feet apart. Sid handed me the underwear, and I slipped them on underwater.

"Do you still want me to come out?" I asked and smiled at Yvonne.

She and the other officer were both smiling now. But I saw that look in her eye. She was screwing with me. She was going to make me get out of the water with my shriveled privates covered in white, now transparent underwear, three sizes too small.

Really?

I slowly climbed out of the water and stood on the beach. Everybody laughed, even Miss Gwennie, from way the hell up on her porch, who shouted down, "Da wa-*ter* be a little cold, Mr. Arlan?"

Yvonne smiled and got back into the police car, and the two officers drove off. Sid and I went behind the boulder to change out of the kid's T-shirt and underwear and into our own clothes. Miss Gwennie had disappeared into her house.

Chapter Thirty

"Humor is tragedy plus time."
Mark Twain

Exactly one year to the day and with no fanfare, Captain Jay returned to the island. It was just like any other day. I wasn't there to meet the boat. He had been gone long enough for most who lived on the island a year ago to forget about the explosion. He had a lot of friends more than willing to help him get back to normalcy, whatever that was. His dive business was operating fairly well with Scott and Gizmo in charge. I never told Jay that I'd shut down his retail store. If he didn't already know he'd learn soon enough.

Jay's old baby-blue Jeep was now a permanent fixture at the resort, used only as a utility vehicle carrying scuba tanks from the maintenance area to the dock. Somebody had given Jay a used Isuzu Trooper. It was in good shape with no dents, until Captain Jay drove it through Cruz Bay the day he got it, waving like a politician to everybody he drove past and forgetting about the utility pole next to the road on the one-way loop. I stood on a corner talking to someone as Jay drove by in his new Trooper with his big Elvis grin. He drove to the dock and around the one-way loop, which took about two minutes. When he passed me again the front right of the Trooper was completely crunched. He leaned his head out of the window and shrugged with an embarrassed grin. "I hit a pole," he said, and drove on.

The day after Captain Jay arrived I went to visit him at the house an off-island friend let him stay in indefinitely. He looked good. He had red burn scarring on his neck, the backs of his hands and particularly on the tops of his feet. His arms and legs looked almost normal. He sat on the sofa smoking his bong and talking to a couple of the island's drug culture guys when I walked in. They weren't normally guys Jay hung out with. I don't know why they were with Jay, and I doubted they were there to sell Jay marijuana. His pot always came from Jost van Dyke, in trade for fish and lobster.

After exchanging a few pleasantries, the other guys left. Jay and I caught up on his treatment and recovery. He pulled out a framed photo of him in full hockey gear, with his Elvis smile. I thought it a strange photo—a Caribbean pirate dressed in a hockey uniform with skates and stick on the ice in a vast empty indoor arena. It turned out the investor from Minneapolis owned a hockey team.

"Wow, a lot of changes on the island, right? Looks like you almost have your project built."

"About halfway," I said with a shrug. I didn't want to talk about my stuff. "How are you?" I asked.

"Shit, Rookie. Never been better. Got a new car, nice house, met a cute girl today. She's comin' by tonight. Life couldn't be better."

He was quintessential Captain Jay on the outside, but something was missing. I couldn't tell what just yet. I had noticed this in several of our phone conversations while he was recovering. But now, face-to-face, it was more pronounced. Many of our mutual friends also noticed this subtle change, but dismissed it as part of his recovery. I thought it was something deeper and possibly permanent.

I invited myself on a couple of his dives over the next few weeks. I'd become such an avid free diver that scuba had lost some of its original glitter. The passion seemed to be gone from Captain Jay, too. His dive instructions were not as commanding or humorous. But, more significantly, the sun was painful for him. His scarred skin couldn't take it. He wore a large-brimmed hat with a scarf around his neck. Instead of the regular Speedo and flip-flops, he wore long pants and tennis shoes. He stayed in the shade of the boat's roof and only tried diving on the first trip. The flippers hurt the tops of his feet. Captain Jay could no longer take divers out by himself. Gizmo or Scott had to come along to take the divers in the water.

Several times when I went to visit Captain Jay, people who I knew were part of the cocaine culture on the island were visiting. For the guy who once fired an employee for snorting cocaine, while he was smoking pot next to him, and who was adamantly against hard drugs, this was a big change. I confronted Jay about this one day.

"What, Rookie, do you think I'm a druggie?" he snarled. He changed the subject. "What's with all of these new sedans and shit? They're all over the place. I don't see how they can even be driven on half of the roads. They have no clearance to get over the damn rocks. Hell, they'll all rust out in six months."

This was true. A hot-shot car dealership owner from Texas had brought his business to St. Thomas. He opened up a dealership that offered the newest cars from the US and Japan. Not island cars, but cars that were typically sold in cities across the US, designed to drive on paved roads and not able to withstand the corrosive atmosphere of the Caribbean. To a lot of young locals, these cars represented everything they had seen in the glossy magazines shipped down from the US. They had to have a new US-style car. Not practical, but flashy. The new dealership offered the cars for no money down and a three to five year loan. The cars were snapped up. More cars were shipped down. They were snapped up too.

Of all of the cars that made it over to St. John, none were operable after their first year. The loans lived on, though.

My concern about Captain Jay grew when the new Caneel manager flagged me down one Sunday afternoon as I was walking to the Caneel dock to help Scott with a dive. He asked me about Jay's health and why he wasn't around much. I knew Jay had become disinterested in his dive operation, leaving much of the responsibility to Scott, who was soon going to take a job as the captain of a large sailboat. I lied and told the resort manager that everything was fine with Captain Jay.

Jay was back to chumming the water for yellowtail snapper two or three nights a week. There were enough restaurants on the island that he could usually sell most of his catch to them before selling the rest from the back of his Trooper. The police never bothered him when he did. He also started to use one of his boats for overnight trips to St. Maarten, ninety nautical miles from St. John. The French side of the island was tranquil at the time. The Dutch side of the island was a busy business hub, and many stores sold electronics—stereos, CD players, speakers, televisions, radios—things that were very expensive on St. Thomas. Captain Jay took orders for electronic devices from people around the island and motored to St. Maarten during the night, returning the next afternoon with a boatload of electronic cargo. I didn't know if either of these businesses was profitable. I doubted Captain Jay did either. I was more concerned that his need for extra cash had something to do with drug use.

Other than the burn scars and the more fragile ego that I had noticed when he returned, there were no typical outward signs of heavy drug use. He wasn't hiding out in his house. He was still somewhat the swashbuckling pirate around town, though fewer people knew him. He had his normal appetite whenever we stopped at a restaurant. But something wasn't right.

There were glimpses of the old Captain Jay, pre-explosion Captain Jay. Every year hurricanes threaten the island, but we had had no direct hits since I'd arrived. We experienced tropical waves and tropical storms and near misses by large hurricanes, all of which can be pretty bad. The odds of getting hit grew with every passing tropical system.

We finally got hit.

Being on an island before, during and after a hurricane has its unique problems. If a hurricane threatens coastal US you can drive inland to escape its force. Even if you choose to ride out the storm in your coastal home you can drive away afterward if there is continued lack of power or communications.

You can do none of this on an island. If you were on an island when the hurricane hit, you were going to be there for a while. After the hurricane passed and it was safe to pry yourself from whatever hole you had spent the previous several hours in, you walked out to see unbelievable destruction. Jungle trees bare of leaves looked more like a winter scene in the Adirondacks than a tropical broadleaf forest. A few days after the hurricane a friend stopped by my house. He looked up the hill above my driveway through the once thick jungle vegetation, saw a house and said, "I didn't know you had a neighbor up there."

"I didn't either."

Days were filled with the sound of chain saws cutting away downed trees so that vehicles could drive more than a few hundred yards. Downed power lines and poles were pushed to the sides of the roads, looking like a giant black spaghetti dish.

Even if the island's generator still functioned after the storm passed, the distribution system was gone. It took days or weeks, and sometimes months to repair.

The first thing missed on a post-hurricane island was ice. Everything in the refrigerator and freezer must be eaten before it melts or rots. Warm beer was the norm for as long as it took to get power back online. The second thing missed were fans to keep the mosquitoes away. Swarms of them hatch three to five days after the torrential rainfall that accompanies a hurricane. There were a few portable home generators on the island. But hurricanes are like sewage—out of sight, out of mind. After years without a hurricane nobody thought to check to see if their generators still worked. Without use they rusted out and seized up within months. As soon as the power went out those who had generators tried to start them and ended up spending the next several days trying to repair them. Few were successful.

A less conspicuous problem left in the wake of a hurricane involved fish traps commonly used by local fishermen. They were wire crates framed with local hardwood branches and baited with goat meat and fish parts. The crate was configured so that a small-brained fish would swim in to get to the goat meat but would not find its way out. The traps were strategically placed at the base of reefs or in beds of sea grass. There were hundreds of them in the water, marked with floating, empty plastic jugs tethered to the traps with as much line as needed so the jugs could reach the surface.

The traps were heavy but usually one or two fishermen could check them by hauling them into their boat by hand. If not checked, or if the plastic jug marker had disappeared, a single trap could sit on the bottom for weeks and could become a solid mass of fish, new ones attracted to the fish already trapped, helping to decimate the nearby fish population.

The heavy surf caused by the hurricane snapped just about every plastic jug that marked the traps in the area and the old Captain Jay showed up to help. He organized the effort to locate all of the fish traps. For several weeks, mostly on weekends, we followed fishermen to where they remembered their traps to be and dove to the traps. We lifted up those that we could, but for those that were too full we cut a hole in the side to let the fish out, patching it before surfacing.

We found scores of traps and released hundreds of fish, keeping any Nassau grouper and a few yellow tail snapper for ourselves. Even after the organized effort stopped, we all kept our eyes open for abandoned fish traps every time we dove and reattached empty, plastic water jugs or laundry detergent jugs to the traps before returning to the island to tell local fisherman where to find the freshly marked traps.

One Saturday, after finding a dozen fish traps, a group of us tied Jay's boat up to the dock in Red Hook and sauntered over to a new bar for some beers. After a couple of hours most of the guys wanted to get back to St. John. Jay and I were having fun, drinking beer and flirting with the girls in the bar. It was like old times. Maybe another bar brawl was in the cards.

"Gizmo, take whoever wants to go back to Cruz Bay. Leave the boat at the dock in there. Rookie and I will take the ferry back later," Jay blabbered, drunkenly staring at a couple of ladies who had entered the bar.

Everybody left with Gizmo, leaving Captain Jay and me to continue to drink and piss off boyfriends and tourists. We stayed at the bar and missed the last ferry. An hour later the bar closed, and we had nowhere to go.

"Come on, Rookie," Jay said and staggered out through the parking lot toward the dock.

"Where we going?"

"We're gonna find a ride," he said, and stumbled onto the dinghy dock.

The only dinghies that had engines and looked as though they could operate had locks on them. A few motorless dinghies were tied up to the dock. They would do us no good. Rowing across the sound was out of the question. One dinghy had an engine and was not locked, but it was really beat-up. It was a rubber inflatable dinghy that somehow held air. The engine was clamped onto an unsteady-looking wood transom at the stern. Jay climbed in and lifted the gas tank.

"There's gas in here. Doesn't look like much, but it should get us to St. John," Captain Jay said with a laugh.

I guess I was too drunk to realize we were stealing a dinghy, though not much of one, and probably had no business taking it out in the open ocean. I untied the dinghy as Jay pulled the rope to start the engine. It started, which made both of us laugh more.

Captain Jay and I made a midnight run across four miles of Pillsbury Sound in a stolen dinghy. It wasn't really stolen, just borrowed. We could tow the dinghy back to Red Hook or ask somebody heading to Red Hook to motor it back the next day or two.

We made it as far as Stevens Cay when I heard a loud "Shit" and turned around to see Captain Jay fighting with the engine, which was no longer attached to the boat. The rotten transom had broken apart as the poor dinghy bounced over the waves in the sound. He hugged the motor like a teddy bear, somehow keeping the prop in the water and steering by rotating his upper body. He was having a difficult time keeping the throttle twisted at the same time.

"I can't see where the hell we are goin'," Jay shouted.

I grabbed the throttle, faced forward and shouted "left" or "right" to Jay, who turned the motor accordingly. A person who is drunk has a difficult enough time discerning left from right. Throw in backward and in reverse, holding onto what must have been a hot dinghy motor, and commands for left and right were a nearly impossible task—only made possible by our massive consumption of beer which I was convinced had helped to keep us from understanding that we shouldn't have been able to do what we were doing.

We made it into Cruz Bay, and I sped through the anchored boats. I didn't try to offer up any instructions that would maneuver the dinghy to the dinghy dock. That would have required far too many lefts and rights. I kept the throttle full and the boat aimed at the beach. Jay couldn't see where we were going, but he sensed that we were close to something.

"Isn't that the end of the dock we just passed?" he asked as we ran full speed up onto the beach.

I flew head-first into the sand. Jay managed to stop hugging the motor just in time to fly on top of me. We heard the motor splash into the surf and bubble into submission.

The next morning Jay and I loaded the now deflated dinghy, its waterlogged motor and the gas tank onto his boat. Captain Jay and Gizmo returned it to Red Hook. Nobody ever claimed it.

***

I spotted Charlie Kline in Cruz Bay later that day. The last time I saw him was the second evening after the hurricane. I laughed out loud to myself remembering the encounter.

The government had placed a curfew on the island immediately after the hurricane, which coincided closely with sundown. I was driving up the hill past Cruz Bay beach just after curfew. My headlights shone on a large, barefoot figure walking on the side of the road ahead of me. It was wearing a black garbage bag and nothing else. As I got closer I recognized Charlie, who wore the garbage bag like a diaper.

I stopped next to him and asked, "What the hell, Charlie? You have a major diarrhea problem?"

He got in, looked at me with his beady eyes and smiled.

I waited for some kind of explanation but wasn't going to press the issue.

With his gruff voice, he finally explained, "You know I keep my catamaran anchored in Cruz Bay. The waves coming into the bay are pretty big."

The unusually large seas still coming into the bay were remnants of the hurricane. I could see the lights at the tops of sailboat masts swaying with the strong surf and waited to hear more from Charlie.

"I decided to swim out to check my anchor. A rogue wave comes in while I'm swimming and sends me in summersaults. My suit comes off. It's gone. It's almost dark, and I know there is a curfew, but I'm wearing nothing, and I need to find something to wear so I can get home."

He paused with a smile and said, "I see the silhouette of my ex-partner's sailboat anchored almost out in the sound. I swim over there. You know Bob?"

"Yeah, I know him. Not well, though. He seems to keep to himself."

"Well, he's recently found Jesus. Spends a lot of time at church. So I am treading water at the stern of his boat and start hollering, 'Bob. Bob.' It's dark now and he can't see me. I hear him run up on the deck and say, 'Oh, Jesus. I can hear you Jesus. You're calling me.' So I say, 'No, it's me, Charlie.' Bob finally realizes that Jesus isn't talking to him and looks down in the water at me. I told what had happened and that I needed some shorts. He told me that he had taken most of his things to the church for safekeeping before the hurricane hit. He disappeared down in the galley, and I hear him banging around for a while. He comes back up on deck in a few minutes. 'All I have are some trash bags' he says and drops one over the side of the boat to me."

I looked at Charlie as I drove, waiting to hear more. He smiled and looked straight ahead.

Chapter Thirty-One

*"The worst loneliness is to not be comfortable with
yourself."*
Mark Twain

The island continued to swell with people, particularly with another tourist season getting underway. Tommy and I were busy with the development of Gallows Point; Tim was busy with his restaurant; Rupert visited often. We saw less and less of Captain Jay, and none of us were comfortable visiting Jay's house and his new friends.

I was surprised when Captain Jay invited me out to Caneel for dinner one night. I accepted. We were the guests of two ladies in their eighties. They were wealthy sisters from New York who were taken in by Jay's charms.

Dinner was embarrassing. Jay talked a lot. He made all sorts of things up about being from a wealthy southern family and how his father was a famous doctor and that his brother was a hot-shot Wall Street lawyer. I just smiled and nodded. Why the bullshit? Maybe he thought he could get the ladies to invest in a new harebrained scheme. I made up some excuse and left early.

I had met Jay's father and brother a couple of years earlier. His father was an angry retired civil service worker. His brother was active Delta Force, a shorter, more chiseled version of Captain Jay, but with insanely mean eyes. He probably excelled at his job. The guy gave me a bad feeling. He got drunk and picked fights the whole time he visited. Nobody was stupid enough to take the bait. Jay's brother and father seemed to have a pretty close relationship. Jay didn't seem close to either one.

Jay continued his St. Maarten runs. Tommy came into my office one day and told me he had seen Jay pull into Cruz Bay with his boatload of electronics. After the crews left for the day Tommy and I went to visit Jay at his house. Nobody was home, but stacked neatly in the driveway were scores of boxes containing the most recent electronic orders, totally unprotected.

Tommy and I looked at each other and smiled, our thoughts the same.

"Let's h-hide them up th-the hill in my buddy's d-driveway," Tommy said with a grin.

Several giggling Jeep trips later we had moved every box. We parked my Jeep up the hill and hid in the bush next to Captain Jay's house, waiting for him to return. We didn't have to wait long, and it was hard to keep our laughs down when Captain Jay got out of his Isuzu Trooper and saw an empty driveway.

Jay didn't think this was funny, as we expected he would. He looked scared. He hurried into the house. Tommy and I shrugged.

"W-what's wrong w-with h-him?" asked Tommy with an incredulous look.

"I don't know. Maybe we should go up to the house."

"L-let's w-wait for a minute," Tommy said with a laugh.

We were about to climb from the bush when a police car pulled up the drive. It was Harry Daniels, a St. Johnian cop whom we had known for years. Jay had come out of the house, his face red, reminding me of the time when the St. Thomas cop slapped a handcuffed Jay around in the back seat of a squad car.

This was no longer the practical joke we intended. Tommy and I stepped from the bush smiling.

"Hey, Harry," I said as Tommy and I emerged from the bush.

"Okay. What you two doin der in de bush?"

Jay looked at us with an unusual expression.

"Th-this was a j-joke," Tommy said and laughed. "All o-of your b-boxes are u-up the h-hill."

Harry laughed. Jay remained silent, looking more desperate than angry.

"Look, this was supposed to be funny. We'll go get all of the stuff," I explained.

Harry smiled at us and shrugged to Jay as if to ask, "What is your problem?" He got into his police car and drove away.

Tommy and I returned with the boxes while Jay made several phone calls from inside his house. We went in to talk to him, but he walked out and started loading boxes into his Trooper. A couple of his drug friends showed up to help him. Tommy and I left, shaking our heads.

"I think we have a problem with Captain Jay," I said to Tommy as we drove away.

"N-no doubt a-about it."

A week later I got a frantic phone call from Gizmo.

"Arlan, me son, listen. Der is a problem wit Jay, he in da house tryin to keel hisself. The door it be locked. I had to run to a neighbor house to call you."

I ran to my Jeep. One of the carpenters who had become a good friend walked by.

"Drop your bags, Jimmy. We need to go to Captain Jay's house. There's something wrong."

We sped out to Chocolate Hole and up Captain Jay's driveway. Gizmo had returned from the neighbor's house where he'd used the phone. We climbed the steps to the entry door, which, as Gizmo had said, was locked. The door was wood frame with clear, glass jalousie panes. We could see into the house, through the kitchen, and into a bath on the far side of the kitchen. Jay sat in the bathtub sawing away on his left wrist with what looked like a steak knife.

Jimmy grabbed a large rock from the drive and threw it through the glass jalousies. We opened the door and ran to the tub. Jay, still sawing at his left wrist, had already cut the right one. We wrestled the knife away and tried to get him out of the tub. It took all of our collective strength to get him under minimal control. As we fought, I glanced around the house to take in as much information as I could. I could see partially empty and empty bottles of liquor on the coffee table. Next to them was Jay's bong, and on the other side of the table was the ubiquitous mirror that accompanied cocaine use. There was an open vial of cocaine spilled onto the mirror. Nobody else was in the house.

Captain Jay was drunk, high, delirious—and strong. On the way out I grabbed a couple of towels to wrap his wrists, which weren't bleeding as much as I'd expected. We wrestled him out of the house and into the Jeep. He fought hard—shouting, crying and kicking.

Fortunately, the island doctor was at the clinic and was able to sedate Jay. The ambulance boat was also working. The doctor dressed the wounds as best he could and prepared Jay for the trip to the St. Thomas hospital. Gizmo went along.

The doctor told me Jay would be sedated and placed under suicide watch in the critical care unit. He asked me what I knew about what had happened. I told him of my suspicion of heavy drug use and what I saw around the house.

"He is in no danger of dying. It looks like he did more ligament damage than anything else. He must have been very drunk and high."

"He was," I replied, sadly.

Gizmo later told me Captain Jay had been holed up in his locked house for two days. Every time he went to check on him Jay sent him away. Gizmo, and the rest of us, had not realized how far he had slipped. But none of us believed that it was a real suicide attempt either. If Captain Jay really wanted to commit to suicide, he would have gone out in a spectacular fashion. He wouldn't have waited until three of his buddies were at the front door before sawing at his wrists. This was desperation and anger exacerbated by the two-day drunken cocaine binge. It was certainly a wake-up call for all of us about his current condition.

After a couple of weeks in the St. Thomas hospital and surgical repair of his wrists, it was back to the US for Captain Jay, this time into a rehabilitation center in Florida—sponsored by one of the other first lien holders on Jay's boat.

Tim came to see me not long after we got Captain Jay to Florida. He said, "I just got off the phone with the electronics store owner in

St. Maarten. It seems that Jay charmed him and received credit for the last two deliveries."

I thought about that and said, "Jay collected money from people before he left for St. Maarten."

"Well, none of it, at least what he got from the last two trips and whatever he collected when he got back, made it to St. Maarten," Tim said.

"How much are we talking about?" I hesitantly asked.

"Over sixteen-thousand."

After a full minute of silence, I said, "I'm starting to think that we are too much of a safety net for Captain Jay."

Tim looked at me in agreement but said, "Let's see what happens next."

Chapter Thirty-Two

"It is easy to make friends, but hard to get rid of them."
Mark Twain

I had assumed Captain Jay spent the obligatory thirty days in one of the country's supposedly best rehabilitation programs, and I thought the stay might save him from further drug use. I was wrong on both counts.

Sometime while Jay was in Florida he ended up on the Panhandle to visit his father. I got word from Uncle John that Jay's father had committed suicide while Jay was there. He had shot himself in the head while in the shower. Evidently, the circumstances were suspicious enough that Captain Jay was taken in and questioned. Uncle John told me that after several days Jay had been cleared of any suspicion, the death ruled a suicide, and that Captain Jay was on his way back to the island.

A week later I came home one afternoon to see an old, light-brown colored, flimflam, man-style suitcase in my foyer. I recognized it immediately. Only one guy on earth had a suitcase this ugly—Captain Jay. It was his one and only suitcase that I think he had owned since childhood. The gate had been locked, so I guess he tossed it over the wall and left.

Captain Jay showed up a few hours later in a borrowed Jeep and his arm around the waist of a cute young tourist he had met earlier in the day. "Rookie, how ya doin?"

I smiled suspiciously, trying to read in him if the rehabilitation had worked. "I'm fine. What are you doing here?"

"Hell, Rookie I'm back. Let's have some fun."

"How are you?" I asked with a serious frown.

"Shit, Rookie, the rehabilitation was a piece of cake. I had them eatin' out of my hand after the first week. They let me come and go as I pleased. I left after two weeks. Everything is great," he said, slapping my shoulder.

We talked a while. Mostly he talked—rambling bullshit loaded with winks to his girl of the day. I turned my brain off to it. In his absence, Captain Jay had lost the dive concession at the resort. It was awarded to one of the new dive shops in town. The three first lien holders on his boats were all frequent guests at the resort and managed to put two and two together. They took the boats, sold one and leased the other to the new operator. Besides the St. Maarten electronics store, who knew how much Jay owed the drug community? There was no remorse for the mess he left us. No mention of his father's suicide. Just bullshit.

I had a tough decision to make, a difficult one given that he'd been a mentor, however unconventionally.

While he rambled on I looked directly at him and said, "You're out of here. When the real Captain Jay shows up I'll tell him that he is more than welcome to stay with me any time he wants. I don't know who the fuck you are."

I grabbed his suitcase and threw it into the driveway. The girl sheepishly walked out of my house and climbed into the borrowed Jeep, never having said a word. Jay looked shocked, like I had slapped him. I felt bad, but couldn't back down. That would have done neither of us any good. I expected a fight.

Jay left.

* * *

Captain Jay spent the next few weeks with various friends, charming his way around the island and selling any of the equipment he was able to salvage from his boats before they were taken from him.

We saw each other a few times. I didn't see him hanging out with the drug crowd. It looked as though he was getting over that part of his life. He was trying to be Captain Jay, but with no boat, no ability to fish or dive, and no other talents, his future on the quickly-changing island was bleak. Not only were his antics helping him to wear out his welcome, particularly with the newcomers, the island had simply outgrown him.

The older locals and continentals were always happy to be entertained if only for a few minutes by Captain Jay. They still saw the old Captain Jay. There was no other personality on the island that came close to matching Jay's larger-than-life, swashbuckling style. Only a few of us knew the real truth. And only one of us knew exactly when and how the king had started to lose his throne.

The cold relationship between us warmed up during those few weeks. We spoke when we saw each other in town. Captain Jay admitted to me that he no longer felt at home on the island. He said he was checking into some fishing camps in the Bahamas and Mexico that he could manage. That was probably a lie, but I was happy he was thinking about the future.

Uncle John called me one night pretty upset. The call was a warning for Jay, whom he couldn't find. Uncle John always liked Jay, but didn't care for his psychopathic brother, Steve. Uncle John told me that he had always thought that Jay's brother was a perfect fit for Delta Force, or any other military branch that allowed him to hurt people.

Steve had never been happy about the outcome of the investigation surrounding their father's suicide. He was convinced that Jay was involved. He took short-term leave to find and confront Jay. The result would not be pretty for either one of them. One, or both, would probably be seriously hurt or worse. Jay was tough, but I didn't think he could stand up to the strength, training and overall meanness of his brother.

When I told Jay of Uncle John's warning about his brother he didn't shrug it off, but he didn't seem overly concerned either. He knew what his brother was capable of, but he also had enough ego left to think that he could survive a confrontation with him, and maybe win.

I didn't think so.

I talked to Tommy and Tim McQuin about Uncle John's call. Tommy had never met Jay's brother. Tim and I had and agreed that we should try to keep Jay and his brother apart, if Steve did show up. How we would do so was not clear.

Later that week Tommy and I were sitting at a table in Tim's restaurant. Jay's brother coincidentally showed up looking for Jay. He had spent most of his previous visit getting drunk at the bar and thought he could find out where Jay was through Tim.

He was wrong.

Tommy and I had left the restaurant and were talking to Tim in the back parking lot when Steve rounded the corner. Tim and I tried to be pleasant, but Captain Jay's brother didn't have a friendly side. He was loaded for bear, on a mission to kick his brother's ass.

"Hi Steve," I said and held my hand out. He didn't take it. I glanced over at Tommy and saw what I was afraid I would see—Tommy instantly didn't like this guy.

Tim waded in and said, "We know you're here to find Jay. Your uncle called us."

"The prick killed my dad, and I'm going to make him pay for it," Steve said and looked at Tim with his cold, shark-like eyes.

"The police don't agree with you. Uncle John sent me a news article about the whole thing," I interjected.

"Fuck Uncle John, and fuck you. I know you're his buddy and will say anything to protect him."

I could see that Tommy was sizing the guy up, getting more and more pissed off. He stepped a little closer to Steve. Tim and I stepped back, knowing what was coming.

"You're right. He's our friend, and we know he didn't do it," I replied, but knew it didn't matter.

"Maybe you should leave," Tommy told him without a stutter.

"Maybe you should fuck off," Steve said as he raised his hand to push Tommy away.

Tommy moved like a blur. Delta Force Steve, pissed off sociopathic brother of Captain Jay, found himself on his back staring up through surprised eyes. Before Steve could react, Tommy followed through by grabbing Steve's hand and twisting his arm within a millimeter of breaking it.

This all went down so fast that Tim and I had no time to react. We looked at each other and smiled. Neither one of us cared too much if Tommy broke the guy's arm. But he didn't. Steve gave up. He had been in enough fights to know when he was out-matched.

"If y-you t-touch our friend or anybody else o-on the i-island w-we are g-going to send you b-back to the army in a b-body bag."

The threat was gone. Tommy had obviously settled down. Delta Force training was the best in the world, and Jay's brother was probably as good as it got. Tommy was better.

Later that week we all met at the ferry dock to see Captain Jay off for the last time. He didn't even know that his brother had been on the island. He told us that he was going to catch the flight to Miami, then hop over to the Bahamas. I have no idea if that's what he did.

I remember that day like it was yesterday and have always hoped that Jay and I would have had a talk or something that would have indicated to both of us that everything was okay. But I don't think that either of us wanted closure to our strange friendship. I don't think either one of us understood the concept of closure. It seemed too close to quitting—giving up. No future. No hope. Regardless of how we might have postured things, giving up was not acceptable to either one of us. I think we both expected that he would be back.

Captain Jay never returned to St. John.

* * *

Life on the island continued as though Captain Jay had never existed. A few weeks after Jay left, Bob Davis approached me with his big voice and smile to match. Bob was another WWII vet and a long-time resident. He was an avid diver and acted like a big kid and was liked by everybody.

"Hey, Arlan, you got my money?" he asked through his big smile.

I had to laugh. I didn't owe Bob any money. This must have been the beginning of one of his jokes.

"What money?"

"Captain Jay borrowed five-hundred bucks from me before he left and told me he would send the money to you when he got back to the US."

I couldn't help it. I laughed hard. This was total Captain Jay.

"Bob, I don't have your money. Jay never said anything about this to me, and I haven't heard from him since he left."

Bob and I parted, but every time I saw him he asked about his money. It never came.

Chapter Thirty-Three

"Nobody comes here anymore, it's too crowded."
Yogi Berra

Several months later I sat in my office and reflected on the past few years. What a ride it had been. There is a philosophy passage that refers to the "owl of Minerva spreading its wings only with the falling dusk," which somehow means that we don't recognize an era until it is over. However, it was clear to me that with Captain Jay gone and with the vast changes in the world and on our island, those of us who were still there were experiencing the tail-end of an extraordinary era.

A new and different era was beginning.

Almost overnight, the world had become travel-happy and had discovered our little idyllic island. Modern technology and transportation made our island more accessible and a much easier place to live.

We built it and they came, in droves, the majority of whom wouldn't have lasted more than a few months on the island that I had stepped onto a short six years earlier when there were Mini Mokes and Jeeps with bodies made of marine plywood, just a handful of bars and restaurants, constant power outages, ancient rotary dial telephones, bakeries that only sold rolls by the dozen, no black lights, presidential roadblocks, high-speed dinghy chases, hand-mixed concrete, attack pigs at the dump, machete-wielding Tarzans, obnoxious parrots, orange-haired massive-breasted police, CIA operatives wearing garbage bags as shorts, exploding boats and, most importantly, a perfect blend of strange characters with magnetic personalities that made up the cultural fabric of the island; a perfect island, the likes of which will never be seen again. Most of these things were gone, and those that weren't would be soon, and in a few years few would know they ever existed.

New and future residents may look upon the new island as a perfect island. For them, maybe it will be. But they'll never miss what they never had.

I felt the presence of Captain Jay during every new adventure. Few were as risky as those we had shared. One, though, was reminiscent of a Captain Jay adventure, and I felt he was with me as soon as the trouble started. It was an adventure that would cost me my beloved blue Sea Craft.

I'd been banging that poor hull through all kinds of conditions for several years, and it still floated. I had taken a couple of carpenter friends and their wives on a spearfishing excursion on the north side of Congo Cay. Because of the depth of the water, and my friends were not expert divers, I chose to dive with tanks.

It was after five in the afternoon, getting close to the perfect, and most dangerous, time to hunt. The daytime fish were going to bed, and the nighttime fish were coming out of their holes in the coral. The big fish all knew about this time of the day. It was their happy hour with hors d'oeuvres everywhere.

The wives chose not to dive. Their husbands followed me underwater. We swam about half the length of the cay. Thirty minutes later I had three fish in the bag and decided to return to the vicinity of the boat when I noticed that one of the divers was pretty low on air. On the way back, I spotted two sharks scavenging the lower reef. I didn't point them out.

We got to the anchor line, and I sent my buddies up with the bag of fish. I had plenty of air and was looking for another fish for dinner. But I really wanted to see if I could find a recent friend.

I kicked further down the reef but didn't see anything large enough to shoot. I did see my friend—a little, tailless parrot fish. I'd never seen a live tailless fish until I spotted this guy several months ago. I stopped and admired the fish for a few minutes and marveled at its ability to survive. I was losing daylight and visibility and decided to swim back to the boat. When I got below it I noticed that just about everything from the boat that wasn't tied down or that could float was sinking past me to the bottom. I looked up and saw four pairs of feet kicking in the water, the bodies they were attached to hanging on to my boat—which was still at anchor and still floating, but upside down.

The hull had seen enough. I'd guessed that during the rough ride to Congo, it had finally cracked. The boat was double-hulled with foam between the layers and would float no matter what. The hull had filled with water, but while I visited my tailless fish friend, it had turtled in the rough seas.

I was just about out of air and swam up to the surface. The carpenters and their wives were doing their best to hang onto the rounded hull but were not panicked, which was good. I dropped my tank and let it sink to the bottom. It was going to do me no good now.

Our predicament would have looked hopeless to most. Nobody knew where we were. We had no radio. We couldn't swim several miles through the currents to a populated island. I thought about Captain Jay and smiled. I didn't have a plan on how to get to safety, but I knew we needed to get to dry land. "We are going to have to swim to Congo," I told the group.

"But we don't have our masks or fins," one of the wives said, with just a little fear as she looked over at the sheer cliff wall sprinkled with horizontal bushes where pelicans nested.

"I'll get some gear from the bottom," I said with a smile. I had no doubt we were going to make it to the rock and find a passing boat that would give us a ride to St. John. I wasn't sure how, but I refused to think it wouldn't be done.

The sun had set but there was still some light. Underwater was a different story. I started free diving the ninety-seven feet to the bottom to find four sets of flippers and masks. The fading light made it hard to see black flippers and masks. I was constantly looking out for the bag of fish that I had seen floating to the bottom along with the rest of the dive gear. Sharks would be attracted to it. I took five trips to the bottom to retrieve flippers and masks.

We swam to the steep rocky north side of Congo and found a flat rock a few feet above the surface.

"What do we do now?" one of the guys asked.

I thought for a moment and laughed, wondering what Captain Jay would do. I smiled and imagined Captain Jay saying with a smirk, "You fucked up this time. You're still the Rookie."

"You guys stay here. There is usually a bare boat anchored on the other side of the island in the lee of Lovango Cay." I looked up the steep rocky cliffs of Congo and said, "I'll climb to the top and try to flag down a boat."

One of the carpenters, Jimmy, wanted to climb with me. The north face of Congo is steep. Unless you have had some climbing experience, you weren't getting to the top. But I knew he could handle it.

The problem was that we were barefoot, and the rocks were covered with small, succulent cacti. By the time we got to the top our feet were full of cactus splinters, which hurt like hell. Added to that were the nesting pelicans we flushed out of the bushes growing horizontally out of the large cracks in the rocks. These birds are huge, particularly when leaving their nests to get away from the intruding humans. I was nearly knocked off of the steep face a couple of times.

One hundred and fifty vertical feet later we reached the thorny summit, where I could see the calm passage that separated Congo and Lovango Cays. There were no boats anchored on the lee side of Lovango. But there was a thirty-foot fiberglass sailboat, the type bare boat companies rent, motoring through the channel. We stood and waved and shouted at the boat. After minutes of acting like complete idiots on the narrow rocky ledge at the top we finally got the boat's attention. Two ladies came to the port side of the boat and waved, toasting us with their beer bottles.

Through many more of our gyrating motions the two couples on the boat all stood at the port side, finally understanding that we weren't waving just to be friendly. I motioned for them to circle to the back side of the island. I wasn't sure they understood. But when they motored to the end of Congo and turned north to the open sea and the back side of Congo, instead of south, and the comfort of several safe anchorages in Pillsbury Sound, I knew we had a ride home.

By the time they got around to the north side of the Cay, and by the time Jimmy and I had climbed back down the pelican-infested north face of Congo Cay, it was dark.

"We're afraid to bring the boat closer," someone shouted from the bare boat.

Not knowing the local waters, whoever was in control of the boat would not venture too close to the cay, which was almost a shear drop-off underwater. They could have come right up to the rock we were standing on, but they didn't know, and it was standard with some bare boat companies to routinely forget to provide things like charts.

"We're going for a swim," I said to the group. We swam through the dark ocean, over the gear and dive bag at the bottom, past my upside-down boat and toward the lights of the bare boat.

The next day I came out and dove for all of my gear at the bottom. The bag and fish were gone. We righted my Sea Craft using a system of ropes and pulleys and towed it back to Cruz Bay. The engine was ruined. I never patched the cracked hull, and my Sea Craft that I'd purchased from the Puerto Rican fisherman a few years earlier at Charlie's insistence ended up in a boat junkyard in Coral Bay.

* * *

Before we finished Gallows Point, Tim came to see me on a hot Sunday evening. He drove up in his small pickup, Blue in the passenger seat, and parked under the shade of a flamboyant tree. Blue stayed in the truck. Tim left after a few minutes. I returned to my work.

A minute later Tim was frantically shouting up through my office window. "Call Chuck. I think Blue is suffering heat prostration or something. I need to know what to do for it."

We had no veterinarian on the island. A St. Thomas veterinarian visited the island once a week in a small wooden building near the dock on land that would later become a shopping center.

While I was building the inn a few years earlier, I was approached for some leftover materials to help build a volunteer veterinary service for the island. One of my carpenters convinced me that he could build a building in a day, so I sent my entire crew and all of the materials necessary to build it. The St. Thomas veterinarian couldn't thank me enough. After that I never paid a dime for veterinary service.

The St. Thomas veterinarian was Chuck Saunders. I tried calling Chuck several times, but he didn't answer. I left a message and then went out to Tim's truck. Tim had Blue out of the truck and was trying to give him CPR. I ran cold water over some towels and wrapped them around Blue. Nothing mattered. Blue died.

Tim was so upset he left without saying a word. The phone rang. It was Chuck.

"Damn, Chuck, McQuin's dog just died at my house. Tim is really upset. Thinks he was responsible," I explained.

"It sounds like it was heat prostration, but could have been a number of other things. If you bring me the dog's head I can find out what caused the death," he said, in typical deadpan medical talk.

I hesitated for a long while and said, "Uh, I'm not going to do that."

It was dark, and I had no idea what I was going to do with a 150-pound dead dog, so I went back into my office. I would figure it out in the morning.

I woke up early, hoping to move Blue's body before too many people showed up. I was looking at the dog's rigor mortised body when Tommy drove up.

"W-what ha-happened to B-blue?" Tommy asked with a surprised look.

I told him the story. "I thought about throwing him in the ocean, but he might just float around and end up on a beach somewhere. That wouldn't go over well with Tim."

"I-I'll get m-my saw," Tommy said, sizing up the problem.

"What?"

"It's d-dry season. It's g-going t-to be a b-bitch di-digging a hole b-big enough to b-bury him. B-but we can c-cut the legs off. S-sometimes there is just s-surface rock. A w-wider hole will be t-tougher."

He was dead serious. That is what I loved about Tommy. You got a problem, he was there to fix it.

"Tommy, we can't cut up Tim's dog."

We finally agreed to tie up his legs tight to his body as best we could and dig a hole down on the flat land near the mouth of the bay. Maybe there would be less rock down there. A pick, a shovel and three hours later we threw the last shovel of rocky dirt on the grave. I kept Blue's collar and gave it to Tim a few weeks later.

Tim and Mary sold their restaurant a year later and moved to Florida.

* * *

I eventually finished Gallows Point and a few other projects on the island over the next several years. Tommy stayed with me on all but the last one. He moved back to the US a few years before I moved on. Other than Rupert and Gizmo, who were "bawn der," I was the last of our close group to leave the island.

Epilogue

"I've lived through some terrible things in my life, some
of which are actually true."
Mark Twain

My time was up on the Stairmaster when the steps came to an abrupt
halt. I stepped off and realized I must have programmed in a second
hour while reliving my first few years on the island—and Captain
Jay. I wiped sweat from my forehead and thought about the first
time I'd heard from Captain Jay after his departure from St. John,
several years after he had left. He'd somehow found my phone
number and called me at my Virginia house. He was in Mexico,
near the Belize border running a fly fishing camp; but, as always,
he had a side-business. He was transporting jungle hardwoods, or
something, by truck from Belize, through Mexico and to the US.
He wanted me to meet him in Brownsville, Texas and return with
him to Belize after dropping off his load of hardwood. I was tempt-
ed, but had a wife and two small children. I thought about Captain
Jay and me, in a truck, driving through Mexico for four days. It was
an easy decision. One, or both, of us would not survive. I politely
declined the offer.

One afternoon, not long after Captain Jay's call, my phone rang.
"Yes?"
"Is this Arlan O'Brien?"
"Who is this?"

"Do you know Captain Jay Travis, or at least that's what he calls himself?"

"Who?"

"Let me explain," he said. "I live in Texas and own a fishing camp near Xcalak on the Mexico-Belize border. I hired him to run my operation. He was using my satellite phone to call you, and others." He paused and said, "Anyway, he owes me a lot of money."

I paused, suppressing a laugh, and said, "I never heard of him."

I hung up and smiled, realizing that at least up until that point in time Captain Jay had survived and the passing of time had no effect on his stellar behavior.

I turned off my stair machine, stretched and thought back to the only time I'd told anybody the many things I'd experienced on the island so many years earlier, especially those involving Captain Jay. A close friend and I were driving across the Yucatan Peninsula, and he asked me about the Caribbean. For the first time since I had left the island I told many of the stories that I thought I would never tell. My friend was a good listener; he needed to be. Three hours later, after a long silence, he said, "That is a hell of a story. You should write it down."

I laughed and said, "Yeah, before I can't remember them anymore."

After a while he said, "You sure learned a lot on that island."

I smiled but had nothing to say in return. I might have learned a lot, but in the end, just like everybody else, I didn't know much about anything—just enough to survive. Thank you, Captain Jay.

I remembered, though, the first time I boarded the jet to the Caribbean. I didn't really know where St. John was. I figured it was somewhere in the Caribbean Sea, which was south of the United States.

That was all I knew.

I know a lot more now.

The End

About the Author

David Culberson grew up in small town middle America. After a higher education in a warmer climate, he spent much of the next three decades living and mixing with the cultures of the Caribbean, Mexico and Lake Superior, where he pioneered sustainable development and built several low-impact resort properties. He keeps a U.S. home on Lake Superior.

www.ingramcontent.com/pod-product-compliance
Lightning Source LLC
Chambersburg PA
CBHW031053020726
47495CB00007B/1851